MW00643270

WHEN THE

SANDMAN MEETS

THE REAPER

12 TALES OF
MAGIC AND TERROR

BY
JEFF DENNIS

A WordCraft Resources Book
Lilburn, Georgia

This is a work of fiction. The events described are imaginary. The characters and settings are fictitious. Any references to real persons or places are included only to lend authenticity to the stories.

WHEN THE SANDMAN MEETS THE REAPER

A WordCraft Resources Book

FIRST EDITION

All rights reserved.
Copyright © 1996 by Jeff Dennis

Author Photo © Morris Haupt
Cover Art © Jeffrey Thomas

This book may not be reproduced in whole or in part, by mimeograph or any other means, without permission of the publisher, except in the case of brief quotations embodied in critical articles or reviews.

ISBN 0-9655522-0-9

WordCraft Resources Books are published by:

WordCraft Resources, Inc.
P.O. Box 1646
Lilburn, Georgia 30226

E-mail : WordCrafts@aol.com

Additional copies of this book are available at $13 each.
Orders shipped within three business days.
Send check or money order to above address, payable to:

WordCraft Resources, Inc.

PRINTED IN THE UNITED STATES OF AMERICA

10 9 8 7 6 5 4 3 2 1

For Cheryl and Ira . . .
My Family and Inspiration

The author would also like to give special thanks to
Suzanne Scarborough Robinson,
for her painstaking proofreading and valued input.

ACKNOWLEDGMENTS

"The Fjords of Vankosh" first appeared in:
RANDOM REALITIES #1 (Summer 1992)

"Last Call" first appeared in:
STRANGE DAYS #6 (Spring 1993)

"Hologram Sam" first appeared in:
RANDOM REALITIES #2 (Spring 1993)

"Sin and Salvation" first appeared in:
THE END (Vol. 1, 1993)

"Wombstone" first appeared in:
THE END (Vol. 2, 1994)

"Insomniacs Anonymous" first appeared in:
RANDOM REALITIES #6 (Spring 1995)

"East of Hades" first appeared in:
A VAMPIRE BESTIARY (Necropolitan Press, 1996)

"Déjà Voodoo" © 1996 Jeff Dennis

"Listening to the Dead" © 1996 Jeff Dennis

"Maricopa Chameleons" © 1996 Jeff Dennis

"Rendezvous at Waldrop Manor" © 1996 Jeff Dennis

"Trophies" © 1996 Jeff Dennis

WHEN THE SANDMAN MEETS THE REAPER

JEFF DENNIS

For Kent,
Inscribed with pleasure
for a fan of the macabre!
All My Best,
Jeff Dennis
Dec. '96

CONTENTS

INTRODUCTION

C⋆   C⋆   C⋆

WELCOME TO THE STRANGE AND EXOTIC WORLDS where my imagination roams unchecked (I'm glad there are no laws governing such things . . . at least not yet!). On the pages that follow, I take you on twelve mysterious journeys where you will experience everything from whimsical dreams and flights of fancy to heartstopping horror and realms of the supernatural and the macabre. Twelve stories—an even dozen tales of science fiction, horror, and contemporary fantasy, all shaken and stirred in a bizarre literary brew.

Much of my fiction is difficult to classify, as I enjoy blending genres and twisting conventional themes into weird new shapes. Having grown up in the 60s, my earliest influence was the late, great Rod Serling, the dark visionary who brought us television shows like *The Twilight Zone* and *Night Gallery* as well as many outstanding dramas presented on *Playhouse 90* (the most memorable being the Emmy-winning "Requiem for a Heavyweight"). Serling was definitely ahead of his time, blending science fiction and fantasy with horror in intriguing ways long before anybody was calling it horror. Serling's stuff scared the bejeezus out of me, but it also made me think and ponder the possibilities beyond the everyday and the ordinary. Today when I see the opening to *The Twilight Zone* on cable, with the door floating through space against a star-studded nightscape, and I hear Serling's voiceover: "You unlock this door with

1

the key of imagination . . . beyond it is another dimension," I still get the chills. Rod Serling opened *many* imaginative doors for me. He taught me how to dream.

Another of my early influences was the Master of Suspense, Alfred Hitchcock, whose work oozed with terror and impending threat. Hitchcock's genius was in his ability to create dark and ominous moods using subtlety. Nobody was better at macabre plot twists and pacing than Sir Alfred.

More recent influences have come from what I consider to be the big three of horror—Stephen King, Dean Koontz, and Robert R. McCammon. King has been heralded as the genius golden boy of horror for some time now, and his reputation is deserved. He is quite simply the best at creating characters who evoke immediate emotional responses in readers. We might love them or hate them or feel sympathy for them, but we always *know* King's characters. He forces us to relate to them because they are real and three-dimensional—no easy feat to pull off on paper, let me tell you. King also possesses a remarkably accessible, chatty writing style that is the envy of most writers, genre or otherwise. This commercial style is a gift he has honed to a sharp edge through two decades of hard work. Dean Koontz, I feel, comes closest to Rod Serling's style of blending genres. Koontz's *Strangers, Dark Rivers of the Heart,* and *Watchers* have influenced me greatly with the way he mixes science fiction and horror. Koontz also creates the scariest psychopaths—I find when I'm reading a Koontz novel at night, I keep quite a few lights burning and the doors double-bolted. Robert R. McCammon is the best there is at making the most outrageous concepts seem real and plausible. His work that has most influenced my style is *Swan Song* (to my way of thinking, the best post-Apocalypse horror novel ever), *The Wolf's Hour* (great stuff with werewolves running rampant in Nazi Germany), *Bethany's Sin* (female ghost riders on horseback, haunting a small town), and *Night Boat* (zombies in a sunken German U-boat in the late-70s Caribbean). I also admire McCammon for his versatility and his willingness to dabble in areas outside the horror genre. His *Boy's Life* is a masterpiece of mainstream/contemporary fantasy, and his last published book, *Gone South,* is a quirky, heartwarming slice-of-life tale about a Vietnam vet trying to cope and survive after discovering he has been poisoned by Agent Orange.

I have had many other influences over the years—too many to mention here. But Serling, Hitchcock, King, Koontz, and McCammon have been my biggest speculative fiction inspirations.

And now, a few notes about *When the Sandman Meets the Reaper*. I wrote the dozen tales in this collection between 1988 and 1996. During that eight-year span, I penned 40+ genre stories. Certainly not a prodigious output, but it made the selection process a bit difficult—kind of like trying to decide which of your children to keep. Due to space considerations, I had to leave some good material behind. But these twelve stories are unquestionably my favorites. Seven have appeared previously in various small-press magazines. Included is my first published story, "The Fjords of Vankosh," though it was not my first sale (that distinction goes to "Hobo Harvest," which I sold to *Eldritch Tales* in early 1991 and is not included here). Also included is my first large-circulation story, "Last Call," and a new science-fiction/horror novella, "Rendezvous at Waldrop Manor." Quite the strange brew. Hope you enjoy the taste.

Jeff Dennis
November, 1996

Leading off is undoubtedly my most widely-read tale. "Last Call" appeared as the lead story in the Spring '93 issue of STRANGE DAYS. This one is a bizarre slice of contemporary fantasy that Editor Peter Bianca referred to in his editorial as 'a great tale about the Nearafter and the Hereafter.' My Rod Serling influences are definitely at work here.

LAST CALL

MORNINGS WERE SO MUCH MORE pleasant now that he had kicked the bottle.

Brad Kissel sauntered down the alley leading from the bus stop to his office, just as he had every morning for the past six years. His head was as clear as the crystalline morning, his stride purposeful and bouncy. Seven months since he had last let alcohol stain his lips. It had been tough, maybe the toughest thing he had ever done. Compared to licking his drinking problem, building his advertising empire had seemed mere child's play.

It had all come crashing home one miserable hung-over morning in January. Brad had awakened on the floor of his bathroom, his cheek pressed against the cool porcelain of the toilet, his mouth tasting of stale gin and puke. Through blurred, crusty eyes, he spotted the succinct message his wife had scrawled across the top of the mirror in her peach-colored lipstick:

Brad,
I can't take this any longer. Have taken
Melanie and Kelly to Mother's. Call me
when you grow up!

That is when Brad Kissel changed, when he realized what was truly important. A thousand Coca-Cola accounts didn't add up to Sheila and his two daughters. *Especially* his two daughters. He decided he had suffered his last hangover. Quit, cold turkey. That's the way Brad Kissel did everything. All or nothing—obsession or denial.

He had pulled himself up off that hard tile floor, determined to redirect his life. And he had done it, though there had been some very dark days indeed. It wasn't until he became active in AA that Sheila and the girls had come back to him. There were still times when it took all the self-discipline he could muster to avoid stopping by a package store or bar after a tough day. Days when he felt close to giving in, going on another patented Brad Kissel bender. But all it took was the vision of Sheila's lipstick-smeared message seven months ago. *Call me when you grow up!* Very direct words that kept him in line.

Brad rounded the corner leading to Peachtree Street and the entrance of his office building. Immediately, he knew something was wrong. Normally, the service entrances lining the alley were soiled and grimy, the paint peeling and rust freckling the naked metal of criss-crossing fire escapes. Today, he saw no service entrances, only shiny immaculate storefronts with unfamiliar names. Brilliant gold and silver facades gleamed in the sunlight. Normally he could smell the faint scent of urine and the reek of rotting garbage. Now, an overpowering perfumed scent filled his nostrils, some sweet fragrance like honeysuckle or lilac.

5

Brad slowed his pace, gripped his briefcase a little tighter. The more he walked, the longer the alley seemed to stretch out in front of him. It was like trying to go up a down escalator; the more he walked the less distance he seemed to cover. He had no idea where the alley ended. His office building was nowhere to be seen.

He grew disoriented and faintly dizzy. The sun brightened, tinged with a strange phosphorescence that gave everything a bluish tint. Oddly, the heat and humidity had disappeared. Brad actually felt cool, which he knew was impossible for Atlanta in August.

He sat down on the curb and shook his head, trying to clear the dizziness. A peculiar tingling buzzed through his fingers and toes. Panic hit him as he noticed the street was paved with glowing gold cobblestones. The curb was a bar of solid silver. A sewer grate was studded with diamonds and rubies.

What the hell is happening here? Brad wondered, squinting against the glare. *I feel like Alice after she tumbled down the rabbit hole.* He looked back up the alley, from the direction he had come. *Maybe,* he thought, *if I walk back that way, I'll be back at the MARTA bus pickup. Then I'll be able to get my bearings again.* Brad took several deep breaths and stood, determined to retrace his path.

He couldn't move.

His feet were rooted to the golden cobblestones.

Suddenly, Brad felt himself being tugged forward, as if he were a tiny scrap of iron drawn to a huge magnet. He was pulled to the entrance of a bar, feeling a pang of dismay as he looked up to read the elegant gilt-edged marquee:

LAST CALL LOUNGE

Great, he thought sullenly. *This is all I need!*

He tried to walk away but couldn't. Dumbfounded, he stood, gazing at his reflection in the mirrorlike face of the building. Not sure what to do, he fidgeted with his tie, fussed with his hair. Weird, disassociated thoughts strobed through his mind.

Finally, the massive gold doors creaked open. Brad peered into the cavernous dark, hearing the usual tavern sounds: glasses clinking, the low buzzing undercurrent of voices. A piano played a soft familiar tune, but Brad couldn't name it no matter how many notes they gave him.

The magnetic pull swept him into the darkness. The doors slammed shut behind him with a deafening thud.

The piano went silent.

Conversation stopped.

Brad blinked, trying to adjust to the dim light. The silence was oppressive. A chill raced through him as he realized all eyes were on him, hundreds of eyes, scanning him with telescopic intensity. Self-consciously, he made his way to the bar.

"Excuse me, young fella," he said to the bartender, a slight black man with beaded dreadlocks. "Something really strange is happening, and I was wondering if you could help me out."

A hushed chuckle spread through the packed bar.

"What problem ya have, mon?" the bartender asked in a thick Jamaican accent.

Brad looked around uncertainly. "Well . . . I seem to have lost my way going to work this morning . . ."

The bartender laughed as he toweled off a cocktail glass. "Most folks in bars . . . they be lost," he said. "Worse the world get, better the business be. What'll it be for ya, mon?"

7

"No, no . . . you don't understand," Brad said, leaning over the bar, his voice a whisper. "You see, normally I walk down the alley out front to get to my office—you may have heard of my company—Kissel Concepts? Fortune Five-hundred advertising firm? We're located on the top two floors of the Equitable Building."

"Heard of it, yah," the bartender said, nodding. "Heard of Kissel Concepts plenty, mon."

Brad was in no mood for this. "Well, if you've heard of it, why don't you be a nice fellow and point me in the direction of Peachtree Street."

"No can do for you, Brad," the wiry Jamaican said, turning his back on him, pouring colorful drinks from a spigot behind the bar.

"How'd you know my name is Brad?"

"No problem, mon. *Everthing* 'bout Brad Kissel be my business." The barkeep turned around and set the tray of drinks on the bar, looked at Brad. "Name's Reggie, maz Kissel. Ain't much in your life is secret from Reggie."

Brad didn't like the way this guy Reggie was looking at him—the weird smile and the familiarity in his rheumy eyes, like they were long-lost buddies or something. "How do you mean?"

The Islander scratched his chin, thinking. "You had younger brudder with name of Billy, no? Die before his sixth birt'day . . . rheumatic fever, I think. Topeka, Kansas, yah? Your faddah, he be machinist for a farm equipment company . . . make big dollars, enough to put you through college at Kansas State. You study Marketing, no? Your beautiful wife, Sheila . . . you fall in love wid her at college. Two lovely daughters—Melanie, age ten, and Kelly, who be eight . . . I right about dis, no, mon? When Melanie is born, you move to Atlanta, you search for golden fleece. Summer, you spend time at cottage on . . . Lake Lanier, I think, and you are big Georgia Bulldog football fan. Right so far, mon?"

Brad could only nod as he listened to this strange Islander and his sing-song dialect.

"You decide you want own company after three years. Make quite the name for yourself, wid all those blue-chip accounts an' such, yah? But it's not all paradise, right, maz Kissel? You be more married to your work an' firewater than to your wife . . . Even few udder women, no? Sheila, she find out, too. Not so good at Kissel house many times, eh, maz Kissel? You want I should go on, mon?"

Brad Kissel was completely stunned. Every fact was pinpoint accurate. Reggie the bartender was the Jamaican version of Ralph Edwards and they were playing some surrealistic version of *This Is Your Life* with him. It didn't make sense. *Nothing* about this made any rational sense.

He looked around the room slowly, searching for answers, but the dull stares of strangers revealed nothing.

"What is this, Reggie?" he asked. "Some kind of sick prank? One of my employees set this up, I'll bet. It had to have been Carpenter. He's a practical joker extraordinaire."

"No prank, mon. We been expecting you some time now. Take a seat . . . Heavy news Reggie 'bout to lay on ya, mon."

"All right, that's it," Brad said angrily as he backed toward the doors, "I've wasted enough time in this dump!"

Reggie snapped his fingers and two burly henchmen appeared from out of the woodwork, grabbed Brad and shoved him down on a barstool.

"You be more comfy sitting, maz Kissel." Reggie's voice was cool, comforting, yet somehow distant. "I make sweet *Slice-o-Heaven* elixah for you to enjoy while we talk,

mon." Reggie slid a tall carafe of strawberry-colored liquid
in front of him. Brad looked at it dubiously. "Bottoms up,
dude," Reggie said, pointing a thin forefinger at Brad's
drink. "No udder beverage here . . . just elixahs. No nasty
firewater . . . no Perrier . . . no spring water . . . no tea or
coffee . . . just this *Slice-o-Heaven* elixah. Take sip. I think
you'll find it quite, um . . . spiritual, mon."

Brad's gaze shifted from his drink to the mysterious
barkeep. Finally he said, "Where the hell is this place anyway? Where am I?"

Reggie emitted a churlish giggle. "You are now in land
of In-Between—the place all God's chillun go before the
changeover . . . before the Day of Reckoning. This pub is
only one of many Last Call Lounges, mon. We be kind of
celestial chain . . . franchise that deal wid spirits of a very
different kind. But don't worry, mon. Not so bad, you see."

Brad looked down at the carafe in front of him. "What
the hell is in this? Heroin? Acid? Something hallucinogenic
to make you dream up this bullshit?"

Reggie kept to his soothing monotone. "Easy, maz Kissel. No need to be so testy, mon. Don't worry, be happy.
Try elixah. I'm sure you like. One carafe increase IQ ten
times . . . strip away inhibitions so you can see the way . . .
God's Way."

I've stumbled into some kind of weird wonderland,
Brad thought. *This Reggie character is the Mad Hatter and
somewhere in the crowd lurks the March Hare and the
Dormouse. Maybe this is one of those alcohol-flashback
dreams they talk about at AA meetings. It has all those
same warped qualities.*

Brad was sure he would awaken from this lunatic
dream momentarily, soaked in a cold sweat. He decided to
play along. "Now let's see if I've got this straight," he said,

"I've been abducted by a UFO and brought here to try out this truth and beauty serum, after which you want me to use my creative talents to come up with an advertising slogan. Well, that's no problem, Reggie . . ." Brad snapped open his briefcase and pulled out a pen and a sheet of company stationery. "I'll just write out a quick ad campaign and you can fly me back to Atlanta. I'm sure quite a few people are wondering where I am."

Reggie sighed. "Ever'body know where you be, mon."

Brad quit scribbling and looked up, uncertain. "How do you mean?"

Reggie hesitated, glancing at the untouched elixir in front of Brad. "You'd make things more easy if you drink."

Brad frowned and pushed the carafe away. "I'm not touching that stuff."

"Jolly well, mon. You want to know the hard way, I'll tell you. Four moons ago you go to sleep at ten-fifteen. You never wake up when the sun kiss the day. Now you're here in the In-Between, waiting for the big cyclone. To you this be reincarnation . . . rebirth . . . life in the Hereafter."

"Come on, Reggie." Brad eyed the barkeep suspiciously. "I've been off the sauce for seven months now. I just had my annual physical, which I passed no problem. I've never felt better in my life, and you're telling me I, um—died in my sleep?"

Reggie nodded. "That's what it be, mon. Your heart stop. Be thankful, maz Kissel. Quick and painless. You're here now in spiritual form. You're a soul, soon you be reassigned to 'nudder physical form. Sometime it take a while for right match. God uses the lounges to store souls like fishermen uses live wells. When the right body and situation come along, you go. Simple as that, mon."

For the first time since entering the lounge, Brad

11

laughed, a mad cackle. "You've flipped your wig, Reggie, or I should say your *corn rows*! You need a rest. A long vacation. You're saying I'm a ghost? If I'm a ghost why can I feel it when I pinch myself . . . Look, I'm pinching myself and it hurts, Reg."

"Mebbe this will convince you." Reggie snapped his fingers, turning on the television above the bar.

Brad looked on in astonishment as the screen filled with familiar faces. There was Sheila, flanked by the two girls, who were clutching small bouquets of flowers. They were all dressed in dark clothing, their faces wet with tears. A melancholy funeral dirge droned from a bellowing pipe organ. People—most of whom Brad recognized—filed past his family, offering their most heartfelt condolences. He sat watching for a few stunned moments, then gasped as the camera zoomed in on a glossy mahogany coffin. The camera dipped over the edge and Brad saw himself lying inside, pale and lifeless against the red satin interior. He nearly choked as he saw that his corpse wore the same gray Brooks Brothers suit he now wore. The camera panned back to Sheila, who was visibly shaken.

Brad's face drained of color. His jaw hung open. Slowly, he got up off the stool and backed away from the bar, his eyes never leaving the screen. "You're all crazy, you know that?" he screamed. "You're all a bunch of morbid maniacs and I want no part of you!"

The two bouncers intercepted him and brought him back to his stool, sat him down. One of them held him still while the other forced the strawberry *Slice-o-Heaven* elixir down his throat. The crimson liquid dribbled off Brad's chin and splattered across the front of his suit.

Reggie watched as Brad slurped at the elixir. The bartender snapped off the television. "This is the way it is, maz

Kissel. Your karma now is in the hands of God. Only way out is through the back doors—Doors of Reassignment. Only God knows where you'll go . . . Only God knows when."

Brad loosened his tie and unbuttoned his top button. He elbowed one of the bouncers aside and grasped the carafe with both hands for some two-fisted drinking—just like the old days. He drained the last of his elixir and slid the empty carafe forward on the bar. "Hit me again, Reg. This stuff's tasting better with every swallow."

The more Brad drank the more unreal he felt. Euphoria and giddiness stroked his senses. He watched Reggie glide around behind the bar as though the bartender hovered half a foot above the ground. He watched a pair of cheap-looking waitresses beat a path to and from the bar, serving the mystical fruity-tasting elixir to patrons at the tables. He saw others enter the lounge in the same confused, pissed-off manner he had, and listened as Reggie gave them the opening orientation. Occasionally, Brad heard names announced over a loudspeaker, and people would disappear through the double doors behind the bar amid shouts of encouragement. The crazy thing was, the more elixir Brad drank, the more legitimate all of this seemed to him. *Maybe I am a spirit*, he thought, watching two more disappear through the double doors to an unknown fate. *Maybe I am about to meet my maker.*

"No offense, Reggie," Brad said when things had slowed down, "but how did you get selected to God's Welcoming Committee? What makes you so special?"

"No offense taken, mon." Reggie smiled warmly. "I was one bad dude in my last physical life. I deal drugs through Caribbean," he said, a faraway look misting his eyes. "On the day I died, I be on my boat between Bonaire

13

and St. Vincent, runnin' a load of ganja up to the Virgin Islands. The Coast Guard, they intercept me—wait 'til we be out of international water, try to bust us, mon. We try to outrun 'em, but we lose. We worse off than a leaky banana boat since we be carryin' more than two-hundred bales of primo Colombian redbud. *Real* stupid we be, maz Kissel. Some shots be fired, and me, I catch two slugs in me head. I come here. God say, 'Reginald, the coconuts, they have fallen, mon. But I can use you here.' God say I be good workin' the Last Call bars. Been here ever since. No regrets, mon."

"But doesn't this place get boring?" Brad asked. "I mean, hanging out behind the bar and serving one kind of drink all the time has to get old fast."

"You jivin' me, mon? It's never boring servin' the Lord. This job is my privilege, an honor. I be on a first-name basis wid God. Get to meet many souls. I be free—no emotional or physical pains of the flesh for me . . . Is wonderful an' spiritual here in the In-Between."

Brad mulled this over. It still sounded like a boring life to him, though the Islander did seem happy. So did the bustling waitresses, the two gorgeous floozies he had come to know as Amber and Ginger. Brad could hardly keep his eyes off their long shapely legs which sprouted from beneath skin-tight hotpants, or the generous cleavage peeking over their tight tube-tops. If Reggie had been a gun-toting drug dealer, Brad could only imagine what sinful past lives these women had lived.

He was checking out the way Ginger's ass moved against the silky cocoon of her shorts when he heard his name announced over the loudspeaker. At first it didn't register. Then he heard it again, and the reality of it filled him with sudden terror.

"LAST CALL FOR BRADLEY LIVINGSTON KISSEL"
Reggie winked at him. "God be waitin', maz Kissel."

Brad grabbed his half-full carafe and guzzled the remaining *Slice-o-Heaven* elixir. For the first time since entering this otherworldly lounge, he wished for a fifth of Johnnie Walker Black.

"No fear . . . don't worry, be happy," Reggie said, reading his mind. "Tough part is dyin' . . . when you separate from physical being. Trust me, mon, the rest is easy."

Brad stood, hypnotized, and grabbed his briefcase off the bar. In a trance, he moved behind the bar, taking baby steps toward the swinging doors.

Behind him, several patrons interrupted their drinking and private conversations to shout: "Good luck, Brad!" and "We'll see ya next time, Mr. Kissel!" He thought he also heard a few faint strains of 'Happy Birthday', but he couldn't be certain.

Boldly, Brad pushed through the grimy doors and found himself smothered in a thick, swirling mist. A soothing harp blended with mellow brass and whining wood-winds. Violins and cellos caressed his ears. Bells chimed from somewhere in the distance. He felt a warmth spread through him, a sense of well-being. *Well, what do you know,* Brad thought, taking it all in. *Miracle of miracles . . . I actually made it to heaven.*

His reverie was cut short by a strong hissing.

The foggy mists parted.

He watched as a stooped-over old woman removed a rack of glasses from a mammoth institutional dishwasher.

This isn't Heaven, Brad suddenly realized. *The mist is just steam from the dishwasher. And the orchestral music, the harp . . . it's just a bad Muzak version of Led Zeppelin's "Stairway to Heaven." This is no spiritual place. It's just the back room of a neighborhood pub.* He slouched his shoulders, dejected.

"Not what you expected, is it, Bradley?" The old woman turned to face him.

He could only gape. The woman was *ancient.* Her face was carved with deep ridges. Patches of pink scalp showed through steely-white hair. Her hands were gnarled and liver-spotted, her knuckles swollen grotesquely.

"It never is . . ." she uttered through a mouth pinched by a lack of teeth, ". . . what my children expect, that is."

"Y-your . . . ch-children?" Brad stammered.

"Come on, Bradley," she said, walking toward him and removing her apron. "I don't have time for doubters. I know Reginald has already filled you in as to my identity."

Brad retreated a few steps. "B-but you ca-can't be—"

"Why not?" she said, reaching out and touching his cheek with a twisted, lumpy finger. "I can assume any physical form I desire. You would never recognize me in my natural state. It would be too difficult to communicate face-to-face."

Brad felt an electric tingle run through his cheek and shoot down his spine. She was close now, and he studied her. This near she appeared even older. Her fetid breath rattled and wheezed in her lungs. Her skin was nearly translucent, like wadded-up parchment. Brad had never seen anyone this old. This woman rubbing his cheek had survived more than a few generations. She was hundreds, perhaps thousands, of years old. Antiquity personified.

But though her physical being was used-up, there was something about the eyes. Something *magnificent.* They were intelligent, all-knowing eyes. Eyes that held all the secrets and mysteries of creation. Eyes that expressed youth and age, naive curiosity and infinite wisdom. Poignant, penetrating eyes. Prismatic eyes that glimmered with the colors of hope and life. As Brad stared into these celestial orbs, he realized he had met his maker. He *knew* he was glimpsing into the soul of God.

God removed Her hand from his face. "Better now?"

Brad could only nod.

She smiled, and he was filled with love and understanding. "Believe me," God rasped, "your reaction is no different from most. I purposely make these meetings challenging, to test my children's faith. We don't have much time, my son. Surely you must have questions for me."

Face-to-face meeting with God? Questions? Brad's mind staggered at the thought.

"I'll help you get started," God said. "A common one I always hear is: with all the billions of people in the world, how can I possibly spend time with each and every one?"

Brad found his voice. "Yeah, that crossed my mind."

"I exist in a very different dimension and time from you, Bradley. I can hold millions of these Last Call meetings in the time it takes you to blink once. Even so, my time is stretched thin. Besides Earth, I have two dozen other worlds to look after. And I'm not just talking sentient life, either. I meet with *all* forms of living things . . . all the way down to the simplest cells and protozoa."

Brad shook his head, the concept much too large for him. "What about all the evil in the world? . . . *my* world, that is. Why do you allow Satan so much leeway?"

God laughed as She grabbed another rack of glasses from the dishwasher. "There is no Satan, my son," She said, steam enveloping Her. "That's just a concept the early Christians employed to represent evil. They refused to believe that I could let wickedness and sin go unchecked."

"So what are you saying? That God has a dark side?"

"No, I'm not saying that at all. I have created so much life that I can't keep watch over all of it all the time. Rapid growth sometimes causes a dip in efficiency. A common misconception is that I can be everywhere at once. Not true. I'm powerful, but I'm not omnipresent. Some of my children can get very peculiar ideas when I am unable to check on them for long periods. Stalin and Hitler come to mind. Of course, there are *many* more, but they are good examples."

"How can you not hate them? How can you forgive all the murderers, rapists, and thieves who have ruined innocent victims?"

"Hatred is so unproductive, Bradley. Like any good parent, I love all my children and I forgive them for their mistakes. After all, we're talking the flaws of humanity. I never expect them to be perfect, though my self-righteous fundamentalists seem to think *they* are . . . they think they have some kind of an 'in' with me, which couldn't be farther from the truth, the obsequious little brown-nosers!" She saw Brad's shocked expression. "I'm just making a point, my son. I love all my children, but that does not mean certain types of behavior don't disappoint me. Those who waste their lives and just go through the motions without using the unique talents I have given them irritate me. And of course, murderers and the wide assortment of nefarious types who do harm to others give me great heartburn. But they *are* still my children, my family. I forgive them all when they come through here. After all, the only way to upgrade a soul is to nurture it."

Brad thought about Reggie. "Is that why you give Last Call bartending jobs to drug dealers and gun runners?"

God frowned as She wiped her hands with a towel. "You're missing the point. Reginald was a very disturbed individual in his last life. By giving him responsibilities here, I have taken him out of circulation while nourishing his damaged soul. There are thousands of Last Call Lounges, and all the employees are children of mine who went very far astray. All of this Last Call business is my way of cleaning up the cosmic environment, though it's getting more and more difficult. There is a restlessness throughout my household that is wearing me down. I need a long vacation, but that's just not possible. Who would take my place?"

"So I guess since I didn't kill anybody and wasn't a real hard case, you're sending me on, right?"

"Yes, my son, it is time . . ." God continued to talk as She disappeared behind the enormous dishwasher. ". . . even though you abused alcohol and cheated on your wife, you will be moving on."

Brad heard God scavenging around in the back of the room. "But what about Sheila? We had worked everything out and things were getting so beautiful between us again. I miss her already. And what about my girls? Melanie and Kelly?"

"You and Sheila will cross paths again. Neither of you will look the same or really think the same, but your souls are forever mated. Your girls? I'm not sure. It depends on so many factors. But I promise to do my best, Bradley."

"Where am I going? What will I be doing?"

More rattling around behind the big stainless steel dishwasher. "You'll see soon enough. All I can tell you now is that you will be born into a loving household and will eventually make a career of astrophysics. You will be instrumental in the first manned flight to Mars."

"Astrophysics?" Brad said, disappointed. "But I'm not interested in physics. I'm an ad man, all the way."

"You *were* an advertising man, Bradley," God said,

19

returning with a large, oddly-shaped plastic dish rack. "In your new life you will be intensely dedicated to physics and engineering." She plopped the rack up on the front end of the dishwasher, on the rubber conveyor belt. "Get in, my son. It is time for your reassignment."

Brad looked down at the dish rack, which was elongated rather than square, and had a large indentation in the center instead of slots or pegs.

God urged him on. "Come on, Bradley, get in and lie down. This is the way it works. Trust me."

Strange request, Brad thought. *But when it comes from the mouth of God, you believe it, no questions asked.*

Brad dutifully got in the plastic rack. God touched him on the shoulder, and immediately he began to feel different. The dishwasher roared to life and the conveyor belt lurched forward. By the time his rack passed under the rubber strips, he had forgotten everything about his meeting with God. When the hot spray washed over his face and the darkness gobbled him up, he began to shrink. His arms and legs withdrew into his body until they were mere nubs. His head became smaller. Steam and coarse brushes whipped at him—a hurricane of heated frenzy *(the cyclone Reggie had told him about?).* His Brooks Brothers suit and Gucci loafers began to disintegrate. But Brad was not afraid. For some reason, this all seemed natural, familiar.

In quick succession, going backward in time, Brad saw key moments of his life play out on the silver screen of his mind. As each brief scene concluded, the memories were wiped clean, never to be recalled again . . .

Signing the Coca-Cola contract . . .

Sheila's lipsticked note on the mirror . . . *Call me when you grow up!*

Melanie's second-grade play, where she played a princess . . .

Sitting in the hospital room, holding Kelly after her birth . . .

Lifting the veil to kiss a ravishing young Sheila at their wedding . . .

Cap and gown graduation ceremonies at Kansas State . . .

Playing bass and singing with the Elastic Band, his high school rock band . . .

Sitting around a campfire on a Boy Scout camping trip . . .

Circling the bases after hitting a Little League home run . . .

Riding his bicycle and tossing newspapers on his paper route . . .

Playing with his little brother Billy, before illness claimed him . . .

His mother and father, reading him bedtime stories . . .

Having his picture taken with Santa Claus . . .

Swatting at a mobile of winged dragons in his crib . . .

.
.
.

Happy fragments of Brad's life zipped past in one-act passion plays.

And then there was darkness.

THICK, GELATINOUS FLUIDS washed over him. He sensed forward movement, like he was swimming through a cylinder of gummy syrup.

The walls seemed to breathe, constricting and expanding in a rhythmic motion, pushing him along.

Far ahead, a small pinpoint of light appeared, wavery at first, then steadying as he pushed closer. The light became his beacon, a lone sun on a dark horizon. As the walls squeezed, he pushed, and the sun became brighter. He kicked and twisted, working his way to freedom.

Another kick and a push, and his head poked through the opening. A final twist and a squirm, and he was freed from his sticky imprisonment.

He felt a painful twitch around his belly. He opened his eyes, squinting in the blinding light, watching as a snaky appendage was cut away from his pink, slippery body.

Masked faces stared at him, nodding, mumbling strange sounds.

Everything was so bright and shiny, foreign and frightening.

He was handed to another masked figure, who ran a loud sucking instrument over his nose and mouth.

He began to cry in long, pealing wails.

The sucking instrument was whisked away and he was turned around. A tired woman smiled at him, uttered some sounds he didn't understand. He stopped crying for a moment and studied her. Her expression of maternal warmth and love transcended all barriers of spoken communication.

He began to cry again. But this time the tears he shed were tears of joy.

He didn't stop crying until he started nursing.

His mother's milk soothed him like a magical elixir.

"East of Hades" is my only story written at the request of an editor. Jeffrey Thomas wrote to me in early summer '95 and asked me to contribute to a vampire anthology he was planning. Of course, I was thrilled and honored that he would want a story from me, but I was somewhat concerned. I am not a fan of traditional vampire fiction for, in my not-so-humble opinion, I feel it is way over-done and has become a very tired sub-genre. But Jeffrey assured me he was looking for different slants and twists on the ages-old 'undead' theme. And got it he did, with seven different writers contributing wonderfully diverse stories to his anthology, A VAMPIRE BESTIARY, published by Necropolitan Press. "East of Hades" was my contribu-tion, a blend of future-Earth science fiction and post-apocalyptic horror. The vampires in this story care nothing about blood. They are after something much more precious . . .

EAST OF HADES

WE HAD BEEN TRAVELING FOR THREE DAYS without incident, and I held that thought close to my jittery heart like a silent, hopeful prayer.

We rode eastward, cloistered in the rear of this win-dowless solar-coach, prisoners of the terrible, perilous world outside. Thick, solar-paneled walls surrounded us, humming a sad tune as they processed the day's dying sun-light into energy, propelling us toward what I hoped would be our safe harbor. I wished I could scavenge a modicum of assurance from the dense alloy walls, but I knew all too well

23

of their impotence against the beings who slinked through the shadows of the foothills outside.

I felt a gentle tug at the hem of my skirt.

"Mommy, are we almost there yet?"

I looked down at Katie and was struck by a pang of familiar melancholy. Unlike her twin brother, Judson—who had come into the world perfectly proportioned—little Katie had been marked by the curse of The Great Change. Her forehead protruded grotesquely on one side, her left eye buried deep beneath the bony ledge, barely visible, twinkling faintly like a distant, milky star. Her mouth and nose twisted around to the opposite side, making it appear as though God had corkscrewed her violently before thrusting her out into the world. The stump of a third arm jutted from atop her left shoulder. There were others on this solar-coach who wore the deformities of The Great Change with self-conscious shame, but none were as disfigured as my poor, sweet Katie.

I brushed long, silky hair off her cheek, careful not to reveal the gaping hole where her left ear should have been. "We'll be there tomorrow, sweetie," I said with forced patience.

"But this is boring," Katie whined petulantly.

"I know, dear. Why don't you pop in another disk and read for a while."

"I'm tired of reading. I just wanna be there."

Six-year-olds could be a handful, especially on a trip of this nature. I smiled at her with a love that transcended my growing frustration. "I want to be there, too, Katie. Why don't you have Grampa tell you another story?"

"Pawpaw is telling Jud about how he used to build car motors and it's stupid! I don't understand it."

"I'm sure if you ask him nicely, Grampa will tell you

lovely stories about how things were . . . things that would appeal to a smart young lady like you."

Katie beamed, a twisted grin emerging from her ravaged face like a ray of sunlight peeking through an overcast sky. She ambled off to the rear lounge to pester her brother and great-grandfather.

I sighed and sat back in my seat, thinking about the events that had led to this journey. During the past six months I had experienced more loss than any faithful, God-fearing person should have to endure.

Last October, as winter's first snow blanketed the hills of our Wyoming ranch, we were visited by a force of evil darker than any moonless night, personified by creatures surely spawned from a bottomless black cauldron of depravity. My parents both sacrificed their lives on that nightmarish eve, attempting to protect us from the marauding gang of aberrant hooligans who overran our ranch.

As though the loss of my parents was not enough punishment, my grandmother, Annabeth Whitney, lost her soul on that fateful night. Though I have tried desperately to forget, I could still envision Nanna screaming as three of the mutants overpowered her, their eyes raging infernos of violent rage and blind lust. I shuddered every time I thought of those animals, taking turns inserting their long, taloned fingernails into the base of her neck . . . her screams, terrified shrieks abating into catatonic murmurs as her eyes frosted over. They thrust their styluslike claws deep into her cerebral cortex, mind-raping her, sucking her memories of a pre-Change world up through those needle appendages like mutant mosquitoes, savoring each impression and experience as it transferred across their diseased synapses. Their pleasure was almost sexual in its translation, and it sickened me to my core.

25

I remember standing next to my husband as we helplessly watched the grisly ordeal unfold, rooted in place as though shackled by the chains of a cruel dream. My father lay moaning in horrible agony at my feet, his neck twisted at an unnatural angle, his spine snapped like a dry twig. My mother lay next to him, gasping her last tortured breaths through a ragged windpipe that had been laid open by these monsters.

Never had I felt so violated. Never had I shed so many tears. Never had I known such anger and outrage. A day did not pass when I didn't wonder what had prevented me from intervening. Why had I been so powerless to stop it? Hysterical fear? Cowardice? The realization that I needed to stay alive for the sake of my sleeping children?

The passage of time had somewhat diminished my anger and brought the tragic events of that winter night into clearer perspective. I now suspected my inability to defend my family stemmed from some type of trance under which my husband and I were placed. I have since learned through my interaction on the GlobalNet that these abominations they call mindmutes possess strong hypnotic powers. There had been a brief moment during the raid when one of the wretched creatures had halted me with his stare, a look of dark seduction that was at once welcoming and blissful, yet treacherous. That one tempting glance held me spellbound, captivated me, drew me into the dusky abyss of his soul and froze the blood in my veins.

I was not able to discern whether my husband had felt the same sense of powerlessness, for William departed the following morning, never to be heard from again. The twins missed him and asked about him on occasion even though he had emotionally left us several years before—six to be exact—with the births of Katie and Jud. William was not equipped to deal with the raising of a severely deformed child and a de-evolutionalized world. The night of the mindmute raid was the exclamation point on his long, unraveling demise, and he had fled into the vast Wyoming wilderness. I thought about him during my more introspective times, wondered where he was, if he still lived. At times I cursed him for leaving me. It wasn't that I needed help with the twins and Grampa. No, my needs revolved around the healing process and having someone around to help mend my tattered, tear-streaked emotions. But I do not blame William for his cowardly response of flight; the post-Change world had broken far stronger people than my husband.

A week after my parents' double murders, Nanna Whitney wandered off from the main house in a daze and fell through the ice on Lisle Pond. To this day I do not know whether it was an accident or premeditated suicide as the result of her heinous mind-rape. I suspect it was the latter, for she had become nothing more than a walking vegetable, incapable of coherent thought, her cognitive processes plundered by the malignant mindmutes. The Annabeth Whitney I had known and loved for all of my thirty-one years had cherished life. Nanna had always been a fighter, a benevolent crusader of causes, giving much of herself and asking little in return. She was a courageous woman, almost to a fault. I had heard the tales of her concern for other ranchers the first two years after The Great Change, times when she would brave the elements and threats of biocontaminated air to venture down into the valley, spreading her cheer, delivering loaves of fresh home-baked bread and bowls of her mouthwatering turkey gumbo to the less fortunate. She had also midwifed me into the world as my mother went into labor on a blizzardy night in

27

January when conditions made it impossible to reach the hospital. Yes, my Nanna Whitney had been my deliverer, my inspiration and hope in a desperately dark world. She had given me life, and her warm light had been snuffed out in the most horrendous manner imaginable.

I didn't expect my agony would ever completely heal, though the wounds had scabbed over. Life went on, as life always self-indulgently does. I began to be thankful for cer-'tain things, which helped to harness the enormous pain and soften the hard edges of my fury. I was thankful for the resiliency of children. Judson and Katie got over the deaths of their grandparents and great-grandmother quickly. *Too* quickly, I often thought, though this cynicism was always followed by a pang of guilt. I had to remind myself that, at age six, death was but a myopic fantasy. One of the things I felt most grateful about was that the children had not witnessed the bizarre intrusion of the mindmutes that frigid October eve. After a time, I was even able to laugh at the little ironies. Due to Grampa's incontinence, he had taken to sleeping in the guest house at the rear of the property so as not to bother Nanna, and had slept blissfully through the carnage. Of course, he had taken the three deaths hard, especially Nanna's, and though I knew he continued to hurt over the loss, he remained outwardly strong, especially around the children. And as was his way, Grampa battled the cold harsh reality of the post-Change world with a delightful sense of humor. Two weeks ago he had told me with a sly wink, "I never thought my chronic bedwetting would save my life one day." He had said it in jest, of course, but I could see sadness pulling at the corners of his eyes. Grampa had traveled a ways up the long, serpentine road to recovery. We all had, but it was still a tough journey.

Wanting to protect what remained of my family, I set about the task of learning as much as I could about the mindmutes—genetic mutants that had evolved from the primordial stew of The Great Change. Thirty years ago, the world powers had unleashed their vile, omnipotent biochemical nerve gases in a final apocalyptic fury. The devastation was immense and billions died in slow, twitching seizures. Much of the world's population was erased in a matter of weeks as airborne toxic fumes swept over the continents with lethal determination. The extinction was grand in scope, mind-boggling in essence. Humanity soon consisted of small pockets of survivors, those like us Whitneys, elevated in the Bighorn Mountains of northern Wyoming, or those submerged in the newer undersea colonies and others habitating in underground dwellings. My parents had told me often they felt lucky to have been spared, blessed to be among the survivors. But most of the time I wondered just who the lucky ones were. My family had lived for years in the post-Change world like human mountain goats, sequestered in the high forests of the Bighorns, cut off from what we once knew as civilization. When I thought back on the bleakness of my early childhood, somehow the word *lucky* did not seem applicable.

I was born the year before the virulent gases were unleashed, and was therefore too young to know of the panic and mass hysteria that gripped humanity. There were times during the loneliest parts of my childhood that I would have given anything for a brother or sister, but it was not to be. I remained an only child. My parents, not wanting to risk bringing mutant children into the desolate new world, practiced celibacy after The Great Change. Being devout Catholics and passionate followers of the papal doctrine, they shunned contraception, and soon, they shunned each other.

Their marriage turned bitter and sanctimonious. When I was old enough to perceive such things, I realized that though The Great Change had not killed my parents physically, it had depleted them spiritually. Their hearts were barren. They were incapable of feelings, of self-expression and tenderness. Being in dire need of attention and affection, I turned to Nanna and Grampa Whitney. They responded with an abundance of love and devotion.

Grampa painstakingly taught me how to read. He instilled in me a love of the printed word and the joy of discovery that lay between the covers of books. I remember him telling me that ideas are the only worthwhile commodity, that I should collect them as I would solid gold medallions and bring them out occasionally to admire their shine. Grampa has shared many words of wisdom with me over the years, but that profound statement is etched in my psyche like a musical mantra.

In my desire to please Grampa, I read voraciously. Since my grandparents had been avid book collectors all their lives, there was no shortage of material at my fingertips. Though organized education was not part of the post-Change world, I acquired a thorough and well-rounded base of knowledge through those dusty paper tomes that I preferred over the newer, antiseptic cyberbooks. Vicarious though it was, I gained an acute understanding of the world in which Nanna and Grampa had lived, developing a distant but faithful sentimentality for the world my grandparents had known.

"You look like you could use some company." A mellifluous voice raised me out of my reverie. "Mind if I join you?"

I looked up to see the dark, serious-looking man I had noticed before. He was unique in that he was traveling alone, the only one on this solar-coach not accompanying elderly kin. Reluctantly, I nodded to the seat next to mine.

"Daniel Eliason," he said, extending his hand. "And you must be Anne Whitney."

Wondering at his easy familiarity with my name, I took his hand, which was small, yet firm and masculine. Strangely, I felt a great energy surge through me. "How . . . how do you—"

"Your grandfather," he said quickly. "He's quite a remarkable man . . . such a zest for life, especially considering what he's been through. We talked at length this morning and you seem to be the centerpiece of his life." He pulled his hand away, and oddly, I felt a crushing disappointment. "Pardon me for my forwardness, Anne, but looking at you now, I can see why he adores you."

His emerald eyes glittered like sun-dappled ponds, arresting, inviting. I blushed and looked down at my hands in my lap, feeling at once self-conscious. His swarthy good looks and easy smile reached inside and grabbed me, but my inexperience with strangers activated my insecurity. I cursed myself for my inconvenient timidness and tried to regain my lost composure, but my gaze remained frozen on my fidgety hands.

Daniel Eliason said, "Your grandfather is excited about going to Daufuskie . . . your children, too. Seems to be a big adventure for them."

"You met Judson and Katie?" I said, alarmed the twins had been talking to a stranger.

He nodded. "You should feel proud, Anne. They're both extremely bright and inquisitive. I can see them someday playing major roles in rebuilding the new world. Your son, Jud, told me that if we met up with any mindmutes, he would, and I quote, 'blast them into another universe.' I

31

asked him how he would do that and he showed me his toy laser rod." Daniel snorted a quick laugh. "His childlike bravado reminds me of myself when I was his age."

I smiled, warmed by this stranger's apparent kindness and interest.

"And your daughter, Katie," Daniel continued, and I felt myself stiffen, "she has the heart of an angel and the intuitiveness of a soothsayer. She's special, that one. Such intelligence and perception for one so young. Do you know that we had not talked for more than five minutes before she guessed my occupation?"

I took note of Daniel Eliason's lustrous white broadcloth suit and dark silk shirt. A bright gold watch sparkled with diamond-cluster inlays on his wrist. His hands were professionally manicured and his midnight-black hair was impeccably styled. His heady, masculine scent—a musky fragrance of expensive cologne and bath oils—left me slightly breathless. He was definitely from culture and affluence, a world very distant from my mountaintop farm life. I should have felt intimidated, but this man's cheerful open face and welcoming sincerity would not permit it. "So, what is it you do for a living, Mr. Eliason?"

"Daniel, *please.*" he insisted. "I make my way as a clinical psychologist. Katie guessed it right off. She called me a head doctor. I hope I'm not *that* obvious," he chuckled.

"So that's why you're making the trip to Daufuskie?"

"Yes. There is a great need for my services at the elderly camps. The old folks who remain lucid and possess an abundance of vivid pre-Change memories—those like your grandfather—are in extreme danger, as I'm sure you know or you would not be making this trip. Even after they reach their safe havens, they need expert counseling as they go through an adjustment period."

"What is Daufuskie like, Daniel?" I asked, wanting some insight about the place I had selected through the GlobalNet as our new refuge.

Daniel told me about the rustic beauty of the tiny island off the South Carolina coast. Being one of the smaller camps for the elderly, its residency numbered in excess of a hundred transplanted senior citizens. There were planned activities, dietitian-monitored meals, and a full staff of qualified physicians. I beamed as I thought about Grampa socializing with people his own age and all of us together and safe.

Daniel talked about his work, which took him to many of the twenty-plus privately-funded elderly camps within the U.S., most of which were located on small coastal islands. His enthusiasm for his work was contagious, and I was taken with his nearly obsessive sense of helping others. I found myself entranced by this interesting and selfless man; his deep, resonant voice soothed my frazzled nerves, his expressive eyes and hands fueled my long-absent fantasies. Listening to him, my cynical opinions about humanity soon evaporated. Daniel Eliason was the sort of man who could make me believe again—in myself, and in a world that by necessity had become withdrawn and detached. I had no doubt that many of the psychologically damaged depended on him, and I envied his importance and unassuming nobility.

"But I fear I'm boring you," he said after a time.

"Don't be silly," I said. "I find your work fascinating."

He smiled and I felt a pleasing radiance wash over me. "Thank you, but I don't want to dominate the conversation, Anne. Tell me about yourself."

"Oh, I'm afraid there isn't much to tell—"

"Nonsense. With two beautiful children and a spry, lively grandfather, you must have volumes of interesting things to talk about."

He sees the beauty in Katie. What a remarkable man. "Well . . . I, uh . . ." My mind stalled in mid-thought. I had spent much of my life in seclusion; socializing with strangers was a foreign concept to me. Finally I managed, "What would you like for me to talk about?" feeling immediately like an idiot.

"Well, I understand from your grandfather you're leaving your tree farm behind."

"Yes," I said, thankful he hadn't brought up the subject of my missing husband. "Investors from Project Rebuild paid us handsomely for our eight-hundred acres. We'll all miss it, but this is best for Grampa. At what price personal safety, you know." I looked down at my hands again. *Damn it, Annie, at least pretend like you know how to carry on a meaningful conversation.*

"It must have been hard on you," Daniel whispered, taking my right hand out of my lap. He held it gently and caressed my knuckles with a tenderness I had never known.

His touch caught me off-guard and I was surprised to realize I liked it, welcomed it even. Warm ripples of comfort and safety traveled up my arm, culminating with a tingle in my chest. "Yes, it was hard . . ." I said, trying to keep my breathing steady. I squeezed his hand, shyly reciprocating his affection, but I did not dare look at him. ". . . The farm had become haunted by nightmarish memories. But somehow I *do* feel like I've left a significant part of myself back in Wyoming, something I'll never be able to reclaim. This new life we're planning at Daufuskie, it . . . well, it scares me, I don't mind telling you. I have no experience dealing with change."

34

"Your fears are certainly understandable," Daniel said. "But trust me when I say you'll love Daufuskie, Anne. You and your family will be able to start anew. You'll be able to sleep at night without fear of those . . . beasts."

"You've seen these . . . creatures, Daniel?" I asked, chancing a look at him.

"Yes. Quite a few times during my travels, in fact."

I thought I felt a small tremor course through his hand. "I've only seen the three murderous monsters who raided our farm," I said, "and I hope to never encounter their kind again."

"The folklore of the nineteenth and twentieth centuries told of dark beasts known as vampires—" Daniel began.

"Yes, I know," I said, eager to share my knowledge of the subject. "I've read about them . . . spirits of the dead who leave their graves at night to suck the blood of the living. They decapitate their victims, or bury them with stakes through their hearts, to prevent them from becoming vampires. I've read Stoker and Rice and a few of the other classical tellers of those tales. I once thought the idea of vampires was ludicrous. Juvenile entertainment at best— that is, until the mindmutes invaded our ranch and destroyed my family. I had never glimpsed evil until we encountered those malevolent beasts."

"I'm sorry for your loss, Anne," Daniel said, squeezing my hand with gentle reassurance.

"You've worked with victims of these creatures, Daniel?"

He nodded. "Indeed. Many have undergone my re-memorization therapy."

"Then perhaps you can enlighten me as to what these things get from pre-Change memories."

"Well, the same way the vampires of ancient folklore

35

gained vitality by sucking the blood of their victims, the mindmutes gain a positive energy from robbing the elderly of their long-term memories. In that respect these mindmutes are intellectual vampires. They gorge themselves on memories of more pleasant times, back when the world was full of wonderful music and art and life bustled in full bloom like the first day of spring."

"But can't they get that through cybermedia the way you and I do?" I asked.

"No. With mindmutes it goes much further than just experiencing the sights and sounds, Anne. They have a powerful need to control and possess their victims . . . to completely *own* their experiences. They're deviants in every sense of the word. They steal something vital from their prey—all the thoughts and images that make up a person's being and uniqueness. In psycho-babble, what mindmutes do is suck the egos of their victims to stoke their own ids."

"You sound like you admire them."

Daniel shook his head. "No, they disgust me. But despite their beastly appearance, they're quite intelligent creatures. Their actions sicken me, but I must admit to being fascinated by them."

A spiraling chill wound through me. "Could we please talk about something else?"

"Oh, I'm terribly sorry, Anne. Please excuse my insensitivity. I wasn't thinking."

SOMETIME LATER, THE SOLAR-COACH came to an abrupt halt, the cessation of movement interrupting my comfortable road rhythm the way a sour note spoils a melodious sonata. Only half an hour earlier the coach captain announced that we had captured sufficient sunlight to travel non-stop through the night and would be arriving at the Daufuskie ferry at dawn.

"What's going on?" I said uneasily. "Why are we stopping?"

"I don't know," Daniel said, his eyes darting around the interior of the coach.

Shouts erupted up front followed by the sibilant *zip-zip* of laser rod shots. Much scuffling and struggle was punctuated by heavy footfalls and tinkling shattered glass. A long, caterwauling scream stabbed me with its razor-sharp intensity. The air in the coach became charged with a supernatural heaviness, and we were chilled by the icy fingers of human fear and beastly rage.

"It's them!" Daniel whispered urgently.

He didn't have to tell me who *they* were. I could hear their sickening snorts. The sounds of mindmutes on a rampage were forever etched in the darkest regions of my brain, my subconscious recalling them as special effects for my most vile nightmares.

Grampa! I thought suddenly.

But Daniel was ahead of me. He jumped out of his seat and grabbed my hand, pulled me toward the rear lounge. "Go round up the twins and your grandfather. I'll be right there."

"Where are you going, Daniel?"

"Just go, Anne!"

My mind was in turmoil as I entered the confusion of the lounge. Fellow passengers asked me rapid-fire questions I couldn't answer. I responded to their pleading, frightened looks with a silent shrug of my shoulders, then gathered Jud and Katie together, pulling them close. We sat next to

Grampa on a sofa along the back wall and waited. I looked at Grampa, who sat with a majestic stoicism, awaiting whatever cruel fate was about to be delivered. For not the first time, I wondered about the curse that seemed to surround our family like a hangman's noose.

A mindmute entered the lounge, and several of the passengers, having never encountered one of the legendary beasts, gasped at the creature's immensity and demonic bearing. I caught a whiff of their odd scent, a powerful admixture reminiscent of wet leather and rank sewage. Standing well over seven feet tall, the mutant had to duck to get through the door. Dead yellow eyes searched the room like spotlights at the Nazi death camps I had read about. As with all mindmutes, this one had no need for clothing—it was covered from head to toe with thick black fur. It flexed the lethal claws of its right hand as if in anticipation. This one reminded me of how much mindmutes resembled the bears I had seen wandering the fringes of our tree farm. In fact, there were those who truly believed that mindmutes had been spawned from couplings between bestial humans and feral grizzlies.

"Your navigator tried to stop us and we killed him," the mutant said matter-of-factly. "We're here to feed so I hope none of you will be that stupid."

The mindmute muttered "You have what I need," and went for an old woman in the corner. "NO!" A young man with a severely deformed jaw and a bald, misshapen head shouted his protest and lunged for the mutant, grabbing hold of its leg. In midstride, the mindmute reached down with his clawed hand and gored the man through the neck, then flung him against the wall as though he were nothing more than a pesky insect. The man slumped to the floor, staining the wall and carpet a bright burgundy.

Screams and shrieks came from all around me. *We are trapped in Satan's Chamber of Horrors*, I thought, terrified. I felt Katie's stump digging into my ribcage and Jud hugging me tighter. I reached over and grabbed Grampa's arm, and was alarmed to feel him shaking.

The old woman who was the mutant's target grabbed a small black canister of pepper gas from her purse and sprayed a stream directly into the creature's eyes. The mindmute merely hissed and pounced on the woman, finding the soft nape of neck under her silver bun and sinking his needle claws deep. The pepper gas canister clattered uselessly to the floor as the beast probed her cerebral cortex for memories.

I turned away from the ghastly attack and shielded the twins from it as well. All of my emotional wounds that had scabbed over had been reopened and were bleeding profusely.

Three other mindmutes entered the lounge, leading the dazed captain of our solar-coach.

The captain saw the dead young man slumped in a puddle of blood and shook his head sadly. "Give them what they want or they'll kill us all."

Upon seeing their cohort feasting on the old woman in the corner, two of the mindmutes went after their own prey. One old man with no hair or teeth held a large silver cross in front of him, as though it would universally ward off all forms of evil. But it did him no good. A second elderly man succumbed without a fight.

Where is Daniel? my mind screamed. *Is he a coward like my poor, fragile William? Or is Daniel just a sweet-talking con artist?*

The remaining mindmute who had been standing behind the captain approached me, and I was immediately trans-

39

ported back to the ranch that hellish night six months ago.

"I have come for your grandfather's memories, Annie Lynn," it said in an eerily accurate emulation of Nanna Whitney's voice. "Or would you rather I call you Stinky?"

Stinky? Only my Nanna Whitney would know about the little-girl nickname I had acquired as a result of my run-in with a very potent skunk.

I looked at Grampa as he eyed the creature with a fearful curiosity. I then gazed back into the frosted tawny orbs of the mindmute and knew without a doubt this was the monster who had stolen all that was precious to my Nanna. A chilling anger flooded me as I listened to the mewling moans of those being violated all around me and the gurgling sounds of contentment from the feasting mind-mutes. I tried to speak but the speech part of my brain felt iced-over and incapacitated.

The mutant turned to Grampa. "It's time to come join me, Richard," it said, still mimicking Annabeth Whitney's voice. "Do you remember the dances at Slattery Park?"

Grampa merely nodded, as though in a trance.

"And do you remember the night you proposed to me in front of the bandstand where the trumpet players sat?"

Another hypnotic nod. I had never seen Grampa this lifeless. His willing submission frightened me.

"You told me that night that memories were the portfolios of human existence, and that your portfolio would only be half-complete without me. You remember that, Richard?"

"Yes, I do," Grampa said, in a monotone.

The mindmute's voice changed back to its usual gruff raspiness. "Well, I'm here to collect the other half of the portfolio . . . *Your* half."

It reached to strike with its clawed hand but stopped

when Katie poked her head out from under my arm and yelled, "Don't you touch my Pawpaw you big hairy creep!"

"Shut up, you little freak!" The mindmute slapped Katie hard across her mouth with its unclawed left hand, then lunged at Grampa and jabbed its memory needles deep into the back of his neck.

I pulled Katie back protectively and watched with impotent dread as the mindmute began in earnest to drain Grampa of his pre-Change memories. "Who are you to call anyone a freak? You goddamn bastard!" I screamed, out of control. Tears spilled down my burning cheeks. Jud and Katie sobbed loudly from within the cocoon of my arms. The horror had returned to claim another Whitney.

Suddenly Daniel appeared, clutching something shiny in his right hand. He ran at the beast who hovered over Grampa.

"Daniel, NO!" I screamed.

But Daniel avoided the mindmute, electing instead to plunge the metallic object he carried deep into Grampa's chest. Grampa let out a startled cry of pain, then went slack.

"What are you doing?" I cried, thinking this man I had trusted had killed my grandfather.

Suddenly, miraculously, the mindmute grunted and disengaged itself from Grampa, then fell to the floor in a heap. The feasting mindmutes looked up, distracted by the commotion of their fallen comrade. Daniel pulled the metallic object from Grampa's chest and held it over his head, showing it to them. It was a hypojet I now saw, and Daniel squirted fluid from it. The beast at his feet twitched several times, took a final enormous breath, then died. Foamy blood bubbled from its mouth. The needle claws curled in rigor mortis. The other mindmutes squawked in fear, pulled their memory talons from their victims, and fled the lounge.

41

"Grampa, are you all right?" I yelled running to him and panicking as I felt his weak, thready pulse.

"He'll be fine in about an hour, Anne."

"Whatever did you do?" I said, looking up at Daniel.

"Shot up your grandfather with a dose of MemoBane-Five."

"Which is?"

"Partly a high-grade memory blocker. We use it for rape victims and post-traumatic stress disorder treatment. By injecting it into your grandfather's heart, it traveled quickly to his brain and short-circuited our overzealous friend here."

"You mean a memory blocker is all it takes to kill these monsters?"

"Not exactly. My special brew also contains electrically-charged microbes that attack the dendrites and neurons in the nervous system, destroying them instantaneously."

"You pumped something that dangerous into Grampa?" I asked, appalled. "Why not just shoot the mindmute with it?"

I listened with rapt fascination as Daniel explained that mindmutes were nearly indestructible in direct confrontations, but that their right arms and needle claws were extremely vulnerable. Their right arms housed a sophisticated nervous system sheathed in thick layers of cartilage and bone. The microbes had to be channeled through the victim and picked up by their claws to introduce the deadly agents directly to their brains. The memory blocker acted as both a cover for the dangerous microbes and a magnet for the mindmute memory probes. "Don't worry, Anne," he said, "the microbes are encapsulated and triggered by the lower body temperatures of the mindmutes. Only if your grandfather's body temperature was lower than eighty degrees would the microbes affect him. In short, Anne, we sacrificed a small piece of your grandfather's memory for his life."

Grampa regained consciousness and leaned on his elbow. "Hello, Stinky," he said, smiling at me.

I didn't understand everything Daniel Eliason had just done, but one thing was certain—Grampa didn't possess the vacant stare that Nanna had after she was attacked. His eyes shone with awareness though the rest of him betrayed his exhaustion.

"Oh, Grampa!" I said, going to my knees and hugging him on the floor where he lay.

Then I looked up at Daniel through a veil of tears and I thought my heart would burst with gratitude. "You've done this before, haven't you?"

Daniel nodded. "I told you they fascinated me."

THE NEXT MORNING we were on the ferry heading east, cutting through placid green channel waters. I stood at the bow, a fine mist spraying my face, listening as the twins marveled at the vast expanse of ocean. This stretch of the Atlantic Inland Waterway was their first exposure to a body of water larger than Lisle Pond.

Daufuskie Island loomed ahead—our Promised Land. Seagulls circled the shoreline, incandescent in the radiant sunshine. They looked like angels to me, welcoming us home.

Though I mourned the losses suffered by other families aboard the solar-coach, I was ecstatic Grampa Whitney had not been taken from us. Grampa couldn't remember any details from his early courtship days with Nanna, but Daniel assured me he would be okay, telling me that Richard Whitney would probably outlive us all.

I could feel the sorrowful weight of my past churning away on the wake trailing the Daufuskie ferry. I looked forward to creating fresh happy memories with Katie and Jud and Grampa at our new island home. And I was sure many of those memories would include Daniel Eliason—the man who had saved my Grampa Whitney's life, and in large measure, a big piece of my own as well.

I have long enjoyed stories about con artists and the clever methods they employ to scam their marks. Once a 'sting' is in process, almost anything can happen. That unpredictability factor seduced me into trying one of my own 'sting' stories. "Hologram Sam" is straight science fiction, set on Earth at the turn of the 21st century. The protagonist uses tactile-sensory motion holograms as his scam. This tale, I feel, is my best plotted story. It is fitting that it appears third in this collection, as it was my third published story, originally seeing print in the Spring '93 issue of RANDOM REALITIES.

Hologram Sam

"SO WHAT'LL IT BE, LADY? A child to satisfy your motherly instincts? A well-hung stud to please your carnal cravings, perhaps? Or maybe you want me to recreate one of your dearly departed?"

He was perched on the rear bumper of a hover-van, wearing a skin-tight tunic and wide-brimmed floppy hat. Eyes like Mexican jumping beans darted under the lowered brim of his hat. He was all motion and verbosity, hands gesturing dramatically, husky voice urgent and solicitous, like some carny side-show pitchman. Experience had taught him that flashy showmanship was more effective than the subdued approach.

Hologram Sam was known far and wide for his work with tactile-sensory motion holograms. As most legends went, he *was* quite talented. His customers could smell and

45

touch and hear his lifelike motion holograms. Nobody did it better. He was an honored *artisan* among artists. But though Sam enjoyed creating his holographic masterpieces, he kept a low profile. That was due to his passion for risk and danger. His thing was working on the wrong side of the law. Confidence games were his true aphrodisiac, and the hotter the sting, the bigger the turn-on.

The woman analyzed him with that familiar glint of amused doubt in her eyes. Most of Sam's marks came to him wearing this same look of disbelief. His less-than-impressive physical appearance came nowhere near matching his immense artistic reputation.

"No," she answered finally. "I don't need anything quite so pedestrian. I've never had a desire for children. My bed has been warmed by a constant parade of lovers. And no one close to me has died . . . at least no one I care to bring back."

The wrinkles on Sam's ancient face creased into a practiced frown, but underneath, he was rejoicing. This woman wore the look of the severely desperate. Her mannerisms and clothing also indicated great wealth. "What is it then, my dear? What is it you want me to create for you?"

She brushed back a lock of salt-streaked brunette hair and stepped forward, lowered her voice. "I want you to recreate me. I want you to make a hologram of my identical twin—sort of my stand-in or body double. I understand you can do that."

The holo-artist studied the woman for a long moment. She was obviously of upscale breeding—the way she carried herself, her expensively tailored clothes, the hint of demand in her honeyed voice. He scratched his stubbly chin, the sound like sandpaper smoothing roughened pine. "There are laws against such things."

She smiled, more of a nervous tic, really. "There are laws against *most* of the things you do, Mr. Sam. I figure you wouldn't be working out of the back of a hover-van like a flim-flam man if your activities were legitimate."

Sam's tone turned apologetic. "You have to understand, ma'am, that I would starve if I had to rely solely on my legitimate artwork. We artists are tossed mere crumbs for our efforts. The public seems to think what we do is trivial."

"I applaud your flexibility," she said. "I'm for anyone trying to get ahead. But the bottom line is, what you're doing out of the back of this van is illegal."

"What's it to *you*? You're not a cop are you?"

She smiled widely, revealing oversized horsey teeth that were not unattractive in combination with her full, glossy lips. "If I were a cop I would have arrested you by now."

"On what charges?"

"Operating without a business license. Failure to pay sales and income taxes. Selling an unlicensed product. Shall I go on?"

"You sure know a lot about the law—and *me*—for someone who isn't a cop. You with the IRS?"

"Hardly." She unsnapped her purse and removed her billfold, withdrew several forms of ID and handed them to him. "My name is Sally Randolph. Monday, I am scheduled to go on trial for the murder of my husband. Perhaps you've heard of him. Quentin Hughes . . . the big interspace shipping magnate."

Sam licked his lips as he looked up from the laminated cards in his hands. In the dim light, he hadn't recognized her. But now he knew she was who she said she was. Before him stood Sally Randolph Hughes, one of the richest women in this part of the galaxy. News of Quentin

47

Hughes's vicious murder had been plastered all over the electronic and print media the past month. Sam had hooked a big fish indeed, and though he knew this could set him up for life, he realized he had to be careful. This fish was a barracuda.

"Of *course* I've heard of him," he said. "A person would have to have been on the dark side of Mundavia the past few weeks to not know about that."

She continued, as though she had not heard him. "I'm really not the black widow the press makes me out to be. Quentin was a brilliant businessman but he was a sorry husband . . . he was unfaithful. He had a little floozy stashed away in every metro on every planet that his business sent him. It wasn't so much Quentin's dalliances that bothered me . . . powerful men are restless, you know. But he became violently jealous when *I* decided to fool around. I got tired of the one-way street so I put an end to it. It was self-defense. You believe me don't you, Mr. Sam?"

Sam was chilled by this woman's nonchalant attitude about murder. "Not for me to say." He tugged on the fabric of his tunic. "This is not a judge's robe."

She shrugged. "Anyway, I'm out on bail, and I've spent a great deal of time looking for you. You are a hard man to locate, Mr. Sam."

Sam's mind staggered at the amount of bail it must have required to set this woman free. He tried to remember what the news reports had quoted—a million? A million-and-a-half? "I'm afraid I don't have the luxury of staying in one place too long. Nor can I buy my way out of trouble the way you can, Ms. Hughes."

"It's *Randolph*! Ms. Sally Randolph," she said, perturbed. "Sally Hughes died along with my husband."

Sam's finely-tuned sense of suspicion gnawed at him.

48

Something about this wasn't right. "I didn't know the authorities let cold-blooded killers run around loose before the trial," he said, testing her.

Sally Randolph didn't even flinch. "I'm *not* out running around loose. My bail-bond deputy is waiting for me on the street, just around the corner."

"And he lets you do as you please?"

"Not hardly. The poor dear is very dedicated to his job, which I find positively gauche. Follows me around like a shadow. But he's young and cute and . . . ooh what buns! When he gets testy I give him a little sugar and he lets the leash out a little. Hot blooded young men like Robert can learn a great deal from experienced women like me. Know what I mean, Mr. Sam?" She winked at him lasciviously.

"Uh . . . yes, I believe I do," he said, handing the rich widow her identification. "And you want me to concoct a hologram of yourself so you can break free of his leash once and for all, is that the plan?"

She nodded. "Yes. You see, I don't have a prayer of acquittal since there were several eyewitnesses to the murder. Also, things look depressingly bad for me since I am the major beneficiary on Quentin's numerous insurance policies. They're going to throw the book at me, Mr. Sam, and I'm scared. *Really* scared. The thought of a women's prison turns my stomach—even the minimum security places where the rich and privileged serve their time. The things that go on in those places would destroy me. I also have no desire to sit through a lengthy trial, having my private life brought before the public like so much tabloid fodder. I'd prefer to have my hologram suffer through the trial and do the time."

This is no empty-headed rich bitch, Sam thought, proceeding with caution. "Surely you know my fees for this

49

type of procedure are enormous."

"I'm prepared to pay you two million for your efforts. This would be doled out over three payments—five hundred thousand today, another half-million when you deliver an acceptable hologram, then the final million once my holo- gram makes it through the trial and is incarcerated. I'm not talking credits, I'm talking cold, hard Federation dollars. I've heard that your work holds up well under close scrutiny, Mr. Sam, and fortunately I am able to pay top dollar. Is this arrangement acceptable?"

Sam nearly choked. He nodded and tried to speak, but thoughts of set-for-life wealth paralyzed his tongue.

Sally Randolph prodded him. "You just give me a verbal agreement to do the work and I'll produce the currency."

He watched her carefully. "Okay then," he said finally. "I agree to create a tactile-sensory motion hologram of you, Ms. Randolph—your stand-in, if you will. And I give you my personal guarantee that it'll be real enough to fool the public. Even your lawyers won't know the difference."

"Splendid," she said, smiling. "You just stay here for a few minutes while I go get the money."

She turned and flounced down the dark alley. Sam watched her as she walked in that high-society kind of *swish-swish* strut. He could hear her heels clicking against the hard pavement. This was one brassy babe.

Two million in cash!

Not knowing with what or whom she would return, Sam got his tri-barreled laser-stun from the van and waited. He didn't have to wait long; she returned within five minutes. But she was not alone.

"There is no need for a weapon, Mr. Sam," she said, leading a tall, muscular man who was toting a large briefcase.

"One cannot be too careful in today's worlds, Ms. Randolph." He pointed the laser-stun at the man. "Is this your bail-bond deputy?"

Sally Randolph introduced Deputy Robert Trask to Sam. The two men eyed each other, sizing each other up like gamecocks before the big cockfight. The air was thick with tension.

"Show me the money," Sam said, getting impatient.

The young deputy set the briefcase down on the pavement and unlocked the hinges. He opened the lid and Sam stared down incredulously at what looked to be genuine Federation currency.

Sam flung open the back doors of the van to throw more light on his newfound fortune. Stacks of neatly bundled twenties and fifties gleamed crisply with the reproductions of galaxy planets—the four major and ten minor—and the serial numbers looked authentic. He picked up a packet and fanned through the bills. They had the right weight and feel. He brought the packet to his nose and sniffed it. The bills had the slight oily smell indigenous to used paper currency.

Sally Randolph spoke to Robert. "You can go now, love. Wait for me out on the street. I'll be with you soon."

Dutifully, bail-bond deputy Robert Trask shuffled off, leaving the holo-artist and the widow alone.

"I think you'll find that everything checks out," Sally Randolph said. "All non-consecutively numbered bills, approximately two to four years old, withdrawn from eighteen accounts at seven financial institutions on four different worlds. In other words, this currency is completely untraceable. Now let's get to work. I'm an impatient woman and we don't have much time until the trial."

51

"Not so fast," Sam muttered as he continued checking through each stack of bills in the briefcase, making sure it was all there and that there were no counterfeits or padding underneath. "What's the deal with this Robert guy? I mean, he brings enough cash to rival the GNP of most off-world nations down a dark alley so that you—a murder suspect whom he's supposed to be watching—can make some kind of a deal. Why does he waste his time watching you? You could just buy him off, or even better, he could have just taken off with your money. Something smells really rotten here, lady, and I don't mean the stench in this alley."

"I admire your precautionary logic—"

Sam cut her off. "I haven't survived this long by taking stupid risks. Now why don't you come clean with me."

"Okay, The fact is Robert doesn't need my money. The Department of Justice makes sure they hire wealthy individuals for their bail-bond deputy positions. Keeps the temptation factor down."

"So what keeps them working then?"

"Applicants for those positions are carefully screened and checked out. They all have obsessions other than money. Power, control, religion, sex . . . sometimes hard-to-find drugs. The courts keep these people supplied with what they want. That way there's very little turnover and no temptation."

Sam finished inspecting the cash. He closed up the briefcase and locked the latches, put it into a safe in the back of the hover-van. "And this Robert character . . . his thing is sex, right?"

"Very perceptive, Mr. Sam. The poor young man has taken quite a shine to me. It's quite obvious he's never been with a woman of the world like me before. I introduced him to the joys of Kama Sutra games. Robert just *loves* Kama

Sutra games. He may be holding the leash, but I'm the one leading him around."

"And what does he think our little transaction is all about?"

"He thinks you're an investment broker. I'm meeting you to appropriate my liquid funds before I trudge off to prison."

"An investment broker working out of a hover-van in a dark alley?"

"I told him you deal exclusively in illegitimate ventures . . . electronic funds fraud, dummy corporations, money laundering . . . that kind of activity. I think he liked it."

"He believed that?"

"Robert's never had to think much. He really doesn't care what I do as long as he can keep an eye on me until the trial. And as long as I play Kama Sutra games with him!"

Sam studied her in the dim light. Sally Randolph's gaze was steadfast. Though the whole thing was ludicrous, she seemed sincere.

And two million in cash was well worth a risk.

"Okay. Let's get going," he said finally.

"Going? Where is it we have to go, Mr. Sam? I thought you could do the work here, out of the back of your van."

"I can only do small jobs here—mostly inanimate objects and scenic reproductions. A job like the one you're talking about requires the full use of my laboratory. To capture you just right requires complex thermal physics and chemical analysis and electromagnetics. I have to be sure that when people who know you are around your hologram, they're convinced it's really you. Your hologram has to smell just right. When somebody touches your hologram, it must have the proper mass and body heat and tactile sense. I have to reproduce your voice and mannerisms and skin tone accurately. This requires feeding massive amounts of data into my computer programs. I can't do all that out here on the street. Even in the lab we're cutting it close if we want to be ready by Monday's trial."

"Okay," she said, reluctantly. "Robert and I will follow you. He's got the transportation."

"And what's he going to do while we're creating a new you?"

Sally Randolph thought for a minute, then said, "We'll tell him we're going to your place to play some virtual reality sex games. Robert will eat that up."

Sam sighed. *The things a man must do for two million dollars.*

THEY ARRIVED AT HIS LABORATORY and went to work. Sam positioned Sally Randolph behind thick sheets of plate-glass and bombarded her with a series of laser beams, capturing her moving images on film. He had her stand in a variety of positions and move in a number of ways to capture all of her nuances and mannerisms. She whirled and pirouetted like a dancer. She posed and primped with the mannerisms of a high fashion model. She went through a full range of facial expressions, like an actress emoting in front of her dressing room mirror. She laughed and giggled the way a little girl would, playing dress-up with her mother's clothes. Sally Randolph was clearly enjoying herself.

Robert sat in a corner thumbing through skin magazines, for the moment completely disinterested in the goings-on.

"Why must I stand behind these walls of glass?" Sally

Randolph's voice was muted from behind her glassed-in cell.

Sam answered while he flipped switches, redirecting the angles of the laser beams. "I must illuminate you with coherent beams of laser light, but the beams must be split into two parts before reaching you. This special prismatic glass does that quite nicely."

"Why do the beams need to be split in two?"

"Because I need to overlap two beams of the same angle and record them on film. The first beam is the reference beam, which is a direct shot of the object. I record that shot directly on the film as is. The second is the reflected beam, or the bounce-back beam. It has a much longer arc. By overlapping the reference beams and the reflected beams on celluloid, we arrive at a foolproof, three-dimensional moving hologram. Later, we feed millions of these laser-light wave-lengths, keyed to the same frequencies, into the computer. This gives us our free-form visual profile, able to pass on-sight inspection through most any trial or prison situation likely to come up.

"You see," Sam continued, "fifty years ago we needed some type of flat surface to project these images on, but Stanley Dumars changed all that with his breakthrough in portable tele-imaging . . ."

"Hey, when does the virtual reality sex begin?" a very bored Robert said, watching his lover cavort under the banks of flashing lights.

"Soon . . . very soon," Sam said, remembering that he had the perfect pacifier for a guy like Robert Trask. "Let's take a break, Ms. Randolph."

They broke for ten minutes while Sam set up some old holovids that he projected on the far wall. "You'll love this stuff, Robert. Nothing but hard-core orgies in all their three-dimensional glory. They're old and a little grainy, but they're a major improvement over magazines."

Robert's bored expression turned to one of awe and respect. He was set for the next few hours.

When Sam returned to work Sally Randolph was full of questions. "What about the remaining senses? My touch? My scent? My voice? What about my *mind*? How are you going to make me talk and respond to questioning? The most perfect visual imaging won't stand up if everything else isn't fully developed."

"First, we'll do a complete mind-scan to collect your memories and thinking processes. Then we'll tape voice prints of words and phrases that contain all possible speech combinations. We'll also record a variety of your favorite sayings, any slang you might use on a regular basis . . . voice inflections those who know you would expect to hear. Then we synchronize all of these phonetics with the physical mouth and head movements to get speech that would fool all but a sophisticated computer or expert speech pathologist. Your hologram will be able to communicate in give-and-take conversations by a voice recognition chip that triggers the speech programs residing in the computer. It'll know through voice inflection receptors whether it is being asked questions to which a response is needed, or just listening to statements.

"The tactile senses, body heat, and physical mass are far too complex to sum up in a matter of sentences, but suffice it to say it involves thermal physics and electromagnetics. In short, we make good use of natural gravity and drawing heat off of nearby objects. Using these processes we can even come close to simulating your skin texture. Your body scents are the easiest to reproduce. We scan you with an olfactory analysis wand to get a complete chemical makeup,

56

analyzing those chemicals that produce odors—phero-
mones, amino acids, dietetic proteins, perspiration content—we even factor in your favorite soaps and perfumes.
In all, a very time-consuming process. I hope you don't
have any immediate plans, Ms. Randolph."

Sally Randolph twirled and preened behind the glass,
the laser lights washing over her. "Be serious, darling," she
said in her pseudo-bored, high society drone. "A woman
who's going on trial for murder in a few days doesn't have a
full social calendar."

They finished up the visual scanning and Sam wired a
series of electrodes to Sally Randolph's head. The mind-
scan took several hours, and when they finished, the wealthy
widow complained of a splitting headache, which Sam
assured her was normal. When Sam told her she could lie
down and rest for a while, she declined, snorting back a
headache ampule and demanding to continue. The hours
remaining until the trial were rapidly vanishing, and she
wanted to see results.

They began recording voice patterns. Sally Randolph
recited a litany of nonsensical rhymes and proverbs that she
read from cue cards, the aural/verbal recognition programs
using the incoming data to create a working vocabulary.
During a break in the recording, while they waited on a
block of data to compile, Sam asked the widow exactly
where it was she had heard about his talents.

"Through the network," she said, filing her finely manicured nails. "You provided the holographic entertainment
for several of my dearest friends' parties on Rabolia. Both
the Creightons and Countess Victoria spoke very highly of
your work. I'm told those androgynous whores you created
were the hits of both parties. After hearing how lifelike and
exciting they were, I was sorry I had to miss those affairs.

But then, last year, I got to taste the fruits of your creations at a society ball on Gobenhaar. What an orgy that was, darling! I didn't even know those extremely well-endowed waiters were holograms until Princess Twila informed me they were your work."

Sam remembered those parties well. He had made some good money and established some top-flight connections. And he hadn't had to scam anybody, either. Since all the action had taken place in one or two rooms at each party, Sam could remain there and control his creations, bringing them to life. The word-of-mouth references from those affairs, however, had fed his sting operation a hundredfold. Now he was inundated with requests for outrageous creations—long-lasting tactile-sensory motion holograms that could move about freely and pass as humans for many months, or even years. These requests were impossible, of course, but Sam hated to pass up an opportunity to separate the rich from pieces of their wealth. He could create a realistic hologram of Sally Randolph in his lab, but there was no way it would ever make it to that courtroom and stand trial.

That's where the sting came in.

After a few hours they were done with the voice recordings and Sam prepared the olfactory analysis wand. "I'm afraid I'm going to have to ask you to remove your clothes, Ms. Randolph," he said, checking calibrations on the long crystal rod. He pointed the wand in the direction of a dressing area off to the right. "You can change into a paper gown in there if you feel intimidated."

"Nonsense, darling," she said, quickly stripping out of her fancy designer threads without a hint of inhibition.

Robert looked on with increasing interest. "Are the sex games about to start?"

"Not yet, Robert," Sally Randolph said sharply. "If you

have a problem with this, then go in the other room."

Robert refused. "I thought we came here to play sex games," he whined. "I wanna either play some Kama Sutra or link into a virtual reality hooker!" Demanding and insolent, like a little kid.

Sam got him fixed up with the VR headgear and gloves, and Robert spent the next few hours moaning and groaning in the corner while Sam got on with the chemical analysis of the widow's scent spectrum. Twelve hours after they had arrived at the laboratory, Sam was convinced he had all the data he needed to begin construction of Sally Randolph Hughes's tactile-sensory motion hologram.

"You and Robert might want to take off for a while, maybe get something to eat while I build your twin," he said to a very tired-looking Sally Randolph.

She clucked her tongue at him, shaming him. "I didn't get to be a multi-millionaire by being a fool, Mr. Sam. I've made a down payment of five hundred thousand, and we're not leaving until I see something for my money. Besides, I want to watch a master artist at work."

"Okay," Sam said. "Suit yourself. This could take me another six to ten hours. Aren't you getting hungry?"

"Very."

"I'm starving, too," Robert said. "Why don't I call out for some home-delivery Mundavian."

All three agreed that was a great idea.

Sam settled in behind his bank of computers and walls of video monitors, Sally Randolph watching his every move with interest. By the time the food came, Sam had constructed her feet and lower legs. While they munched on fried chispin and biddletips, Sam added her thighs and hips. He was focused, engrossed in the task at hand, piecing together the wealthy woman's holographic alter ego. It was

59

an excruciatingly slow process, the repetitive trial and error of the color shading and figure shaping enough to drive a less patient man insane. But Sam was an artist in his high-tech element, and Sally Randolph and her young lover/guardian watched in curious fascination as he barked verbal commands into the voice-activated system, twisted knobs, and scrawled designs with his plotter.

"What exactly are you doing?" Robert asked at one point.

"I'm designing you the most incredible virtual reality lover you've ever had, my man."

Gradually, the tactile-sensory motion hologram of Sally Randolph took shape. Finally, after hours of displaying bits and pieces of her holographic anatomy, Sam looked up and said "Okay, here we go," and commanded the system to assemble his creation. A slight buzzing sound filled the lab as the full-formed hologram wavered into view—shakily at first—then solidified into three-dimensional shape. Sally Randolph and Robert stood transfixed, mouths open, eyeing the second-coming of the wealthy widow with a sense of amazed wonder.

Robert muttered, "But that's . . . that's Sally!"

Sam looked back at the hologram and pursed his lips, not satisfied. "The image is too jittery," he said.

Robert shook his head as though he couldn't detect the problem.

"The flesh tones are a little off, too. Give me a minute while I correct the tracking and soften the skin color a bit."

It took the holo-artist a few minutes to make the necessary adjustments. "Okay," he muttered. "Now for the big test." He turned to Robert. "Go over and give her a hug and a kiss."

"Are you serious?"

"Go on," Sam urged. "She's waiting."

Reluctantly, Robert walked toward the hologram, and pulled up short when it spoke to him.

"Come on, Robby-boo, I don't have all day," it said in a perfect recreation of Sally Randolph's demanding whisper.

"I don't know if I like this," Robert said.

"Don't be ridiculous," Sam said. "Give it a chance . . . You'll love it."

Robert awkwardly reached out and put his arms around the hologram's waist, bent forward and gave it a kiss. A look of distress crossed his face as the hologram slipped its tongue into his mouth. But the shock passed quickly as Robert threw himself into the heat of the moment, bringing his hands up to its breasts and squeezing them.

"Owwww! Not so hard!" the hologram shrieked, stepping back from him. "You'll bruise the merchandise, darling."

Robert was not to be put off. He moved in for more. "God, she smells great! And she feels so . . . lifelike," he said dreamily, reaching up under its skirt. "She even kisses like you, Sal."

The hologram kneed Robert in the balls, and the big man dropped to the floor in a pained, embarrassed heap. "What do you take me for?" it said, standing over him. "A slut?"

Sally Randolph emitted a hoarse laugh from behind him. "Yeah, let's cool those gonads, lover boy!"

Sam smiled and stood. "So now that I've delivered my end of the bargain, how about the second installment that's due me?"

"Not so fast, Mr. Sam." Sally Randolph pointed at her holographic twin. "It *is* quite the impressive facade, but I'm not completely convinced."

61

Sam glanced down at Robert, who was still doubled over in pain. "I believe Robert can vouch for its authenticity."

She approached the hologram and ran her hand through the silver-streaked, wavy brunette hair, then pulled it back from the neck and saw the two moles beneath the left ear. She saw the pupil of the right eye that was slightly smaller than the left, and the aristocratic nose that turned up a little at the tip. She put her fingers on the full lips and separated them, saw the large pearly teeth, the chip in the upper right eye tooth, and the expensive bridgework along the back. The subtle lines that streaked her own forehead and framed her mouth were even etched realistically. Her index finger traced a rim around the small cleft in the narrow chin, then slid down the long, willowy neck and rested on graceful shoulders. The hologram didn't flinch or twitch a muscle. It just stood there, subservient, hands at its sides, eyes watching intently as Sally Randolph ran her hands down the front of its blouse, giving off a soft gasp as she slowly brushed past its breasts. Her hands traversed the slim waist, flaring out as she fondled the perfectly proportioned hips and buttocks that resulted from many rounds of plastigenetic surgery. She took its hands in her own and examined the perfectly manicured crimson nails.

"Do I pass inspection, Ms. Randolph?" her own voice asked from her mirror image.

She grasped the hologram's hands tightly in her own and gazed straight into its eyes. "What will you plead on Monday when you take the stand?"

"That I killed Quentin Hughes in self defense, of course. Just like the attorneys have instructed me."

"Good. *Very* good. Now when and where was I born?"

"2053 at the Randolph Plantation . . . Quigley Province

on Gobenhaar."

"Fantastic! And who is that sex maniac lying on the floor?"

"That's Robert J. Trask, my bail-bond deputy and current bedmate."

"Beautiful . . . I think you'll do quite nicely, darling." Sally Randolph turned to Sam, who was beaming like a proud new father. "You've done an incredible piece of work here, Mr. Sam. It's eerie just how perfectly you've recreated me. My look, my voice, my scent, my . . . *essence!* You've even got my sweaty palms just right. You're every bit as good as your lofty reputation."

"I knew you'd be pleased. Now how about that second payment?"

"Sure." She looked at Robert, who was just getting to his feet. "Are you capable of going to fetch Mr. Sam's money, Robert dear?"

Robert blushed with embarrassment. "Of *course* I am," he grumbled, hunched over and rubbing at his groin area. "But I'm not going anywhere without you."

"Well then, let's not keep the man waiting. Mr. Sam has earned his commission."

Robert got to his feet. "I thought you said this Sam dude was an investment broker, Sal . . . that he worked with wire fraud and other shady dealings."

"You're right, I did say that."

Bewilderment washed over Robert's haggard face. "Then how come we didn't see any of that going on here? Why are you paying him all this money?"

"My dearest Robert. What Mr. Sam does here is far more shady than mere wire fraud. He creates duplicates of humans. You can't get much shadier than that. In case you've forgotten, there are stiff prison sentences for such activity. Now come on, let's go get the man his money. He's earned it."

Sally Randolph headed for the door. Robert shook his head in confusion, following close on her heels.

"Hey, not that I don't trust you," Sam yelled behind them, "but I'm coming with you."

They went down to the street together, to where Robert had docked his hover-car. The trio returned a few minutes later with another briefcase that looked identical to the one containing the first payment—the one safely tucked in Sam's safe.

"Here it is," Robert said, unlocking the briefcase and setting it on the table in front of Sam. "Another five hundred thousand in untraceable bills."

Sam went through the same process as before, counting and checking each bill to be sure the payment was all there and that it was legitimate currency. Sally Randolph's hologram looked on in mute disinterest while the real widow and her lover shuffled restlessly, trying to hurry him up. But Sam was not to be rushed. He had nothing but time.

"It's all there, Mr. Sam," Sally Randolph said impatiently. "Now show us how to control my hologram. You said there was some kind of remote control pad or something, didn't you?"

Sam finished counting and, satisfied that everything was on the up-and-up, placed the briefcase in the safe on top of the other briefcase. He then presented the widow with a small remote control device. "This works primarily as an on-off switch. The green button activates your hologram, the red button makes it vanish. When you're ready for the permanent switch, you break through this little seal, and presto! You're free. Your body double takes over."

Sally Randolph held the device in her hand and admired

it with the reverence one might bestow on the Holy Grail. The little remote and the tactile-sensory motion hologram standing nearby were her tickets to freedom.

Suddenly, the front door buzzer sounded, making everyone jump.

"Who the hell could that be?" Sam said, commanding the hologram to go answer it.

Three red-suited Federation policemen rushed into the lab, brushing the hologram rudely aside.

"This is a bust!" the captain snarled. "Everyone freeze!"

The two cops in back trained huge laser bazookas on them while the captain showed them a warrant.

"Ah! We're just in time, I see," he said, spying two of Sally Randolph. "I'm sure everyone here is aware of the laws against creating motion holograms of living people. You're all under arrest for felonious commerce."

"But this is my twin sister from Arasmus," Sally Randolph protested.

"*Sure* it is, lady," he said gruffly. "Now everybody produce some identification . . . NOW!"

The real Sally Randolph's face had gone ashen. Sam watched as she fumbled through her purse for proof of her existence. A Federation offense while she was out on bail for murder about sealed her fate. Robert didn't look much better. This would certainly mean his job with the Justice Department and all its perks. For Sam this was but a minor inconvenience. He had been through this quite a few times before, and he wasn't too worried about the outcome.

Robert and Sam handed over their identification, the information of which one of the cops fed into the Intergalactic Crime Network System, checking for previous raps.

"My, my, my!" the captain said, shaking his head. "If it isn't the Black Widow. Once a bad girl, always one, eh?

65

You just can't seem to keep your snooty nose out of trouble, can you, Ms. Hughes?"

"It's *Randolph!*" she said adamantly. "Sally Randolph."

"Whatever. And what about your twin sister from Arasmus?"

"Uh . . ."

"That's what I thought." The captain turned to his backups. "Read 'em their rights, then cage 'em in force-fields and let's run 'em in."

One of the cops knocked the remote control from a stunned Sally Randolph's hand and the invisible force-field cage closed around her, locking her in. The other cop began reciting their rights.

The captain turned to Sam. "I'm getting tired of running *you* in. Don't you ever learn anything?"

Sam smirked. "I've learned plenty from our little get-togethers."

"Why don't you stick with legitimate artwork then?"

"Why? So I can live in near starvation like you cops do?"

That one stung. The captain slapped the force-field cage around Sam so fast it literally made him dizzy.

Soon, the Federation Police led the four caged partners-in-crime from the laboratory. Sally Randolph tried her damnedest to bribe the captain with a major payoff, but Sam knew it was useless. Sam knew this was one cop who was immune to the temptations of hard currency.

THE LABORATORY WAS SILENT.

After a short while, a man in his mid-fifties emerged from one of the back rooms and began to pick up the greasy refuse from the Mundavian takeout feast. He spotted the remote device for Sally Randolph's hologram on the floor and he bent to pick it up. He took it over to the huge console where Hologram Sam had performed his illusionary magic, and sat down.

They'll be just about out of range now, he thought, and he pressed the red button on the remote, making Sally Randolph's hologram vanish somewhere several klicks away.

He barked three commands into the system, eliminating the three Federation policemen in quick succession.

Then he issued one final command, which erased his own holographic alter-ego—Hologram Sam.

Marvin Newburgh, one of the most gifted holographic engineers in the galaxy, threw his head back and laughed uncontrollably. *This Hologram Sam scam is getting almost too easy*, he thought between fits of laughter. *Those three Federation cops I created were a lot of work, but they've paid huge dividends.*

And this is my biggest payoff yet!

Marvin could just imagine the startled looks on Sally Randolph's and Robert Trask's faces when the three cops detaining them vanished into thin air, disappearing along with Hologram Sam and Ms. Randolph's own hologram. His only regret was that he couldn't witness that final part of the sting.

He licked his lips, thinking of the million in hard cash he had just earned. All for only eighteen hours of work.

He went to his safe and enunciated the combination clearly. The heavy door swung open.

Marvin pulled out the two briefcases and took them to his work table.

He flipped open the latches and was aghast at what he

saw.

He knew immediately what was happening, and his jubilant mood quickly soured. "NO!" he screamed as he watched the stacks of bills flicker and waver like broken images on a defective monitor screen. He reached into one briefcase, trying to save some of his booty, but what was left of the bills crackled like dead autumn leaves, then disappeared altogether.

He had been foiled by a perfectly crafted tactile-sensory hologram.

Marvin Newburgh, known in intergalactic crime circles as Hologram Sam the Flim Flam Man, had been beaten at his own game. He stared down at the now-empty briefcases and wondered who had created such a remarkable illusion. His practiced eyes and hands had told him the currency was real.

The con game was getting almost as competitive as the art world. Marvin smiled, appreciating the genius behind the return scam.

Easy come—easy go he thought while contemplating his lost fortune.

Sally Randolph Hughes would be going to prison and would serve the time herself, the way it should be. Marvin detested murderers.

But he felt sure he would see Robert J. Trask again. *Guys like him think with their peckers,* he reasoned. *While his high society lover is serving time behind bars, he could still be making love to her somewhere more convenient. He knows Hologram Sam has Sally Randolph's identical twin stashed away here in these banks of computers. After all, he seemed quite taken with my creation. But he'll pay through the nose for it—oh yes he will! And this time I may insist on credit transferred through some off-world finan-*

cial institution that specializes in laundering and creative investment schemes. It's a little difficult to conjure up holographic magic with that type of payment plan.

Marvin Newburgh leaned back and yawned. It had been too long since his last shuteye. After a few minutes he got up and walked back to his bedroom. Though he was exhausted, he found the strength to set his alarm.

He didn't want to sleep too long. The galaxy was swarming with an infinite number of potential marks. In fact, he was sure there were quite a few suckers searching for Hologram Sam at this very minute.

He sighed wearily. A con artist's work was never done.

Being primarily a novelist and feeling infinitely more comfortable writing lengthy fiction, one of the more difficult tasks for me is writing effective and entertaining short-shorts. I find it tough to pack much plot and/or character development into the short ones. This next tale is the shortest piece I have done, and ironically, was accepted by the first magazine to which I sent it. "Sin and Salvation" first appeared in the premier issue of THE END in '93. This one is for all of you who like your horror rough and nasty. It deals with a society in which church and state govern moral issues in a decidedly heavyhanded fashion. Here's hoping "Sin and Salvation" will grab you by the throat . . .

SIN AND

SALVATION

THEY LED ME THROUGH A CAVERNOUS BARN, my nose assaulted by the stench of rotting hay and decomposing corpses. A shotgun dug into my back, the cold twin barrels pushing me along. No chance of making a run for it, not with manacles pinching my wrists and chains clinking around my ankles.

High in the rafters, along either side of me, hung hundreds of bodies, swinging from the end of thick ropes in the fetid breeze like bloated, fleshy pendulums. The ropes groaned and rasped against the gnarled wooden beams, protesting the weight of their burdens. I gagged, knowing a similar fate awaited me, but I managed to hold back the bile.

One of them spoke, his voice harsh and hateful. "You know you're gonna die, sinner . . . and you'll take all your atrocious evils with you!"

I chanced a look at the speaker, who was garbed in the maroon cloak and hood of a guard. Across his chest was emblazoned a bloody crescent moon cradled in a noose— the logo of the terroristic Rightists. Fear spread through me like a quick-infecting virus.

A bloodcurdling scream pierced the heavy air, startling me. "What was that?" I dared ask.

A guard snorted behind me. "A heathen homosexual separated from the tool of his sins," he said arrogantly. "Be thankful your crimes warrant only a hanging."

Thankful? I shuddered. *How is it that the world has come to this?*

I trudged through the gauntlet of swinging corpses in a disbelieving stupor. Each victim stared at me through milky, lifeless eyes. Their necks were crooked and scarred, their stiff bodies disjointed like marionettes hanging in a closet. Flies buzzed excitedly around them, darting in and out of noses, ears, and open mouths in unsettling necrophagic flight-dances.

The guards directed me to a large plywood platform, over which was constructed a crude gallows tree. A man stood beneath the crosspiece with a noose tightened around his neck. Terror and hopelessness dominated a face that had seen too much . . . a youthful face etched by thick lines of despair.

The executioner released the pulley and the trap door sprung.

71

The man plunged through the scaffolding, jerking violently as the rope went rigid. He gagged and gasped, eyes bulging in horror as he fought for air. His feet kicked and his arms went to his constricted throat, trying in vain to loosen the noose. Quickly, his arms fell to his sides and his body twitched spasmodically.

And then he was dead.

This is madness! my mind screamed. I fell to my knees and vomited my disgust.

"Whatsamatter, sinner?" the guard to my right said. "You see your life flash in front of you?"

I watched as couriers cut down the victim and dragged him off to be strung up with the other so-called sinners.

The executioner smoothed his ceremonial robe and opened the Doctrine—the voluminous, blood-red tome that served as the Rightist Bible. "Bring forth the next sinner," he boomed.

The guards pushed me up the rickety steps as my shaky legs and infuriated will refused to cooperate.

"What has this sinner been convicted of?"

The lead guard propped his shotgun against the gallows tree and put his right hand on the Doctrine. His voice was muffled through the hood. "Father, I swear on the holy book that this man has violated several of our most sacred principles."

"Such as?"

"Cohabitation without proof of a marriage contract, failure to tithe thirty percent of his income to the Rightist cause, and possession of pornographic materials."

"And what is the nature of these pornographic materials?"

"Father, we found materials of the most offensive nature in the convicted's home—tapes and picture books depicting lewd sexual couplings . . . horror magazines which glorify despicable acts, and science fiction novels that question our origins. We have dispensed with these vile and amoral objects in appropriate fashion."

Memories of Rightist guards dragging my lovely Susan out of our house by her hair and torching my humble bungalow were as fresh in my mind as the bitter smoky scent of their destruction. "Father," I spat venomously and without respect, "in my book I have committed no crimes. Release me this instant."

The executioner glared at me with naked hatred. "Your book is not the *good* book, sinner! Not only have you violated the sanctity of the Doctrine, you have questioned my authority." He waved to the guards. "Prepare to hang this blasphemous fool!"

Roughly, they positioned me under the gallows tree and lowered the noose. My bowels loosened as I felt the coarse rope dig into my neck. Sweat trickled down the small of my back. *What a wasteful, insane way to die,* I thought, my mind racing to keep pace with my galloping heart. I tried to envision what death would be like, but couldn't.

From up here on the scaffolding, I could see a glorious orange sliver of moon through the hayloft doors. Its brilliance beckoned me . . . a guiding light on a nightscape of demented darkness. I whispered a prayer to it—for me, for my beloved Susan, for all the others so harshly judged and humiliated and strung up in death barns such as this.

And then, the trapdoor snapped open beneath me and the moon turned crimson.

Intense, buzzing pain shot through my spine like a scorching electric current.

I panicked, struggled for air, tried to move my useless limbs.

My brain went black.

I dangled from the gallows . . . a dead vine on an evil tree.

Soon, I floated out through the hayloft doors and became one with the moon.

I gazed upon the carnage scattered throughout the barn below me, watching as the couriers cut my body down and dragged it away. A peaceful calm swept over me, intense and surreal.

A thought of profound worldliness invaded my celestial mind: I had lost this battle but had won the war.

I had finally escaped from Hell.

Sweet, sweet salvation.

On my 40th birthday, I began to write the following tale. On that day, I found myself making assessments of my life, as most of us do on the big birthdays . . . Where have I been? Where am I going? What have I accomplished? To ease the anguish, I dreamed up a character who had failed miserably in life, a protagonist who had also just hit the big forty and had yet to get his act together. After a few weeks of writing, I came up with "Wombstone," a piece that began as a character sketch and ended up a dysfunctional family supernatural horror tale garnished with snippets of black humor. Compared to Phil Cales, my life is orderly and hugely successful. Compared to Mr. Cales, my life is a joy-filled carnival. "Wombstone" was great therapy, getting me through one of the more mind-blowing milestones of my life. It also got me a sale shortly thereafter, as it appeared in the second issue of THE END in late '93.

WOMBSTONE

PHIL PLACED THE BOUQUET OF roses at the base of the headstone. His fingers traced the engraved inscription lovingly.

HERE RESTS AMANDA BRYSON CALES
B — 1913   D — 1953

Hell of a way to spend your 40th birthday, he thought, kneeling and beginning a silent prayer. *Depressing enough to turn 40, let alone trek out here to Whispering Oaks to stir up old demons.*

Since he'd been old enough to contemplate the enormity of it all, Phil Cales had been visiting his mother's gravesite every year on his birthday. Why? He had asked himself that question nearly every day since his first visit as a hormone-crazed, wide-eyed teen. He wanted to think it was a mourning of lost love. But how could you love a mother you never really knew, a mother whose breast you had never suckled? How could you have feelings for a mother who had never changed your diapers or wiped your nose or bandaged your scrapes? Oh, Phil had seen many photos of Amanda, as well as a handful of her flickery images on grainy 8mm films that he'd had converted to videotape. In his lower moments, he would go through a twelve-pack of Beck's Dark, the photo albums spread out on his living room floor and the tapes rolling through his VCR, his youthful mother starring in ten-hour marathons while he watched in a drunken depression. After years of torturing himself, Phil came to the conclusion that he couldn't love a mother who existed only in Polaroid snap-shots or on celluloid. There was too much distance to it. Too frustrating, like when he used to lust after the air-brushed fantasy women in his father's men's magazines. It wasn't love that brought Phil out here to this lush green graveyard. No, it wasn't love at all that drew him to this ornate slab of marble the way migratory birds were drawn south for the winter. It was guilt, and lots of it.

When you murder your mother, you spend a lifetime in guilt hell.

Phil sat down on the damp grass and leaned back against the headstone. He took a deep breath, the spring-time aroma of newborn pollen and perfumed honeysuckle filling his head. Life bustled all around him. Squirrels scampered across the green velvet grounds. A pair of robins frolicked in a graveside puddle. Birds chirped beautiful melodies from distant treetops. Insects buzzed and clicked in a rhythmic cacophony. The irony of it struck Phil every time he made this sad sojourn: Mother Nature celebrating rebirth while he revisited his own mother's death.

He spoke, a litany to his long-dead mother that had remained pretty much the same all these long years. "I never meant to kill you, Mama . . . surely you know that. How could I have possibly known what I was doing? I sit at home and watch those silent films Papa took of you and I cry until my tear ducts're all dried up." Phil sighed and closed his eyes, rested his head against the gravestone.

"I've got every frame of those old home movies committed to memory, at least the ones you're in. In quite a few of them you take that long cigarette holder out of your mouth and point it at the camera, mouthing words I so desperately want to hear. Wherever you are right now, I'll bet you've got that black-lacquer cigarette holder clenched between those pearly whites. Before Papa ran off to parts unknown, he told me they buried you with it, that you had requested it since it had been passed down from your grandmother. I'll never understand the importance of a silly cigarette holder, but then there's so much I don't understand. Every time I see you with it I think of that ad for Virginia Slims—the one with the beautiful babe in the flapper dress and the bouffant hairdo who's waving one around and the caption that reads, 'You've Come a Long Way, Baby!'" Phil's voice became choked. "That model looks so much like you, Mama. I can't stand to see that ad."

He sniffed back oncoming tears and shifted to talk of himself. "I'm forty today, Mama. How did I *ever* get to be forty? Where has it all gone? There is so much I thought I would have accomplished by now, but it just snuck up on me too fast. I've tried, lord how I've tried to make a success of myself, but everything I do seems to end up in failure. There was that T-shirt company Petey Griggans and I started up just out of high school. Bad time to try mail order with shopping malls popping up all over the country, selling the same designs for a whole lot less. Next was commercial printing, working as a crummy press operator for Janson Litho. Five years of my life wasted in that ink-stained hellhole. Of course you remember my disastrous stint in construction. That ended when I fell off the roof of a house we were shingling. Got me a severe concussion and damn near killed myself. Wasn't a day that went by when I was laying in that hospital bed that I didn't wish for God to just take me . . . bring me closer to you, Mama. But of course, that wasn't meant to be. Then I tried driving for a courier service, but that didn't last long, either. I totaled three Post Haste Courier cars before I lost my license and ultimately, the job. I used to space out at intersections and traffic lights. One doctor said I was partially color blind . . . another said it was the lingering effects of the concussion. I think it was Papa.

"Before he left he took great pleasure in letting me know what a loser I was. He always held me responsible for your death. Of course he was right, Mama, I *did* kill you . . . I'm not denying that. It's just the *way* Papa went about laying into me all the time. When he wasn't beating me or yelling at me, he would ignore me, which was just as bad. That kind of treatment when you're a kid has a lot to do with the adult you become, Mama." Phil paused and scratched at his chin. "Yeah . . . I think it was Papa who caused me to space out at those traffic lights.

"I think things might be starting to turn around for me,

though. Yeah, I'm still workin' as a stockboy at Kroger—"
Phil chuckled, though it was a hollow laugh, "—it's really
humbling to be ten years older than the oldest floor man-
ager. But the pay is good and the hours are regular. And
Mr. Hollander likes my work. Somehow, I've managed not
to screw up too bad . . . though there was that time I left a
delivery of frozen meats out over the weekend. Mr.
Hollander reprimanded me pretty good, and they deducted
the amount of spoilage from my paycheck, but I didn't get
fired. Thank, God, too, since I was already a month behind
on my rent. But anyway, I'm getting it together now,
Mama. I'm studying for the CPA exam. I figure accounting
is the perfect field for me. I don't have to deal with people
much . . . only numbers. And how much can a person screw
up numbers?

"I guess my biggest disappointment is that I don't have
a family of my own yet. A man ought to have a family by
the time he's forty. I'd love to have a son I could take to
ball games and a daughter to spoil rotten. But I just can't
seem to interest a woman for very long. I've had a few
sorta-kinda relationships over the past couple of years. I
told you last year about Polly. She even kinda looked like
you, Mama. But she got turned off and left when I bought
her a cigarette holder and a flapper dress and one of those
pearl-bead necklaces like you used to wear. Yeah, Polly left
me real quick after that. Said I needed professional help.
Maybe it was because the pearls were fake . . . I don't
know.

"This year I joined one of those exclusive video dating
services. Cost me an arm and a leg, too. Met some nice
girls, but none of them stick with me long after I introduce
them to my 'home movies'. Even the nicest one, Valerie,
got really weird after I showed her my photo albums and

videotapes. I just don't understand it, Mama. I thought relationships were supposed to be a mutual opening of the souls, a sharing of intimate details of our lives. But every time I open up, women run for the hills . . . even faster than Papa did. Maybe my problem is that I open up to women *too* much. They all tend to freak out when I tell them I killed my own mother. You should see the looks on their faces when I tell them that."

Phil began to cry, tears streaming down his cheeks. His voice cracked and his shoulders shook as the gentle crying accelerated into wracking sobs. "I'm all alone, Mama. I'm forty years old and I have *no one!* You're the only one I can talk to, and that scares me half to death. I come here every year on this day to tell you what a success I've become, but I can't lie to you, Mama. I've never been able to lie to you because I know you can see right through it. I'm nothing but a confused, bitter loser. I don't want to be that way, believe me, but no matter what I try, I fail. I *am* a loser and I'll always *be* a loser. It's my lot in life, Mama . . . my destiny. I'm so lonely and scared and desperate. Oh, God, I'M. SO. TIRED. OF. LIVING. THIS. WAY!" he cried, banging his head against the gravestone, emphasizing each word.

A voice broke through his sobs. "Your losing days are over, son."

Phil stopped his self-pitying sobs. He shook his head, bewildered, not sure if what he heard was real. Frantically, his eyes searched the immediate area. "Papa? Is that you?"

"Do I *really* sound like your father, Philip?"

The voice, distinctly feminine, came from behind him. Phil scrambled to his feet and couldn't believe what he saw. His mother—or at least a very real apparition of her— leaned against the headstone. A soft breeze ruffled the hem of her flapper dress. A pearl necklace adorned her graceful neck, several beads sparkling in the bright sunlight. She brought the black-lacquer cigarette holder to her mouth and puffed slowly, the smoke spiraling lazily in front of her face.

"M-Mama?"

She approached him, and Phil backed off a few steps, not sure of what he was seeing. She moved in a weird, herky-jerky way, as though she had arthritic joints or something.

"Happy birthday, Philip," she said, stopping, looking him over.

Phil could smell damp earth and something like rotting leaves. An icy dread filled him. *You've Come a Long Way Baby! Oh yes, indeed.* "Mama?" His voice was as weak as his legs. "Is that really you, Mama?"

"Who else were you expecting? Your father perhaps?"

He rubbed at his eyes, trying to clear what surely was another post-concussion hallucination.

She smiled, showing straight, slightly smoke-stained teeth. "It's really me, Philip. Your father has no need to visit my grave anymore. He got hooked up with a rich showgirl in Vegas. He's been enjoying the life of sin for all these many years, though the poor dear is getting a little long of tooth now. He can't use women the way he once did."

"How . . . How d-do you know that?"

"We who live in the Beyond have a very wide perception of things."

Phil shook his head, but the image of his long-dead mother remained.

She fluffed her hair with her free hand. "You'll see what I mean soon enough, Philip dear."

"W-wh-whaddaya mean?" he said, resisting the urge to turn and run.

81

"I'll get to that," she said, taking a leisurely draw on the cigarette, then tapping the holder against the gravestone to knock off the ash. "You see, Philip, your father never wanted any children. Said they would cramp his style. Couldn't handle the responsibility. I, on the other hand, wanted children very badly. Unfortunately, I didn't become pregnant with you until I was forty. The doctors informed me of the risks involved, but my desire for a family out-weighed those risks in my mind. In the end, I sacrificed my life so that you could have one. I never held you responsible for my death, Philip. We Brysons have always been strong-minded and I have paid dearly for this strength. Conversely, your father has always been weak, running from everything that is difficult. It's a Cales family trait, I'm afraid, and I'm sorry to say you have inherited the Cales weakness rather than the Bryson strength.

"For the better part of forty years I have listened to you whine and carry on about being a loser and how unfair the world is. I have watched you pay homage to a mother you never saw alive, and while I am flattered by your dedication to my memory, I am disgusted by your refusal to get on with your own life. You are truly pathetic, Philip! You have built a shrine to me that is stuck in a 1953 time-warp. And while I do not condone the treatment your father subjected you to, there comes a time when you have to put things behind you and move on. No matter how bad they were. For forty years I've watched you squander your life . . . waste a gift for which I gave my life. I sacrificed the last half of my life for you and you have wasted it. Do you under-stand what I'm saying, Philip?"

Phil didn't like where this was heading. This specter which so resembled his mother was becoming more mean-spirited as she went on. He nodded, not really sure of any-

82

thing much at all, and began backing away from the gravesite.

She advanced on him, jabbing the cigarette holder at him to emphasize her points. "And now you will return the gift, son. Now you will give me the last half of my life that you stole from me with your birth."

Phil stumbled across a grave marker, fell to the ground. He looked up at her in sheer terror.

She was yelling at him now, smoke pouring through her mouth and nostrils as she took on the appearance of an enraged dragon. "You will die so that I may live, Philip. You will die so that I can enjoy the years I was cheated out of! You will die . . . Die . . . DIE!"

She jumped on top of him and everything went dark, as though God had extinguished the sun. He felt no physical weight come down on him, only a weird chilling sensation, like being spritzed from head to toe with a freezing mist. Phil struggled for breath as something clamped around his throat, squeezing off his windpipe. He smelled something akin to the rotting meat he'd been responsible for at the Kroger.

And then he lost consciousness.

HE AWOKE, THE SUN BLINDING, burning. His head pounded with the fury of a rampaging stampede. A quick glance to his left told him he was stretched out alongside a gravestone. His mother's?

Bits and pieces came back to him as he lay there, trying to gather the strength to move. He had experienced something strange, but what? The last thing he remembered was talking to his mother's grave. But wait . . . there was something about his mother wishing him a happy birthday. He couldn't quite piece it all together. His mind had a habit of going on the fritz since his fall. Had he blacked out again? The only thing he was sure of was that he felt an enormous change deep within himself. He felt *different*. It was hard to explain, but he felt infused with a new courage he had never before known.

This new courage prompted him to sit up. God how he ached! Especially around the groin area. But for some reason, the pain down there did not surprise him. It was as though he expected it.

He stood, moving as though someone else was controlling his body. He spied a lit cigarette in a black-lacquer holder on top of the headstone. He picked it up and placed the lipstick-stained stem in his mouth, took a long, deep drag. Exhaling, he felt the burdens of a thousand lifetimes lifting away from him. The guilt that had haunted him for so long was finally gone.

And then he saw the inscription on the headstone:

HERE RESTS PHILIP J. CALES
B — 1953   D — 1993

He reached over, traced the engraved words with his finger and whispered, "Goodbye, dearest son. I will miss you."

Alien abductions have been a fascination of mine for years. Contrary to popular belief, I cannot claim to have had any close encounters, but I do believe they are out there, monitoring humanity, shaking their heads in puzzlement, laughing their asses off (do aliens really have asses?) at the strange foibles of our species. There is just too much evidence to ignore. The following novella, "Rendezvous at Waldrop Manor," is the story of a most bizarre alien abduction. Though the tale is fiction, I have based the characters and situations on several true-life case studies, incorporating years of research to give the story a sense of contemporary realism. This is one of my personal favorites, as it blends elements of speculative fiction that appeal to me: science fiction, dark fantasy, horror, action and introspection, in-depth character development. I shall delay no longer . . . the aliens don't like to be kept waiting . . .

RENDEZVOUS AT
WALDROP MANOR

"ARE YOU NERVOUS?"

Rita Davies cast an irritated glance at the burly man behind the wheel. "I kept it together when I interviewed Jesse Jackson," she snapped. "Jimmy Carter was a breeze. My Julia Roberts segment went without a hitch, even though she was an hour-and-a-half late. I got high marks for my Ted Turner special, and he's made quite a few women correspondents look bad. Why should I be nervous *now*?"

Bobby Dustwood kept his eyes on the road, his pudgy hands on the wheel. He grinned. "You *are* nervous! You give yourself away when you start reciting your past successes."

Rita relaxed her thin shoulders. "Well, maybe I *am* a little on edge." She pulled her long blonde hair back over her head, out of her face. "Very few people have seen the Saucer Queen the past ten years, let alone interviewed her. I don't know, Dusty—" She gazed out the window, taking in the fragrant pine forests and climbing kudzu as the South Georgia landscape whizzed past. "I don't really know what to expect. I don't feel . . . ready."

The beefy cameraman pulled a Marlboro from his top pocket and lit up. "Let me tell you something, love." Tendrils of smoke coiled through gaps in his yellowed teeth. "You're the most *ready* person I've ever known. You've been eating, sleeping, and shitting that wacky UFO lady since you got the call. I figure by now you probably know more about her than she knows about herself."

"I don't know," Rita said doubtfully. "Laura Waldrop seems to be pretty much in touch with herself, even if she *is* out of touch with the rest of the world."

Bobby snorted. "I still say anybody who claims they were abducted by a UFO ain't in touch with much of anything. And then that bullshit about aliens kidnapping her hubby and daughter—"

"Well, they *have* been missing for ten years, Dusty. What do you think happened to them?"

"I think the goofy bitch offed them both and buried them up there in the mountains, where they were camping.

After all, her husband was some kinda big-time surgeon. She had a lot to gain from it."

"Dusty, why is it you always think the worst about people?"

"Shit, love. I've been behind a camera for going on twenty years now. The worst of folks is mostly what I've seen. You've been in this business long enough . . . you oughta understand that by now."

Rita frowned. "I mostly try to give people the benefit of the doubt."

"And that, my dear, is why you ain't got your own syndicated show. You ain't enough of a hard-nosed bitch. Too many soft spots."

Rita slinked in her seat, ran her hands down her sides. "And you'd just love to get those grubby paws of yours on these soft spots, wouldn't you?"

Bobby grumbled, took a heavy pull on his cigarette and gave her a lingering look that was naked with suggestion.

Rita snickered, made a show of smoothing down her skirt "Keep your eyes on the road, you lecherous old coot."

"*Old?* I ain't much older'n you, love."

They both laughed, free and easy. They had worked as a team the past two years and had been comfortable with each other from the beginning.

Rita watched Bobby crush out his cigarette in the ashtray and light another. "Well, I don't know that I agree with your cynical viewpoint," she said. "The authorities grilled Laura Waldrop long and hard, and she retold her story exactly the same way several times, even under deep hypnosis. Anyway, she was cleared from any notion of possible homicide. As far-fetched as her experience seems, I'm willing to go into this with an open mind."

Bobby exhaled a huge plume of smoke that mushroomed off the windshield. He shrugged his broad shoulders. "Have it your way. I made sure to tell my family and drinking buddies where I was going tonight . . . y'know, in case something happens."

Rita shook her head. "In addition to all your other shortcomings, you're also paranoid, Dusty. Nothing's going to happen to us . . . that is, nothing but an interview that just might be our ticket to the major networks in New York. I'm tired of Atlanta. Local news is starting to feel too small-time, too confining. I want bigger horizons. Don't you? You've been playing this game longer than I have."

"You're too ambitious for your own good, Rita. No offense, but I still don't know how *you* got this exclusive. The big boys—Brokaw and Rather and Jennings—they ain't been able to pin down this crazy bitch."

"That's because they don't need to. They have little to gain and everything to lose. They'd be crazy to touch anything that smacks of tabloid."

"Well, I hear she's turned down all the big talk shows, too. Most recently, Geraldo. And if he ain't tabloid, nobody is."

Rita grimaced. "Who in their right mind *wouldn't* turn down Geraldo! And thanks so much for reminding me of my lowly status in this business, buster." She rapped him playfully on the arm. "You're such a jerk sometimes."

Another wide grin. "It's my job to keep that pretty little head of yours from swelling up like the Goodyear blimp," Bobby drawled in that Alabama twang Rita had come to find so endearing.

"I think we're going to have to check your job description again," she said, and they shared another carefree laugh.

Bobby Dustwood (or Bobby Joe as his drinking

buddies referred to him) was a sexist good old boy, but he could work miracles behind a videocam. Rita knew she owed much of her recent success to him, with the infinite ways he made her look better on tape. He was a genius with angles and lighting, and though he could be insufferably crude at times, he usually treated her with a delicate respect.

Rita settled back in her seat. Truth be known, she, too, wondered just how she had lucked into this highly sought-after interview. She thought about the call she had received on her home answering machine last week—the one she thought was a prank. A Ralph Masterton with the prestigious William Dixon Agency wanting to arrange an interview with one of his world renowned clients. Didn't say who the client was. And Masterton's phone number *did* have a New York exchange. Her curiosity about to overwhelm her, Rita had called the agent. She remembered last Friday's conversation with a sense of shocked glee.

"Thank you for returning my call so promptly, Ms. Davies. I have a proposition for you that I'm sure you'll find impossible to refuse," Ralph Masterton had said without preamble. "One of my most famous clients has insisted on a videotaped interview with you next Thursday evening, at six."

"And who might that client be?" Rita had asked, still skeptical.

"Laura Waldrop, the fantasy artist."

"You mean the Saucer Queen? *That* Laura Waldrop?"

"Yep. One and the same." .

Rita's suspicions grew the more the man talked. She wanted to believe, but surely this could be nothing more than an elaborate prank "But why me?" she had asked. "Laura Waldrop hasn't spoken to the press since her husband—"

"I know that, Ms. Davies. But Laura has decided that now is the time, and she likes your work. She told me she thinks you're more on her wave-length than most of the national network correspondents . . ." Rita hadn't known quite how to take that. ". . . and she insists on next Thursday evening. I don't know, there's no understanding the whims of these artsy types. Off the record I'll say that my client is one bizarre individual. But who cares so long as she produces. I just make the deals and collect my cut, don't ask too many questions. So how about it? Can I tell her you'll do it?"

"I still can't believe it," Rita had balked. "*Me* getting an exclusive interview with Laura Waldrop? I mean, she's refused *Sixty Minutes* and *Entertainment Tonight*. She's said no to Barbara Walters and Jane Pauley and Connie Chung. She's turned down *everybody* . . . everybody who's anybody."

"I understand your disbelief, Ms. Davies, I really do. I wish I knew what the urgency was. But one thing's for certain—when Laura asks to see someone from the television media, it's got to be something big. This could be the scoop of your young life, darlin', so I suggest you go for it. I'm going to give you her private number. She gave me permission to do that. You call her and get directions to her place, you hear? And please . . . this number is not to be distributed. My client is bothered enough by the lunatic fringe as it is. *Comprende?*"

So Rita had called the Saucer Queen and was surprised when one of the artist's staff put her through directly. Laura Waldrop had been pleasant but brusque, giving her directions to her sprawling 210-acre estate on the fringes of the Okefenokee Swamp. Just before Rita hung up the artist had said, "Bring plenty of videotape. I'm eager to talk."

90

That's when the enormity of it all hit Rita.

This could be the break that gets me my own nationally syndicated show!

I'm ready to talk, the Saucer Queen had said!

Shortly after she had hung up the phone, Rita went into panic mode. Ever so obsessive about preparation, she had rushed to several bookstores, bought the artist's autobiography and every collection of her artwork she could find. Not stopping there, she ventured to the downtown library and looked up the newspaper reports concerning the traumatic incident that had so dramatically changed Laura Waldrop's life. Rita had devoted a majority of the past week to studying the artist and her highly unusual life.

Laura Waldrop's autobiography, *Abduction at Dawn: Confessions of the Saucer Queen,* told of the artist's young adult years as a frustrated graphic designer for an Atlanta advertising sweatshop, her happy years with her physician husband, and the birth of her daughter Corinne, in 1980. The last half of the book described her struggles in the aftermath of the strange event that occurred on a weekend camping trip in the summer of 1986. Allegedly, a gargantuan spacecraft had hovered over their tent in the North Georgia mountains, taking the three of them aboard, where they were poked and prodded and examined in great detail. When the incident was over, Laura found herself alone in a burned-out section of woods. Her husband and six-year-old daughter, the tent, and all their supplies were gone. She remembered nothing but bits and pieces of the strange medical exams. She had wandered for two aimless days through the Georgia forests before she was discovered by a pair of hikers, who led her to civilization. A doctor who examined her discovered a rude bump on the back of her neck, punctured by a two-inch incision that was lined with an unknown chemical substance.

Of course, no one believed her claim of alien abduction, no one, that is, except for the most whacked-out of the UFO and New Age cultists, and the tabloids, who had a field day with it. She promptly lost her job at the ad agency, and began living off of her meager savings. She received money from her husband's substantial insurance policy, but only after vigorous investigations that left her exhausted and questioning her own self-worth. Laura Waldrop wrote the book as a kind of catharsis, trying to understand the event that had suddenly and rudely shattered her existence. *Abduction at Dawn* was published in December of 1987, a year-and-a-half after the incident, and surprise of all surprises, it climbed onto the bestseller lists and was now in its twelfth printing.

The success of her book, the sale of her condo, and life insurance money collected on her presumed-dead husband's policy, allowed Laura Waldrop to buy substantial acreage among the Georgia pines near the Florida border. She returned to her art in a ramshackle farmhouse, painting and drawing and sculpting round the clock, attempting to forget a life that might have been. She churned out hundreds upon hundreds of pen-and-inks, watercolors, acrylics, and oils, all depicting mammoth flying saucers and exotic alien creatures. Her trademark became the small graves of her husband and daughter, some immediately visible, others well camouflaged.

Rita had ripped through the autobiography in quick order, trying to gain insight into this perplexing and complex woman. Next she studied the artist's work— elaborately detailed pieces that evoked a sense of photographic realism. Many had been used as covers for science fiction novels, rock-n-roll compact discs, and promotional

92

art for fantasy movies and videos. Laura Waldrop had churned out a monumental body of work in the ten years since the incident that had forever altered her life. The artist had not communicated verbally with the public since her book was published, but she had left her unique and indelible mark through thousands of otherworldly images and sculpted pieces. In one short decade, the once-struggling graphic designer had worked her way to several fortunes and equal billing with such fantasy artist luminaries as Frank Frazetta, Michael Whelan, and Boris Vallejo. And all the while the Saucer Queen had shunned the media.

But now she wants to see me! Rita Davies shook her head, wondering if she was worthy of the task.

Bobby turned off the interstate onto a rutted two-lane, heading west into the low-lying sun. The Georgia pines gave way to sprawling poultry farms and horse ranches. The pungent odors of grazing animals, fresh-cut hay, and cow manure wafted through the van.

Bobby interrupted her thoughts. "It ain't like you to be so quiet, love."

"Just thinking," Rita said. "I take it from your opinions about Laura Waldrop that you don't believe in flying saucers, Dusty."

"I don't know. Ain't never thought about it much. It all seems like a buncha made-up fantasy, I reckon. Makes for great movies, though. How about you?"

Rita thought about her childhood, living on various military bases throughout the Deep South and Southwest, the times she and her friends would sit transfixed, while meteors flamed across the broad night skies, burning trails through her active imagination.

"I always wanted to be an astronomer when I was a kid," she said. "*Dreamed* of being an astronaut, but Daddy

93

informed me that was a man's job and I shouldn't get my hopes up. So I set my sights on astronomy because I knew I was destined to prove that one—just *one*—of those shooting stars was actually a flying saucer from some distant galaxy filled with little green men. I was quite the dreamer back then," she said wistfully. "Still am, I guess. But I think it's pretty smug of us humans to think we're all there is."

"So you believe this Saucer Queen character then?"

"I don't know, Dusty. I want to, but . . . it's awfully hard to grasp. I mean, *something* profound happened to her out there in those woods ten years ago. Her husband and daughter are still missing without a trace, but I don't know about a UFO abduction. Even we dreamers have our limits. I know professionally that I should remain unbiased, reserve judgment until after the interview, but it's difficult in this case. One thing's for sure. The woman is a master at self-promotion. She's parlayed this quite nicely into celebrity status. But I'll tell you what's got me *really* freaked about all this, Dusty."

"What's that?"

"Tonight marks the ten-year anniversary of the alleged abduction."

"Exactly ten years ago tonight?"

Rita nodded.

"Holy shit!"

"My sentiments exactly."

They rode in silence the rest of the way.

BOBBY PULLED THE CHANNEL 2 NEWS VAN off the two-lane onto a narrow gravel road, following directions they were given. Huge oaks and maples draped with Spanish moss and creeping kudzu vines shut out much of the sunlight, creating a green canopy overhead. They rounded a bend and came to a tall wrought-iron gate with a sign overhead:

WELCOME TO WALDROP MANOR
No Appointment — No Entrance
Trespassers Will Be Prosecuted

Bobby drove the van up to the gate and stopped. A hard-looking security cop wearing mirrored sunglasses emerged from the guardhouse and walked to the driver-side window.

"State your name and purpose," he said in a strangely stilted monotone.

Bobby looked him over, trying to decide if he was for real. Finally he said, "This here is Rita Davies, correspondent for Channel Two News outta Atlanta. I'm her camera technician and jack-of-all-trades stud gigolo, Bobby Dustwood." Rita punched him in the arm. "Laura Waldrop is expecting us."

"I need two forms of picture ID from each of you."

This man certainly is lacking in the social graces, Rita thought as she dug through her purse. *Probably a necessity to keep all the kooks away from Ms. Waldrop—the 'lunatic fringe' is how the agent had referred to them.* She handed her press pass and driver's license across to Bobby.

The security guard took his time examining the IDs. Finally, he bent down to look through the window, presumably to match faces with photographs, and when he did, his sunglasses slipped down his nose. Rita felt her heart go frigid. The man's eyes were lit by strange fires—orchid-tinged laser beams that burnt through to the tender part of her soul. She shuddered and looked away.

"You're early," he said in the strangely-cadenced monotone that further unsettled Rita. "The Lady prefers people to be on time," he said matter-of-factly, though his tone bore a hint of menace. He handed back their identification.

"Did you see that guy's eyes?" Rita said after they were through the gate.

"Yeah," Bobby said, looking up in the rearview mirror. "Creepy as hell."

Rita watched the gate and guardhouse get smaller in the side mirror. "I wonder how he would've reacted if we'd been *late*."

They drove another half mile, winding through the dense foliage. Gravel pinged the underside of the van with a loud, percussive rattling. They entered a sweeping bend, then broke out into a clearing. Sunlight greeted them. Ahead of them, on top of a subtle bluff, sat Waldrop Manor.

Rita had seen some stately mansions before, but Laura Waldrop's estate pulled the breath from her lungs. An enormous structure, the mansion blended Southern Gothic and futuristic architectural styles which Rita found jarring, yet oddly captivating. Wide porticoes surrounded the house and ornate Doric columns gleamed in the early-evening sunlight. Tall mullioned windows of subtle stained glass reflected tiny rainbows. Rita counted five floors in all. The roof peaked into a huge charcoal-tinted dome, looking like the black beady eye of some gargantuan insect.

They drove up the winding driveway and parked in the circle. As she and Bobby got out and stretched their legs, they were met by a slender bald man with a protruding forehead. Rita noticed he had the same spooky orchid eyes as the security guard they had encountered earlier.

"Rita Davies and Bobby Dustwood, I presume," he said in the same awkwardly-clipped speech they had heard at the front gate.

Does Laura Waldrop's staff take lessons in weirdness? Rita wondered. "Yes, that's us," she said, studying him. A chill ran through her as he focused his eerie eyes on her. They weren't just Liz Taylor orchid eyes, but rather a kind of phosphorescent purple neon that electrocuted her senses.

"Please, gather your equipment and follow me," the odd-looking butler said without emotion.

Rita and Bobby looked at each other. Momentary doubt passed between them, then Bobby shrugged, opened the rear of the van, and gathered his equipment bags.

The nameless butler led them through a maze of corridors and up meandering staircases. The spacious hallways were crammed with original works of art: busts in window sills, framed oil paintings on the walls, life-size statuettes in the corners. Banisters on the staircases were elaborately carved marble with sculpted brass fittings. Handsome Persian rugs added splashes of color to the hardwood floors. The overall effect was tasteful, though somewhat cluttered, and made a statement about the proprietor's fussy cultural tastes. The faint scent of lemon polish hung in the air along with something else, another vague aroma that was not unpleasant, yet foreign to Rita.

Rita could hear Bobby huffing and puffing behind her, trying to keep up. She was sure this was the most exercise he had had in years. She heard a slight clicking sound and was surprised when the butler stopped at the foot of a staircase and turned around. He looked past Rita, glaring at Bobby with his frightful eyes.

"I must ask you to refrain from filming here, sir," he

said. A threat, not a request. "The Lady authorizes no photographs outside of her studio. She will be very perturbed about this."

Bobby shrugged his heavy shoulders and flicked off his videocam. The red light darkened. "Well *excuse* me, Lurch!" he muttered under his breath, but the butler was oblivious to his sarcasm. Rita did her best to suppress a laugh.

They traipsed up two more flights of stairs, coming to the top floor and Laura Waldrop's studio. The butler knocked on a set of double doors. "Your visitors are here, Madam."

From behind the massive doors came, "They're early! I *will* not have my work schedule interrupted by media people who cannot tell time. Have them wait."

Rita glanced at her watch. 5:54. Six minutes early. *This is going to be more difficult than I thought.* Her mouth was dry and her stomach rumbled.

THIRTY MINUTES LATER they were admitted to The Saucer Queen's lair. They entered Laura Waldrop's studio, both gazing around in awe. The impressive charcoal-tinted dome they had seen driving up arched overhead. The late afternoon sun illuminated the spacious room with fluttery gray ribbons of light. Works of art in various stages of progress were scattered everywhere. Oils, water colors, and pen-and-ink sketches were propped on a batallion of easels. Several shelves held drying clay busts. One long worktable held numerous wire mobile creations and ceramic figurines. The acrylic smells of paints and turpentine blended with the earthier scents of pottery clay and drying greenware to assault their nostrils. Rita figured nearly five hundred works in various stages of completion cluttered the expansive studio.

And every piece centered around an extraterrestrial theme.

The busts were of huge alien heads with wide, wraparound insectile eyes. The mobiles and ceramic pieces were of saucer-shaped spacecraft. The paintings and sketches were all variations on the alien invasion motif.

Rita looked at Bobby, surprised to see his expression of utter disbelief, a look that mirrored her own. Bobby Joe Dustwood prided himself on his jaded outlook. He liked to tell people that he had been in the news business so long that *absolutely nothing* surprised him anymore.

But this was not just *absolutely nothing*.

They had entered the hideaway of a mad genius.

The Saucer Queen certainly has earned her nickname, Rita thought, looking at several of the nearby paintings. She shuddered as she saw the twin graves in all of the paintings. The headstones read the same on each:

DAVID R. WALDROP   CORINNE A. WALDROP
B — 1943 D — 1986   B — 1980 D — 1986

Of course, Rita had seen these symbolic depictions of Laura Waldrop's loss of family in the artist's work before, but standing here facing all of these extraterrestrial works-in-progress and seeing the side-by-side tombstones had a disconcerting effect on her. Decades of research could never have prepared her for this. She began to feel the self-doubt creeping back like an obsessed stalker.

"Good evening, Ms. Davies."

Rita and Bobby looked up in tandem. Shock spread across their faces as quick as fire over oil slicks.

"Oh, don't look so surprised," Laura Waldrop said, emerging from behind a partition. "You didn't *really* expect me to look like those promo shots from all those years ago, did you?"

Rita couldn't help but stare. The artist bore scant resemblance to the photographs in her book and those snapped of her before she turned reclusive.

Laura Waldrop was gaunt, a pale skeleton of a woman. Her cheeks were hollowed out, her eyes sunken in a haunted stare. Her head was shaved, and a spiky mohawk dyed a gaudy indigo streaked over the top. At the back of her neck she had let the hair grow out into a brilliant crimson fantail, cascading down her back like a bursting supernova. She was naked from the waist up, her ribs looking as though they might burst through nearly translucent skin. Her breasts were small and shriveled, like two dried apples, and both nipples were pierced with tiny gold rings. A number of flying saucer tattoos decorated her belly and arms. The Saucer Queen would have no trouble passing for an alien herself.

The artist extended her hand and Rita took it. Her handshake was dry and limp.

"What's the matter?" Laura Waldrop said to Bobby "You've never seen a topless woman before?"

For the first time Rita could remember, Bobby was speechless. He began unpacking his indoor lighting gear, trying to keep from looking at the outrageous woman.

The artist threw her bony elbows back, stretching in a languid feline motion. The little gold rings in her nipples jingled. "I *always* work topless," she said. "Sometimes completely nude. Clothing tends to restrict me . . . strangles my muse. I need to be free and unencumbered when I create."

They didn't prepare us for this in journalism school, Rita thought. "Um, I think we might have a little problem with this, Ms. Waldrop."

"Please. Call me Laura. And why would you have a problem with my nudity? Isn't television news built on sensationalism?"

"It is . . . I mean, no . . . not really . . ." *Quit stammering like an idiot,* Rita told herself.

The Saucer Queen helped her. "What you really mean is that your employers offer *selective* sensationalism to your viewers. The news is packaged in such a way as to shock and horrify, and Mr. and Mrs. MiddleAmerica sit in front of the boob tube taking it all in like it's gospel. Doesn't matter that there isn't a shred of journalistic integrity in most of it, just so the ratings are high. But it *has* to be safe, doesn't it, Rita? There're some stories they won't report in a straightforward manner, for fear of appearing *too* sensational. Even though I routinely work in the nude, you can't show me that way, because that's a shock that might actually move Mr. and Mrs. MiddleAmerica to action. That might make them light up your switchboard with complaints, or boycott your sponsors, or worse, cause them to switch the channel.

"Your employers did their best to assassinate my character . . . to make me into some kind of cheap joke. After all these years I'm still angry about that. They treat alien abductions like they're nothing but the delusional ravings of leftwing maniacs. I came forth and told the truth after losing my husband and daughter, and the press held me up for further humiliation. I may be an eccentric artsy type, but I have always been truthful. I stopped talking to the media when I realized they weren't interested in truth."

101

Rita became indignant, but she held her temper in check. "Well then, I guess I have to ask the six-million-dollar question. If you have such a low opinion of broadcast journalism, why have you summoned us for a taped interview?"

"Because tonight I aim to prove to the entire world that I spoke the truth about my experiences ten years ago." Laura Waldrop smiled, an unsettling grin full of dark secrets. "Tonight I redeem myself and win back my honor and self-esteem."

"And just how do you aim to do that?"

"Don't you think we should be getting this on tape? This is going to be the scoop of your young career, hon."

Rita hated the patronizing tone. She looked at Bobby who was busying himself with light readings. "You about ready, Dusty?"

He nodded.

Laura Waldrop disappeared behind a partition. "I'll tell you, Rita," she said, rummaging around, "I'm in such a good mood that I'll even wear a sweater during the interview, so I don't offend your little sadsack viewers."

Five minutes later, with Laura Waldrop properly clothed, Rita's hair and makeup right, and Bobby's equipment set up, they were ready to roll the tape for the historic interview. After taping the lead-in and the introduction of the world's most reclusive artist, Rita got down to business.

"Why is it, Laura, after ten years of silence—actually eight-and-a-half since your book was published—you've decided to come forward to tell the public your story? And why me? I'm sure America would like to know why you didn't go on the talk-show circuit or why you've refused some of the big names in television."

"Don't sell yourself short, Rita. You're better than

most of the so-called big names. Most of them wouldn't be worth a crap if they couldn't read from teleprompters. Your special segments are fresh. They breathe with the essence of life. You interview from the hip and you seem to have some empathy for your subjects, a characteristic most of your contemporaries lack. Simply put, I'm a big fan of yours."

Rita hoped the makeup hid her blush. "Why, thank you, Laura. I'm flattered. But how can you possibly know much about my work? My segments only appear on Channel Two in the Atlanta area."

The artist waved a bony hand. "I know *everything* about you, sweetheart. You were a military brat. Your father is now a retired colonel and lives with your mother in Arizona. You graduated third in your class at University of Georgia, received your degree in Journalism in 1989. In 1990 you went to work for the CBS affiliate in Nashville as a stringer, but you were too bright and ambitious to remain a flunky for long. You moved into the weekend anchor slot, but quickly bored of being confined to the studio. You started doing some human interest pieces on your own time, a few of which aired and impressed some folks. In 1992 you got your chance and moved to Atlanta to take a special assignments position. My favorite piece was the one you did with Ted Turner. You did a good job keeping him under control. No woman's been able to do that, at least not until Hanoi Jane came along!"

Rita tried to sound professionally cordial. "Most of that is already public information. And I guess maybe you *could* pick up Channel Two broadcasts with a satellite dish. Or maybe a friend sends you videotapes or something."

"Not convinced?" the artist said, scratching the back of her neck. "How about I let the world in on more private things about Rita Davies? You're a natural brunette who dyes her hair blonde so that—and I quote you on this—you appear younger and more photogenic on camera, and, you will be at an advantage since most people underestimate blondes. You've been seeing your fiancé for almost three years now, a big corporate tax lawyer by the name of Thaddeus Cromwell. It seems Thad is a traditional old-liner who wants to be the sole breadwinner. He wants you to be his agreeable little housewife who stays home and takes care of domestic duty. He's jealous of your rising star and all the men who hit on you. It also occurs to me that there is a little friction between you two because he wants a brood of future legal-beagles and you wish to pursue your own career. It's a typical battle many women fight these days. But here's the shocker. I have it on good source that you're so worried about getting preggers that you use both a diaphragm and the pill."

Rita was astounded. Only Thad knew about *that*. And even their close friends thought she and Thad had the model happy relationship. "How did you—I mean, that's not true—"

"Oh, yes it is, Rita."

Rita turned and waved at the camera. "Dusty, rewind the tape and edit that part out."

Bobby laughed from behind the viewfinder. "Like hell. This is getting good."

To Rita's chagrin, the red light stayed on. "Okay, damnit," she said, trying to regain some composure, "I confess. How'd you know about *that*?"

"I told you. I know *everything* about you. You prefer the missionary position and you like to receive rather than give oral—"

"Okay, okay! Enough already." Rita shook her head, not believing this woman's vulgarity "How do you know these things?"

"Through the Network."

"What network? Surely you're not talking about the Internet."

"No, no," the Saucer Queen said impatiently. "ETIN"

"What is ETIN?"

"It stands for the Extraterrestrial Intelligence Network. It's an organization of a dozen alien races that communicate through a digitized network. I've been in touch with them for about eight years—ever since I moved down here. There are quite a few humans on the Network, also. Humans who have been abducted and examined the way I was."

Rita hoped the smirk she felt coming on wasn't evident. "And how do they communicate with you? And you with them?"

"Through a titanium chip they planted in the back of my neck. At least the casing is titanium. The chip itself contains some alien silicon-based polymers that are sophisticated transmitters and receivers. They have language translators that convert binary digits to human languages, then back to binary so alien cultures and humans can understand each other. It's all done through a compact little chip. These races are thousands of years beyond us in technology."

Laura Waldrop faced away from the camera and swept her bright red fantail of hair up off her neck. Rita saw the nasty two-inch scar perfectly centered at the base of her skull, which was swollen and infected. "At first, I wanted to have it surgically removed, but a couple of surgeons—two of the best in the States—said they wouldn't touch it for fear of doing permanent damage to my spinal cord. They said there was a ninety-five percent chance it would kill me. I didn't much like those odds, so I left the damned thing in."

"Fascinating, really. But you didn't explain it that way

in your book," Rita said, more serious now. "You wrote something about puncture wounds with traces of unknown chemicals."

"That's as far as one doctor would go. Though every physician who examined me knew I had an object of alien origin planted in the back of my neck, none of them would vouch for me. None of them would back up my story for fear of being labeled quacks. Too much of a risk of losing their practices. Doctors are very self-centered personalities. I should know . . . I married one. I wanted my book to be taken seriously. Without backup support from the medical profession, that information would make me come across as a nutcase, even though it was the truth. And that leads me back to your original question, which we've been dancing around. Tonight I aim to prove to the world that my story is true. Tonight I come clean with every last detail of what happened in the North Georgia mountains ten years ago to the day. That's why I told you to bring plenty of tape."

"And what sort of proof will you give us, Laura?"

"Ah!" The artist threw up her hand. "I think it best that we start from the beginning. I remember it like it was yesterday," she began, her red-rimmed eyes acquiring a far-off look. "We were in the tent. The campfire had just been doused and the lanterns turned off. David was snoring and Corinne was fast asleep. I remember hearing a strange rustling through the treetops—not wind really, but something else. And then there was this incredible stillness. It was weird how the nocturnal animal sounds just disappeared all at once. I recall slipping out of my sleeping bag to investigate, and when I threw the flaps back, I became aware of an enormous presence overhead. I heard a faint buzzing sound, like high-tension wires after a rainstorm. I looked up and was nearly blinded by a bright blue-white light. The entire campsite was lit up like it was high noon. The next thing I knew, I was stretched out naked on a cold metal gurney. I felt things sticking in me and leathery hands running up and down my legs. I turned my head and saw five or six alien creatures standing around me, inserting long clawlike fingers into my skin. One of them had a tubelike extension on his arm that he poked down my throat, all the way down into my esophagus. The strange thing was how calm I was, like all of it was the most natural experience I've ever been through. I didn't even gag. Normally, if a doctor comes at me with a tongue depressor, I start to gag, but not that night. They had to have drugged me or something because I felt so . . . so peaceful.

"I kept pretty calm until I saw David and my Corinne strapped to tables, being examined by other aliens. I couldn't stand the sight of these weird-looking creatures inserting things into my sweet little baby like she was some kind of voodoo doll or something. That's when I started to freak out. And then I passed out, thinking as the wooziness overtook me that maybe this was to be the death of me.

"I woke up back at our campsite and saw the tent stakes still anchored in the ground, though the tent and all the supplies were nowhere to be found. I saw the charred remains of our campfire. I remember looking at my watch, and what felt like ten minutes had actually been more than twelve hours. I started looking around the clearing, feeling an itchy ache in the back of my neck. I felt as though I'd been shot with a bullet full of itching powder. I couldn't stop scratching at it . . . rubbing it, which only made the swelling worse. Anyway, as I wandered around the clearing, shouting for David and Corinne, I realized that a perfect circle had been carved out of the forest. I noticed the burnt bark and the fried leaves on the surrounding trees. That's when it dawned on me—I had been abducted by some . . . some supreme force. That's when I realized the enormity of it all.

"I tried to make some sense out of it, but couldn't. My short-term memory slate had been wiped clean. Finally, I left the site, hiking through the woods in a daze, not knowing where I was headed or where I had been. I probably walked in giant circles, I don't know, but I kept calling out for my husband and Corinne until my voice was shot. Time was completely out of whack. It seemed like I traipsed through the Georgia mountains for weeks when actually it was less than two days before those hikers found me."

Rita spoke and Bobby swung the camera her way. "Can you give our viewers a description of the inside of the spaceship, Laura . . . maybe tell us what the aliens looked like?"

"Sure," the artist said agreeably. "But do you mind if I work while we talk? I have *so* much to do before the big moment arrives."

"The big moment?" Rita asked, feeling lightheaded.

"I'm leading up to that," Laura Waldrop said, dabbing a thick brush on a pallet, then making bold strokes across a canvas, quickly creating a dazzling nightscape. "I couldn't see much of the craft's interior," she said while painting. "As I said, I was in some kind of waking dream state, maybe even drugged, so everything was a little foggy. Everything had a kind of surreal curtain pulled over it. But I do remember seeing quite a few blinking lights and hearing beeping sounds, not unlike those on our own computerized medical equipment. The gurney I was on seemed to have properties of both steel and hard rubber and I couldn't tell if it was hot or cold. My senses were all screwed up. Everything inside the craft was built on a miniature scale—

everything except the gurneys. They were built *human* size. And I remember there being a strong odor—sort of a mixture of cinnamon and ammonia, though distinctly unique. The alien creatures were eerily like those reported in most other abduction cases—short and squat, maybe three-feet tall with bulbous, hairless heads and huge black eyes that wrapped around back to where the ears should have been. They had slits for nostrils and tiny openings set above sharp pointed chins. Their skin was dark gray and mottled, tough and leathery like elephant hide. As far as I could tell they were indistingushable from one another, like they had been cast from a single mold."

"Did they communicate with you in any way?"

"No. At least not directly, though somehow I kept getting reassuring vibes through it all, like in some telepathic way they were telling me I was safe."

"Laura, let me play devil's advocate for a moment," Rita interjected. "I'm sure quite a few of our viewers out there are looking at you and saying to themselves that this is an elaborate put-on. You even said you were in some kind of waking dream state. Isn't it possible that this is the result of a deep psychosis that surfaced? Some kind of mind meltdown that happens to exceptionally creative people from time to time? After all, very few people can claim to have seen a legitimate UFO, let alone a close encounter of the fourth kind . . . an abduction. Even those who believe in extraterrestrial races and *want* to have an encounter I'm sure are quite skeptical. How would you answer the skeptics?"

The artist stopped painting in mid-stroke. Her washed-out eyes filled with liquid fire. "This is *not* an elaborate hoax, Ms. Davies."

Rita thought she might have gone too far. The last

thing she wanted was to have the interview of her career cut short. But she noticed a hint of respect behind the artist's glaring eyes, like the Saucer Queen *knew* it was a question any self-respecting journalist *had* to ask.

Laura Waldrop scratched at the back of her neck. "I may look like a complete fruitcake on the outside, but let me assure you, on the inside I'm more stable and sane than most of your precious viewers. When you refer to a mind-melt experienced by exceptionally creative people, you're talking about what psychiatrists call fantasy-prone personality disorder or psychosocial hypotheses. I've been through a most extensive battery of psychological tests and have passed all without a hitch. Time and again I have related the details of what happened on that night, both awake and under deep hypnosis, and my reports have always been consistent. Oddly, they are nearly identical to what other abductees have reported. I have copies of all the test results and transcripts of the hypnosis sessions should you care to see them."

"No. I don't think that'll be necessary—"

"Well, let me throw this interview back in your direction then, Rita. I know you were raised a devout Catholic, so that must mean you have an unflagging faith in God. Am I right?"

"Yes, of course."

"And have you ever *seen* God? I mean up close and face-to-face?"

"Well . . . no, but—"

"Nor have I. And I doubt any of your viewers have, either, yet over thousands of years hordes of worshippers continue to blindly believe in a Supreme Being that they've never seen, or, through self-delusions, think they've communicated with. But they don't believe in the existence of extraterrestrial life? They accept the most outrageous claims in the scriptures while writing off the scant hundreds of us who have had encounters with alien beings? They're willing to believe that Moses parted the Red Sea but they scoff at me? I find it ludicrous, not to mention shortsighted."

"But you can't compare your experiences with religion."

"Can't I? Both involve faith. And the strength to believe in your convictions, what you know to be truth. I'm just saying I have more proof in my faith than do millions of Bible thumpers in theirs."

This was heading in a direction in which Rita did not wish to go. She redirected the questioning. "So I take it that you view this experience as a negative one, that since you've lost your husband and daughter and have been driven to seclusion, you wish this thing had never happened."

"In some ways it's been extremely tough," the artist said, returning to her work. "I have suffered through long stretches of depression and insomnia. I don't much like the migraine headaches caused by this damn plug they sunk in my neck. As you can see by this wasted body of mine, I don't have the healthy appetite I once had. Sure, I've gone through some traumatic changes in the past decade, but not all of it has been negative. Before my abduction, I was an insecure woman, living in the shadows of a skilled neurosurgeon husband. I was a mediocre graphic designer with an attitude problem. I hated my work—creating print ads for cheap grocery fliers and coupon inserts. I hated the whole corporate structure and though we didn't need my income, there was something that rankled me about David being the sole breadwinner. I mean I loved him dearly, but I was one of those wives who desperately wanted her own identity."

She spread her arms, indicating the unfinished artwork in her studio. "I never could have done work this sophisticated before my encounter. No way did I have the skill or self-discipline for this. But they gave me the talent. It's kind of like artwork by numbers. I'm just a medium through which they work. But I haven't minded taking the credit for it. Oh sure, living within a fortress like this, not having close friends and not being able to trust anybody has its drawbacks. Quite a few of them, in fact."

"What do you mean you can't trust anybody?"

"Just what I said. Humans live in tight little boxes, and they tend to point fingers at anybody who lives in a different kind of box. They think people who live in similar boxes are all right and everybody else is screwed up. Humans fear what they don't understand and usually hate what they fear. And since most don't even understand themselves, this planet is awash in paranoia and unfounded hatred. It was bad in the beginning, especially right after my book was published. The kooks were bad enough, but the government agents were unbelievable. They dropped in at all hours of the night, trying everything from blackmail and bribery to outright threats of physical violence to get me to keep quiet. I was roughed up . . . even raped twice by government goons. My condo in Atlanta had more bugs than an entomology lab. I lost track of how many times my place was ransacked. The CIA, NSA, FBI, Naval and Air Force Intelligence personnel . . . I saw them all, Rita. And they all redefine the word paranoia. They wanted me to issue a retraction, stating that I had perpetrated a fraud. But you know what? They all *knew* I spoke the truth. They didn't even mention anything about a retraction until they got all the information out of me they thought they could get. Oh, yeah. Our wonderful government is one of the sleaziest, most underhanded strongarming agencies on the face of this Earth. They're masters at disinformation and keeping Mr. and Mrs. MiddleAmerica off guard. They manipulate the media and have no regard whatsoever for the common voter who elect their useless asses. Certain factions are well aware that what I say is true. Have you ever heard of Project Blue Book, Rita?"

"Yes," Rita said, glad to be able to slip in some of her research. "That was the government agency set up to study UFO sightings. It was shut down in 1969 even though they had over seven hundred cases they couldn't verify as explainable."

"That's half right," the artist said, looking at Rita with a hint of admiration. "Washington announced the closing of the project at the end of 1969, but really it just went underground. The seven hundred cases you cite made the Blue Book people nervous. They didn't want a mass public panic on their hands like *The War of the Worlds* fiasco. They also didn't want the Russians and other world powers knowing about all the alien technology they were collecting." Laura Waldrop shook her head in consternation, her red fantail swishing, brushing her shoulders. "The Pentagon is like a huge classroom full of armed juvenile delinquents, Rita. You'd best believe that, hon."

The interview went on for several hours in this fashion. The Saucer Queen had not issued an idle threat when she had told them she was ready to talk. Ten long years of pent-up verbiage came rushing out of the artist's mouth in lengthy misanthropic monologues. Rita could only sit back and marvel at her voluminous recall. Laura Waldrop rambled on into the night, painting and sketching all the while she regurgitated details of her chosen obsession. She related incident upon incident of UFO sightings, alien contact, abductions—close encounters of all kinds—most of which she claimed worldwide governments had done their damnedest to cover up.

Since 1960, more than 70,000 UFO sightings had been reported. During their Apollo 11 mission, Neil Armstrong saw two unidentified spacecraft and Buzz Aldrin actually photographed one on the Moon, which was quickly given highest classification upon their return. On a Project Mercury flight over Australia, Gordon Cooper encountered a large UFO and recorded voices speaking languages unknown on Earth. Laura Waldrop rattled off countless other in-the-air encounters by other astronauts and jet pilots, where strange saucer-shaped craft would appear suddenly, moving at speeds far greater than the speed of light and defying all laws of modern physics. Most included major glitches in the electronic navigational equipment and jammed radar.

Between 1982 and 1988, twenty-three scientists who worked on Star Wars-like projects that included top-secret UFO research, died under questionable circumstances.

Of course, she spent a lot of time discussing the 1947 Roswell, New Mexico UFO crash, where quite a few eyewitnesses saw the wreckage before the Army moved in and sealed off the site. A few onlookers were even treated to four alien corpses matching the description of the dwarf-sized, gray-skinned, almond-eyed beings that most abductees claim to see. At the site were thousands of half-inch squares of parchment-like balsa wood etched with strange pink and purple hieroglyphics. These squares could not be bent, broken, or burnt. Pieces of lightweight foil also littered the site, and could not be dented, torn, or cut. The U.S. government immediately began a disinformation campaign, stating it was a weather balloon, and going so far as to

114

threaten and intimidate eyewitnesses who tried to talk. But enough of them did talk, beginning the suspicions about government cover-ups.

Then came the Saucer Queen's favorite subject—abductions.

There was the Betty and Barney Hill abduction case in 1961, the first of the 'medical examination' abductions. Under hypnosis the New Hampshire couple told of seeing a flying saucer following their car on a dark country road and then being beamed aboard, undergoing physical exams given by the big-headed, humanoid aliens that hundreds of other 'medical exam' abductees describe. Betty Hill even went so far as to recreate a star chart that she said one of the aliens had shown her when she asked them where they were from. Top-notch astronomers went to work assembling a three-dimensional model of the chart and discovered the view of the Hill map actually existed. Several light years beyond the star systems Zeta 1, Zeta Reticuli, and 82 Eridani are planets the astronomers agreed could support sentient beings.

"In fact, Betty Hill didn't know just how accurate she was," Laura Waldrop said. "Three of the dozen alien races I know about are from that region."

Another case that captured the Saucer Queen's interest was the 1975 incident involving seven Arizona loggers, who saw a UFO and began to run. One of the men, Travis Walton, ran toward the craft and was hit by a brilliant beam of light, disappearing along with the flying object. The remaining loggers sent out search parties, but they could find no sign of Walton. Five days later, the missing logger turned up, talking about strange happenings aboard an alien saucer and undergoing examinations by prototypical humanoid aliens. He was amazed that the misadventure had spanned five days, saying the entire affair seemed like only a couple of hours.

Another bizarre event was the 1983 abduction of an Indianapolis woman, Kathie Davis, who was taken from her back yard and subjected to medical tests where probes were inserted into her nose and ears. When she was returned, she was partially deaf and had a hemorrhaging nose. She also had burned spots on her skin and was losing patches of hair due to radiation burns unlike any doctors had ever seen. Investigators were later even more startled to discover the burned-out patch of yard where Kathie said the spacecraft had landed. Attempts to reseed the area failed as that patch of earth stubbornly resisted growing new grass. Soil samples showed the turf had been nearly crystallized by some unknown chemical-heat reaction well above 800 degrees Fahrenheit. Several neighbors also reported hearing a thundering noise on the night in question as well as experiencing weird electrical problems.

Laura Waldrop had many more abduction stories, and Rita was amazed by her breadth of detailed knowledge on the subject. But it was getting late and Rita and Bobby had more than enough fascinating case studies on tape as it was. Rita was eager to get back to the Saucer Queen's own life story.

"Let me ask you, Laura," Rita said, watching as the artist finished up another intricate painting in quick order. "Most of the abductees seem to have had negative experiences . . . physical impairment, emotional instability . . . But most, if not all, were returned to the place where they were picked up. How do you explain the loss of your daughter and husband?"

Laura Waldrop tilted her head to one side and scratched at the back of her neck furiously, something she had been doing more of the past hour. "I have learned that the Mundavians took David because they needed expertise in neurosurgery. For years they've been experimenting with the cross-hybridization of human and alien races. As advanced technologically as the ETIN cultures are, they are fairly ignorant in human physiology and biology. After all, we humans are complicated little machines in our own right. I still have no clue as to why they took Corinne, though. I shudder to think."

Rita *did*, in fact, shudder at the implication. "Forgive me for saying this, but you don't seem too . . . destroyed over losing your loved ones."

"I haven't lost anybody, Rita. At least not permanently."

"How do you mean?" Rita felt that creepy sensation again as she studied the Saucer Queen.

"I mean that tonight, I will be reunited with my husband and daughter. I have missed the intimacy with David and have missed watching Corinne blossom into young womanhood, but they have been doing important things. And tonight I will be joining them."

"What?" Rita glanced around at the gallery of paintings and sketches, saw the twin tombstones prominently displayed in most every one. "But what about the things you wrote in your book and the—"

"The graves? At the time, I needed the insurance money. And surely you, Rita, being in the business you're in, can understand the need for sensationalism. The graves became my trademark . . . my identifying signature."

"They're alive?" Rita exclaimed, though she really didn't believe it. In fact, she thought things were getting more preposterous by the minute. "You put me down for crass sensationalism then you tell me this? This is all a lie, then. How are we supposed to believe you about *any* of this?"

"Not a lie, really. I've lost ten years of life with the only two humans I've ever loved. I'd call that a death of some sort." The artist smiled, and for the first time in hours, she looked like she had found some inner peace. "Tonight I'll be joining them, finally escaping the petty insane asylum of humanity—"

Suddenly, without warning, Laura Waldrop dropped her paintbrush and clutched at the back of her neck. Her eyes crossed and she toppled forward, bringing a canvas and its easel crashing down with her. A tray of paints tumbled to the floor in an explosion of color.

Rita sat, stilled by the suddenness of the attack. *Is she dying?* she wondered. *Is she having an epileptic seizure or something?* Rita willed herself to get up and go to the woman, but her legs would not cooperate.

Bobby, ever the alert professional, kept the videocam rolling. "This'll be good for a few rating points," he drawled, moving in for a closeup of the fallen Saucer Queen.

One of Laura Waldrop's servants materialized from out of nowhere, a middle-aged woman wearing an apron over an orange jumpsuit. Rita was alarmed to see that she, too, had the eerie neonlike purple eyes. The woman bent over Laura Waldrop and rubbed a metallic wand over the back of her neck, which hummed when it made contact with the skin around the implant. As the artist's breathing became less ragged, the servant spoke to her. "The time is near, M'Lady. Should I prepare your things?"

"Yes, please do, Alannah," Laura Waldrop said in an exhausted voice. "The anticipation is getting to be too much for me." From her supine position on the floor, the artist wiped perspiration from her haggard face and looked directly into the camera. "The world is about to experience a first-hand encounter with an alien race known as the Mundavians."

Rita watched this from her chair, feeling like maybe she had been transported to a Steven Spielberg set. Or maybe she was an innocent bystander in a Phillip K. Dick novel. She wondered whether her viewers would buy any of this. She wondered whether *she* believed any of it.

WITHIN AN HOUR LAURA WALDROP had regained some of her earlier composure. She threw a canvas overnight bag in the Channel 2 van and directed them out to a small clearing in the thick Georgia pines behind the mansion. The only part of Waldrop Manor still visible from out here was the charcoal-tinted dome. It loomed over the treetops, the moonlight reflecting off the Plexiglas like the pupil of a huge onyx eye.

For all Rita knew, the dome *was* an eye, keeping watch on the dark skies overhead for signs of approaching visitors. This was all too much for her ordered sense of logic. A large part of her just knew that this was all scientifically impossible, that nothing would come of this. *You're a gullible fool, Rita Davies,* she chastised herself. *You've got yourself a great interview on tape, but you're chasing illusive rainbows out here, tromping through the woods with a madwoman.* And yet, something primal, something buried deep within her subconscious told her that Laura Waldrop was telling the truth, and that they would see something spectacular out here tonight.

"What do you think, Dusty?" she whispered to Bobby.

119

The glow from Bobby Joe's Marlboro threw faint orange light across his face. He exhaled, watching Laura Waldrop through the windshield as she fiddled with something in the ground nearby. "I think the crazy bitch deserves Oscars for Best Actress, Best Supporting Actress, and Most Original Screenplay. Hell, her case alone could rewrite most of those psychiatrist textbooks! And to think I'm missing my poker night for this."

Rita ran a hand through her hair, pulling it back over her head the way she did when perplexed. "I don't know, Dusty. There's something peculiar about all this that makes me feel like I . . . I *have* to believe her or something."

"Of course you do, love. You're a reporter, remember? Reporters are dreamers. We camera techs are more rational."

"Bullshit, Dusty. It's more than that."

"Believe me, Rita. The woman is crackers."

"Maybe she is . . . but I have a hunch she's telling the truth," Rita said, observing the artist through the window. "It's weird, I know . . . I can't explain it, maybe it's journalistic foresight or something."

Bobby shrugged his massive shoulders, tossed his cigarette butt out the window. "Have it your way, then."

Laura Waldrop stormed back to the van. "Pick up that offensive thing right now, you disgusting slob!" She pointed at the burning butt on the ground. "You start a goddamned forest fire now and I'll never make my rendezvous with the Mundavians."

Rita knew it took a major effort for Dusty to keep his tongue.

Dutifully he got out and picked up the cigarette, put it out in the ashtray. "You can have my seat," he said to the artist. "I'm going in back to do some editing work."

Laura Waldrop slid in behind the wheel. "You better have a camera ready," she said to Bobby's back. "They'll be here soon." She turned to Rita. "We should be all set now."

"Set for what?" Rita asked.

"The landing. I set the infrared guidance sensors around the landing site to help them with their navigation. The sensors are set to a frequency that is undetectable by military and commercial aircraft."

Rita stared across the seat at her, watching as Laura scratched at the back of her neck. Her spiky mohawk and bushy tail made her look like a plucked chicken in silhouette. *Is this woman serious? Maybe Dusty is right. Maybe this woman is crackers!*

"If these Mundavians are so advanced, why do they need your help with landing?"

The artist quit rubbing the back of her neck, turned to look at Rita. "What do I look like, a rocket scientist? You think I'm smart enough to build infrared guidance systems? This is *their* work. *They* instructed me on that part."

"So they've landed here before?"

Laura nodded. "Five times since I've lived out here."

"Why? What do they do when they come?"

"Exchange servants. The Earthly life span of Huma-Mundavian servants is only one to two years."

"HumaMundavian servants? You mean your staff? The ones with the spooky purple eyes?"

"Yeah. They're genetic Mundavian clones cross-hybridized with humans. That's what much of the human abduction research has been about. HumaMundavians are dependable and tireless, but for some reason they don't adapt well to Earth's gravity and atmosphere. Hence the short life spans. And they have trouble getting the eyes right, too. Those are some of the things my husband has been helping them with for the past ten years."

"But he hasn't returned? You haven't seen him?"

"No. Nor my daughter. But I've communicated with them through this chip in my neck."

They fell into a lengthy silence as Rita tried to absorb what she had just learned. She heard sounds coming out of the surrounding woods—the scratch of locusts, the chirp of crickets . . . owls and other nocturnal animals communicating—and the occasional *screeeeech* of rewinding videotape from the back where Dusty worked. A fragrant mix of blooming dogwood and pollinating pine wafted through the van on the thick summer night air.

Rita thought about the bizarre woman sitting across the front seat from her, trying to make some rational sense out of it all. An alien race from the planet Mundavia abducts Laura Waldrop's husband and daughter on a camping trip ten years ago. In exchange they give Laura prodigious artistic talents through some kind of paint-by-numbers system that elevates her to cult status as one of the world's foremost fantasy artists. The Mundavians also plant a small device in her neck that allows her to communicate with a dozen alien races through some kind of extraterrestrial binary network. To complete the package, they supply her with alien-human hybrid servants who have to be changed out every couple of years. And tonight, they were coming for her, to reunite her with her husband and daughter.

Far-fetched? Absolutely.

Implausible? Highly.

But strangely, the implausibility of it all didn't strike Rita with the same magnitude as her willingness to accept it.

She glanced at Laura, who sat so still Rita thought she might be asleep. "Why didn't they just take you with them, Laura? Seems to me that would have been a lot easier."

The artist stirred. "Oh, it would have been. But alien races want humans to know they exist, they really do. They just prefer to be subtle about it. That's been my job for the past ten years, along with people like Whitley Strieber, Travis Walton, Barney and Betty Hill, Kathie Davis, and a host of other contactees and abductees. It's a huge burden to bear, being mediums the way we are. We've had to suffer the finger-pointing paranoia of people who live in those tight little boxes I talked about earlier. We can put the proof on the table, but we can't make the public eat."

Rita mulled this over. Strange how the square pegs seemed to be fitting into the round holes. Inexplicably strange.

"Let me ask you something," Laura said, breaking Rita's reverie. "You suffer quite often from bleeding nasal passages, don't you?"

"Yes. My doctor says it's due to an allergy to pollens and inhalants."

The artist laughed, as if Rita were a stupid little girl. "Of *course* that's what your doctor tells you. That's because he doesn't know any better."

"What do you mean?" Rita asked, not liking the tone of this.

"I mean that your bloody noses are not from allergies, dear. You were visited when you were a little girl—when you were three years, seven months, and thirteen days old, to be exact. They planted a microscopic probe deep in your nasal passages—a tracking device. They've been keeping tabs on you all these years."

"What?"

"Yeah. You'd best believe it, Rita. Why do you think I called for *you* to do my interview instead of one of the national network stars? We're kindred sisters, dear. We

123

have a lot more in common than you think."

Rita was aghast. "No! It can't be. You're insane! You're completely certifiable."

"I'm no more nuts than you are, as you will soon find out."

"No! I refuse to believe it. Nothing like that ever happened to me. I would have remembered something like that."

"You're a bright woman, Rita, but memory has little to do with intelligence. Most people have faint recollection of their lives before their fourth birthday. Advanced alien species know this. Ninety percent of adult abductees are visited and marked before their fourth year. I always thought a tiny bump on the side of my knee was the result of the broken leg I got as a child, when I fell out of a tree. Not so. It was a Mundavian tracking device."

As the Saucer Queen spoke, Rita began to feel an intense dizziness overtake her. The inside of the van began to go topsy-turvy. An unbelievable pressure built up behind her eyes and a gut-wrenching nausea rolled through her stomach.

"Holy shit!" Bobby Joe yelled from the back of the van. "The editing equipment's going haywire!"

Damp with queasy perspiration, Rita let herself out of the van, and immediately felt the presence of some fantastic force. She neither saw nor heard the overpowering energy, but rather *felt* it.

The night had taken on an unnatural stillness.

The chattering, clicking night sounds had died away in the forest.

The soft breeze had disappeared.

Something big had come upon them. The air hung heavy with anticipation, electric in its intensity.

"They're here," Laura Waldrop said, and got out of the van on the far side. In a daze, she walked to the edge of the clearing and then stopped, waited, tilted her Mohawk-coiffured head and watched the skies.

Soon, red and blue lights danced along the treetops far to the east, swirling at first, then consolidating into discernible objects as they moved toward Waldrop Manor at impossible speeds. The objects darted and weaved in gyro-scopic patterns—sharp, drastic movements Rita would have thought impossible. The saucer-shaped glows jerked through the Georgia night skies, silent in their approach, making severe ninety-degree turns, then looping back around, all the while maintaining a loose-knit formation. Even to a layman like Rita, the movement and speed of these objects defied all laws of physical flight. These were no meteors. These were not weather balloons or communication satellites or even the result of some weird atmospheric conditions. These were not conventional flying craft of any kind.

The enormity of it all struck her. Rita was witnessing the approach of alien spacecraft. *They really do exist*, she thought with sudden clarity and awe. But then the moment of import gave way to the implications of what it meant, and icy dread consumed her.

In a matter of minutes four large saucers ringed the perimeter of the clearing, hovering over them. Remarkably, no sound accompanied their arrival, though their presence kicked up a brisk breeze.

"Jesus Christ!" Bobby said in a wondrous whisper from behind her. "Laura Waldrop also gets an Oscar for special effects!"

Rita looked over her shoulder and noticed Bobby recording the proceedings with his shoulder-cam remote.

"I'm quite sure this is no movie, Dusty." She turned back and witnessed the spectacle taking place in the clearing.

Laura Waldrop stood with arms outstretched, illuminated by banks of spotlights trained on her from the undersides of the saucers. Her white cotton skirt billowed in the breeze. Her mohawk bristled.

"What are they waiting for?" Rita called out.

"The flagship. These are just the scout ships."

Soon, the flagship appeared overhead, and it put down in the center of the clearing, perfectly, noiselessly. This craft was much larger than the scout ships and had no visible windows or doors, just rings of red and blue lights running around its periphery. The hull was sleek and streamlined, appearing to be constructed of shiny dark metal. Rita could see scuff marks and dings around the edges and she wondered just how many billions of miles this craft had traveled. The bleachy smell of ozone became overpowering.

"My drinking buddies won't ever believe this," Bobby whispered in open-mouthed reverence.

Everything Laura Waldrop told us is true, Rita thought. And then she shuddered as she remembered the artist's words—*Ninety percent of adult abductees are visited and marked before their fourth year.*

On the far side of the clearing, a handful of the neon-eyed servants walked toward the spacecraft as if in a trance. *HumaMundavians* is what Laura Waldrop had called them. They walked in a straight line, their incandescent purple eyes glowing like the orbs of rare nocturnal animals. Rita recognized the security cop, the stuffy butler, and the nursemaid named Alannah. As they got close to the ship, they simply disappeared, one by one.

A flash of greenish-white light erupted in front of the flagship. Slowly the light faded and two human figures

126

appeared. One appeared to be a teenage girl, the other a middle-aged man. Though they were dressed in extraterrestrial tunics with high collars and hooped belts, they were definitely human. They and Laura Waldrop stared at each other for long moments, as though hypnotized.

Then the girl broke the spell. "Momma? Is that you?"

"Corinne? Is that you, baby?"

Laura Waldrop and daughter Corinne rushed together and embraced. David Waldrop quickly joined them. They hugged and kissed and carried on, oblivious to the strangeness of their environment, letting out emotions they had kept bottled up for ten long, lonely years.

And just as quickly as it had all happened, a blinding white light zapped them—presumably teleporting the reunited Waldrop family back onboard—and they were gone. Rita Davies and Bobby Joe Dustwood stood alone in the clearing, two humans staring with wide-eyed amazement at five alien spaceships.

The flagship's running lights changed hue and the craft lifted off. Bobby rushed out from the edge of the woods to get a better shot, and as he ran underneath the departing craft, the flagship dipped and unleashed a powerful beam of light that gobbled him up, videocam and all.

Stunned, Rita stared at the scorched plot of earth where Bobby had just stood. "NO! YOU CAN'T TAKE DUSTY!" she screamed. "YOU CAN'T DO THAT!"

The flagship seemed to hover in place for a minute, creating distorted ripples in the lights of the surrounding scout ships.

Then the flagship dipped and came for her.

Terrified, Rita jumped into the van and started the engine. Her hands shook on the wheel as she floored the accelerator, clipping two small trees and shattering the right

127

headlight in the process. Adrenaline surged through her exhausted body as she drove helter-skelter toward Waldrop Manor, the moon-flecked dome her target. She glanced in the side mirror and felt panic swallow her up as she saw several scout ships zig-zagging over the treetops, keeping pace close behind her.

She hit the back lot of Waldrop Manor doing seventy, audio-visual equipment coming untethered and smashing into the walls in back as she careened left and right, trying to throw off the overhead pursuit.

Bright lights swept over her like searchlights in a prison yard.

Her pulse pounded in her aching temples. Fear clutched in her throat.

The pain behind her eyes intensified. Rita felt as though her head was coming apart at the ears. She felt a harsh stinging in her nose and watched in horror as large amounts of blood exploded through her nostrils and splattered against the windshield.

She couldn't see.

Her mind was a kaleidoscope of chaos, images and thoughts forming, then breaking away and leaving streamers and trails in their wake.

If only she could get to the woods and the road leading down to the interstate.

Through the blood-smeared windshield, Rita saw her destination and went for it.

Something heavy pounded against the roof of the van—

once . . .

twice . . .

Rita yanked the wheel hard to the left, trying to evade whatever they were lobbing on her. Loose equipment crashed around in back. The van lurched back to the right as a third blow landed, this one crushing the passenger side ceiling and exploding the glass on that side. Rita ducked, screamed, felt her bowels begin to loosen. The steering wheel flew from her hands. The van pitched out of control.

And then she felt her stomach as it left her, sucked away from her body with a monumental force. A light and airy feeling breezed through her. Rita looked up, and gasped. The van was airborne! They had abducted her *and* the Channel 2 News van!

A stiff wind whipped through the shattered windows, stinging her damaged nose. Far below, the treetops were a fluffy deep-piled shag. Rita looked off to the right and saw a miniature-scale Waldrop Manor, and she became overwhelmed by a crushing sense of vertigo. They were taking her to higher altitudes very rapidly. She began to strap herself in with the shoulder harness, then stopped, realizing the futility of it. If they decided to drop the van from this height, the lack of a seatbelt would be the least of her problems.

Rita began to scream in a bansheelike wail.

She screamed until she was hoarse, until her parched vocal cords could emit nothing but a raspy wheeze.

Strange memories and images began to solidify in her mind. Her mother's cherubic face and warm smile, always helpful and willing to be the big sister Rita never had. Her father, stubborn as a mule with an obsessive self-discipline that allowed him to accept nothing less than perfection from his daughter. Rita and he had been through some major rifts over the years, but Rita loved him in ways that only daughters could fully understand and appreciate. She tried to remember the last time she had told him she loved him, and the last time Rita had heard those magical words from him, but couldn't. And Thad. *Oh, my dear sweet Thad*, Rita thought forlornly. *I have been so selfish. If I ever get out of this in one piece I'll have all the children you want, my loving hubby-to-be. I'll even take fertility drugs to speed the process. I promise. If . . . only . . .*

Everything was becoming dreamy, slowed-down.

I . . . can . . . get . . .

Her thoughts were spacing out.

back . . . to . . . you . . .

A weird, animated haze permeated everything, as if she was in a cartoon. She wondered whether it was the lack of oxygen or something the Mundavians had done to her. Rita dreaded being out of control like this.

She thought she could touch the moon, and tried. It seemed to dangle just beyond her reach. She tried again and the moon turned into her mother's face. "Don't worry, Rita dear," her mother's moon-face said. "They're taking you to see Dusty. Everything will be okay. Your father and I will be seeing you soon."

Her mother's moon-face faded away.

"Mother! Don't leave me now!" Rita screeched through croaking lungs.

And with her mother, so went Rita's consciousness.

SHE PASSED THROUGH ALTERNATE realities and hypnotic dream states, falling . . . sliding . . . cascading down a strangely-woven tapestry of rainbow colors and sensual sounds. Rita felt hot and cold flashes that seemed to correspond with these aural murmurings. She experienced a wonderful melange of extraterrestrial tastes and smells. The journey was like a deep dream, where the details are vivid and sharply sensual at the moment of inception, but then scatter a second later, filtering down into some locked region of the subconsciousness, never to be recalled again.

Though much of Rita's dream was this bombardment of flickering sensory stimuli and illusive images, she moved back and forth between two "realities" that stayed locked in her waking consciousness.

The first was obvious, and it evoked in her both a comforting reassurance and a pain-filled terror. She lay naked on a metal gurney as three alien creatures examined her, the experience matching Laura Waldrop's description. They were short with huge hairless heads and worked with gnarled, clawlike hands. They reminded Rita of the Mr. Potato Head toy she once played with as a child. She would have found that amusing if only the alien eyes didn't strike such fear into her: almond-shaped wrap-around eyes that dominated their faces—black, unblinking insectile eyes that unsettled her. Their brownish-gray faces, which had mere slits for noses and mouths, remained expressionless as they worked. One of them bent over and inserted tubes up her nose, which brought her a modicum of discomfort. It was then that Rita spied a tattoo just above one of the alien's wrist joints. It looked like a multifaceted diamond. She looked around the interior of the ship and saw variations of the same design throughout, accompanied by some very unearthly hieroglyphics. Then she felt major pain in her navel and uterus. She tried to squirm but couldn't. Nor could she look down at her belly. She heard a human voice, cussing, a familiar drawl, and Rita was able to look to her left to see Dusty. She tried to call out to him, but couldn't.

And then she was transported through tunnels of colorful prismatic lights and whooshing sounds, to another "reality."

She hung as though suspended from the ceiling, gazing

down at a little girl as she slept. Rita recognized the room with the teddy bear wallpaper and Captain Kangaroo alarm clock. The Mickey and Minnie Mouse nightlights were also familiar to her. She knew the little girl with dark curls who slept so soundly, a thumb and index finger in her mouth, the other arm wrapped protectively around her stuffed sleeping companions—Raggedy Ann and Ellie the plaid elephant. Rita became filled with nostalgic warmth and sentimental loneliness, the way people get when they look at their children growing and realize how quickly life's unique pageant is passing them by. But Rita was not looking down on her child. She was gazing at herself. Twenty-six years ago in the Spartan two-bedroom tract house on the base at Fort Bragg.

Suddenly, two aliens materialized around the girl's bed, and began probing her with instruments similar to the ones they had used on Rita moments before. Rita felt an eerie chill as she spotted the familiar diamond tattoos above their wrists and watched them go to work on the sleeping girl's nose. Young Rita slept through the alien surgery until the very end, when she woke up crying. The aliens vanished as quickly as they had appeared. Lights came on in the hallway, followed quickly by the entrance of Rita's mother. She was tying the belt of her bathrobe. Her face was unlined and though obviously tired, she carried herself straighter and walked with more bounce to her step than she did today.

"Aw, is my baby having a bad dream?" Grace Davies said, sitting on the edge of the bed and swooping young Rita into her arms.

The adult Rita's heart nearly broke. She wanted to reach down and hug both her young mother and the child version of herself.

"Yeth, Mama. I dweamed there wath thome funny men

132

. . ." young Rita sniffled, "and they were real ugly and they played real rough."

"You look like you're coming down with a cold, sweetie. Your nose looks swollen and all stopped up. I'll go get some medicine, darling."

Young Rita clutched desperately at the hem of her mother's robe. "Pleath, don't leave me, Mommy! I'm thcared!"

And then it all evaporated as the adult Rita was transported back to the present and the Mundavian flagship.

RITA AWOKE IN THE VAN, sitting behind the wheel with the shoulder harness firmly in place. Shards of broken glass littered the front seat. The dashboard and remnants of the windshield were coated with dried blood, as was the front of her blouse. She looked down in her lap and noticed her open notebook, a pencil in her right hand. Sketches of peculiar-shaped multifaceted diamonds and bug-eyed alien creatures covered several pages. Her mind was a fog.

Did I draw these? she wondered. *Heck, I can't even draw a straight line with a ruler.*

Her head throbbed and her sinuses burned. She tried to reconstruct what had happened, how she had come to be here. She looked at her watch and nearly shrieked. 11:32 Monday morning—more than three days since the interview with Laura Waldrop! She did some quick calculations and came up with nearly 82 hours of missing time.

Rita got out of the van, her joints achy, her legs weak. Scorched foliage surrounded her. Large sections of treetops appeared to be twisted and mangled. The grass beneath her feet was trampled and crystalized, hard as green asphalt.

Bits and pieces came back to her, stubbornly, slowly. The Mundavian scout ships. The flagship. The parade of HumaMundavians, like orchid-eyed lemmings on a death march. Laura Waldrop's reunion with her husband and daughter. Dusty shooting incredible footage of it all and getting zapped in the process. Her own horrific attempt at escape, alien searchlights stabbing through the forests, tracking her like a hunted animal. Her damaged nose . . . blood everywhere. Her abduction with one of the saucers swooping down and leeching on to the roof of the van, carrying her high into the moon-drenched skies—an alien raptor taking away its human prey. And then . . . *what?*

Rita's mind was a blank beyond that.

She noticed a charred object on the ground in the middle of the clearing and walked toward it. She bent to retrieve it and felt something clutch in her throat. A scorched pack of Marlboros crumbled in her hands.

"Dusty?" she called out, her eyes scanning the fringe of the woods. She called out a second time but knew there would be no reply. Bobby Joe Dustwood was long gone, probably on his way to Mundavia with the Waldrops and the HumaMundavian servants.

Rita walked back to the van, shoulders slumped, head bowed. She was overwhelmed with sadness. The disappearance of the earth-shattering footage was one thing, but the abrupt departure of one of the few human beings Rita could genuinely call a friend carved a huge void in her heart.

Wherever you are right now, Dusty, I hope you're not in any pain, she thought. *I hope they're taking good care of you.*

Though the flying saucer videotape was gone, Rita

prayed that the Laura Waldrop interview tapes were still intact. She opened the rear doors of the van and looked in on a chaotic jumble of electronic equipment. Cables snaked every which way. Several tape editors had dumped into the middle of the floor. Pieces of glass from a shattered monitor screen lay scattered across the worktable. Rita got down on hands and knees, searching through the rubble. A quick search revealed five plastic tape cases. She pulled out the tapes and inserted them, one by one, into a VCR, spot-checking them on the remaining monitor.

Thank God! They're all here! Rita sighed in relief. *The Mundavians didn't think to take the Saucer Queen's true confessions.*

Suddenly, Rita became very dizzy. A sharp, biting pain developed in the back of her neck, stabbing, gouging, twisting. She grabbed at it as an uncontrollable itching sensation accompanied the relentless pain, then she fell to the floor in a gasping heap. She felt a cool wet perspiration envelope her as she struggled for air. Rita thought she would be okay if she could just stop the incredible pain in her neck, which shot down her spinal cord like itchy lightning.

What's happening to me?

And then Rita heard Laura Waldrop's voice and she knew what this attack was all about.

I told you, Rita. It's like being shot with a bullet full of itching powder. You're one of us now . . . Welcome to the Network.

Soon Rita's delirium passed, and even though the itchy pain persisted in the back of her neck, it was diminished by the knowledge she had acquired. She had a clearer understanding of what had transpired during her missing 82 hours. She knew that Dusty was very far from home, but safe.

But most importantly, Rita had discovered a newfound sense of purpose.

She drove the van back to Waldrop Manor and let herself in the eerily deserted mansion. She called Thad's office, but he was in court this morning, so Rita left word with his secretary that she was okay and on her way home. She phoned her boss, and Peter Heller was relieved to hear from her. When the News Director pressed her on Bobby Joe, Rita told him she'd explain everything when she returned, that she had a story too incredible to sum up in a five-minute phone call. She called her parents out in Arizona, interrupting their breakfast with words of love for both. Her father had been most surprised. Then she pitched her blood-stained clothes and took a hot shower.

Within the hour, Rita Davies was on the road, speeding back to Atlanta with five videotapes that would forever alter the direction of her life. She was a True Believer now, and her mission was to convince the masses of The Truth. She only wished that Dusty could share the glory with her. A lone tear trickled down her cheek. But then she realized that in a remote way, Dusty *would* be sharing this with her.

Her thoughts turned to her fiancé. Rita couldn't wait to make love with Thad tonight. *Oh sure, he'll have been plenty worried about me and will probably play twenty-questions, wanting to know which man I've run off with for a weekend fling. But I'll make Thad see the truth tonight. I'll be extra special to him under the sheets tonight, make him see that he is the sole object of my desires.* Rita smiled deviously at the wicked images running through her mind.

But before she made any carnal advances, she would toss the pills and the diaphragm.

Time for her and Thad to start a family.

Sure, it will be tough, balancing child-rearing and a career that will become increasingly demanding, but I know I can do it, she thought while scratching the painful itch in her neck. *We'll soon be facing great scrutiny from the disbelievers and the stress will be difficult, but not impossible. I can handle it, Dusty and Laura Waldrop assure me of that. But though their votes of confidence provide me with a steady rudder, I realize I have no free will in this matter.*

After all, I am one of the Chosen Ones, a child of Mundavia.

The plight of Southwest Native American tribes has long been of interest to me. The white man killed off their buffalo, stole their land, murdered large numbers of them, then banished those remaining to the depressing and claustrophobic confines of the reservation. I wrote "Maricopa Chameleons" as a kind of Indian revenge horror tale and started sending it out to various magazines. It came back time and again with basically the same comments: 'Great story with the exception of the ending, which is far too political and preachy.' Finally, I set my stubbornness aside and completely revamped the ending, making it much more experimental and supernatural. Trouble was, the new version was too long for most magazine formats, so I kept it in my archives. In the spring of '95, I met William Raley, (editor of the west coast horror magazine AFTER HOURS) at the World Horror Convention here in Atlanta. He remembered "Maricopa Chameleons" and two of the characters by name, telling me how close I had come to a sale at his publication. This blew me away, seeing as how I had sent him the original version more than two years before. I figured that if an editor remembered specific things about the tale for more than two years, it must have something going for it. So here, for your perusal, is the new version of "Maricopa Chameleons," a macabre blend of Indian mythology, terror, and supernatural metaphysics.

Maricopa

Chameleons

The chameleon is a deceptively powerful warrior,
for it moves swiftly,
undetected and all-knowing,
through multi-colored spectral worlds.

— Maricopa Indian Proverb —

THIS WAS THE STRANGEST CARGO Harley Ordner had ever hauled.

Caskets.

Two-hundred-and-fifty of them. Everything from the most expensive satin-lined mahogany and cherrywood coffins to the cheap pine box variety. Close to twenty tons of product manufactured by Dallas Casket, Inc., to be delivered to West Coast Mortuary Wholesalers in San Diego.

At least they were empty.

Just another load of freight.

Might as well be tires or produce or appliances. That's what Harley told himself when he started getting spooked about it.

It was late—3:14 AM according to the digital clock on the dash. He yawned, feeling the twenty-two straight hours behind the wheel in his stiff back and sore shoulders. His eyelids felt gritty, heavy. The eighteen wheels beneath him met the asphalt with a monotonous hum. Broken lines on Interstate 8 had him hypnotized. Two hours west of Tucson and he was starting to nod off. He was pushing it, he knew, and the logical side of his mind urged him to pull over and take a nap. But his entrepreneurial side won out, as it usually did, telling him to keep rolling, to keep ticking off those miles toward his final destination. In the trucking business time was money, and when you were an independent like Harley Ordner, an idle truck was costly.

He spied the spray bottle on the seat next to him and grabbed it, squirting stiff shots up both nostrils. Nothing like a few burning snorts of crystal meth to keep a trucker alert and his rig rolling onward.

Harley lit up a smoke and clicked on the CB radio, searching for some semblance of civilization out in the vast Arizona night. Maybe he could find another tired and lonely trucker to talk to—a kindred spirit. But a quick run through the stations revealed nothing but static. He sighed and crushed out the cigarette in the ashtray, slipped a tape in the cassette deck. Creedence Clearwater Revival. *His* kind of music. Not that faggy heavy metal noise and rap drivel his two teenage sons listened to.

Thinking of his sons, he flipped down the visor and turned on the cab light, looking at the photographs of Tim and Bobby and his wife Sharene. He cringed every time he saw his boys' vacant and petulant stares framed by shoulder-length hair and gold earrings. Sharene let them get away with hell. That was one of Harley's chief regrets. He just couldn't be home enough to be sure his sons grew up proper. His wife was a wonderful woman, beautiful and caring, but discipline wasn't her thing. In Harley's day, any guy with long hair and weird clothes got his ass pounded on a regular basis. Earrings might have been grounds for murder.

Harley was buzzing now, the crystal working on his senses like thousands of tiny electric nerve prods. He was one with the road, tapping the wheel in time with the music, tooling along at a rapid clip, the dark curtain of Arizona nightscape whizzing past in a blur. Interstate 8 had become almost surreal, winding through the foothills like an asphalt serpent. His mind raced nearly as fast as his Peterbilt. He felt free and easy, stoked up, hyper-alert.

He had just gone through Maricopa Pass when he saw the sign:

ROAD CONSTRUCTION AHEAD — DETOUR 4 MILES

"Shit!" he muttered. A change to back roads would kill his schedule.

He rounded the bend and saw the barricade with the flashing yellow lightshow, the small army of graders and land movers. He slowed, following the blinking arrows to the alternate route, a rutted two-lane on which it was impossible to build up much speed. Dark and desolate, not a sign of civilization save for the occasional mailbox perched atop wooden fences that staked outer boundaries of enormous spreads of ranchland.

He had gone several miles and was thinking about pulling over to take a leak when, unbelievably, he saw two Indians dressed in full ceremonial garb, standing smack in the middle of the road, starch-straight, unflinching, like a couple of cigar store Indians placed in his path as a prank.

Were they real? Was his road-weary mind playing tricks

on him?

Harley blinked several times, trying to shake away what was surely a crystal-meth hallucination. But they remained, daring him to run them over.

"Jesus!" he screamed, literally jumping on the brake pedal.

The brakes locked up and Harley Ordner's multi-ton Peterbilt went into an uncontrolled slide.

He could smell the sickening stench of burnt rubber and fried crankcase oil.

Time crawled and he could see everything in intricate, slow-motion detail: the trailer careening wildly out to the left, the cab pulling to the right; knotholes on fenceposts whizzing past; the Indians' bright blue and red beads woven into their buckskin vests; the greasepaint slashed across their high cheekbones and broad foreheads; their stoic expressions of defiance.

Why in the hell weren't they moving?

What in the hell were Indians doing out here on a deserted road a few hours before dawn?

The inside of the cab became a carousel of swirling night sky.

Harley heard the pings of gravel pelting the under-carriage, felt his rig lean precariously to one side. A large, spiny cactus and sandy earth raced toward him. The trailer slammed into a fence or a row of trees, Harley wasn't sure which. A gnarled tree branch swooped out of the night and cracked the windshield in front of him. He screamed, hoarse cries of fear, but the splintering wood and shrieking metal drowned him out.

When it was over, he dared to open his eyes and peer through the webbed glass. Dust swirled through the head-light beams as he gazed up through a network of tree limbs to the bright orange crescent moon beyond. Disoriented, Harley looked out the side window and realized with dismay that his rig had become wedged in a deep drainage ditch.

Anger flushed away his fear and he reached under the seat for his sawed-off double-barrel and a flashlight.

He had a mind to kill a couple of Indians. That is, if he hadn't already. Dumb bastards! They have a death wish or something?

Harley kicked the door open and stepped down from the cab, the shotgun out in front of him like an Indian divining rod. He climbed up the embankment and searched the dark road, north . . . south.

Nothing.

He walked across the road and searched the ditch. Again, no sign of them. Where could they have gone? He pointed the flashlight beyond the post of a low barbed-wire fence.

The silence was eerie, closing in all around him.

Harley didn't normally scare easily, but this silence had a disturbing quality to it. A pair of Indians in facepaint didn't just disappear into the night air.

An owl hooted its mournful cry and he nearly jumped from his skin scrambling back across the road.

He went to the far side of the ravine, shaking his head in consternation as he inspected the damage to his rig. Quite a bit of rubber lost from the tires on that side. A lot of structural damage to the lower trailer wall. Probably a bent axle as well. To complicate matters, it appeared as though he was hung up on the fence and jammed in pretty good. More than likely he wasn't getting out of here without some help.

Shit! Where were those two idiotic Indians? They would pay dearly for this.

He started thinking that maybe the Indians were nothing more than a crystal-meth illusion when he heard a thumping inside the trailer. Temples pounding, he put his ear against the wall and listened. His heart nearly jumped into his throat as he heard what sounded like coffin lids opening and closing. Quickly, Harley raced to the rear of the trailer and noticed with relief that the seal remained intact and the locks were still secured. Couldn't be anything happening inside. Just his drug-drenched imagination playing games with him again. He'd have to quit doing so much crystal.

Well, best to try driving the truck out of this bog and submit insurance claims on any structural damage. Thankfully, the cargo had been well padded and strapped in.

He rounded the corner, returning to the cab, and pulled up short. Sitting in the driver's seat with the door open was a squat man with a feathered wide-brim Stetson tilted down low over his forehead. Harley couldn't see his face—the man was turned away from him, studying the pictures of Harley's family on the sun visor.

With his left hand, Harley shined the flashlight on the stranger while training the shotgun on him with his right. The man had distinct Indian features, though he was not one of the two he had seen in the middle of the road.

"What the hell are you doing in my rig?" Harley's voice echoed strangely.

The man's eyes remained trained on the photographs. "This is quite a good-looking family you have here, Mr. Ordner."

At first, Harley was startled that the stranger knew his name, but then realized he could have read it off the registration. "I'm giving you three seconds to get your ass away from my truck. After that, I pull this trigger." He lifted the barrel as the man turned to look at him.

The man smiled, showing brown, stumpy teeth. "That won't accomplish anything. It'd just jack up your insurance claim on this beautiful truck of yours."

Harley took a few steps forward, hoping to scare him off.

"One . . ."

The man sat like a statue.

"Two . . ."

The man yawned, not the least bit concerned. This was getting too weird.

"Three."

Harley fired. Twin cannon shots reverberated through the canyon. The first shot he aimed high, bringing leaves and twigs raining down on the roof of the cab. The kick from the first barrel knocked Harley to the ground as the second shot peppered the trailer wall, just behind the cab where the man in the Stetson sat.

The guy didn't flinch. Surely some of the shot had hit him. But he just looked down the length of the trailer and whistled. "That was *very* unnecessary, Mr. Ordner. Your insurance adjustors won't like this one bit." He patted the seat next to him. "Come on up here and let's have us a little chat."

Harley looked up from his position on the ground. Something was very wrong here. People on the receiving end of double shotgun blasts usually crapped their pants. At the very least their speech was shaky. This guy was calm and collected. A chill of uneasiness wriggled through him.

From behind, two pairs of hands helped him up and guided him toward the truck. Harley glanced to either side and noticed greasepainted faces—the two Indians he had nearly flattened on the road! They dragged him up into the cab and pushed him into the passenger seat.

Harley observed the arcane little man sitting behind the wheel. The guy was definitely an Indian. He wore turquoise rings on most fingers and a pale goatskin vest that matched his rather sickly complexion. Some kind of animal foot hung from a rawhide necklace. Black chino pants were studded with turquoise and silver. The bone handle of a large knife protruded from his belt. The man pushed his hat back and turned his dead-looking eyes on Harley. He didn't look well at all.

"Just who *are* you?" Harley asked. "And who are those Indians out there?" he said, pointing through the cracked windshield.

"The name is Nicky Stillbrook—*Chief* Stillbrook of the Southern Arizona Maricopa. The two you met outside are Maricopa Indian warriors . . . or at least they were. I guess I'm not really a chieftain anymore, either."

"Oh? So what are you guys now?"

"Dead."

A feeling of intense anxiety gripped Harley. Yes, indeed, this guy was a bonafide nutcase. For the first time Harley noticed the yellow blotches all over the Indian's face and hands. "Dead, huh? If you're so dead how can you be sitting here talking with me?"

"We're spirits. More precisely, we're chameleon spirits."

"Spirits? You mean like ghosts?"

"Something like that, though chameleon spirits are different from normal disembodied spirits. You see, Harley . . . may I call you Harley?" the strange little man asked rhetorically. "The Maricopa believe that any human being not receiving a proper burial ceremony becomes a chameleon spirit, because the soul never separates properly from the physical being. Like the lizard that changes color to blend in with its environment, so are we chameleon spirits able to change so that we can move between dimensions. We have powers the living cannot fathom. We can conjure up our old physical shells when we want to be seen and heard, then change into a disembodied force that is not detectable. We sleep with the dead and move among the living."

"Yeah?" Harley snorted. "And I'm Tom Cruise, pal! Get the hell outta my truck. Now!"

The Maricopa's leathery face registered surprise. "I thought you might not believe the truth. You don't think I'm *really* a chameleon spirit, do you, Harley?"

"You got that right, Jack. You ain't even a real Indian, let alone some lizard ghost. You talk more like a big-shot politician than an Indian. I ain't the world's smartest guy, but even I know Indians don't get buried in caskets."

Nicky Stillbrook laughed. "You white folk have a strange perception of Indians. Many of the Southwest tribes have adopted the white man's ways . . . more because of lost heritage than any desire to emulate the so-called civilized world," he said, sadness lending a heaviness to his voice. "And as far as me talking like a politician, well, that's not far from the truth . . . or at least it *wasn't* far from reality. I was educated at the University of New Mexico—Anthropology with a minor in Business Law. I handled most of the high-level Maricopa negotiations with other tribal communities and the U.S. government before I met my untimely demise. So if I sound more educated than your average Sitting Bull, it's because I am."

Harley stared at him, mouth open. "What happened, you and your friends get a little too juiced at a masquerade party or something? Get lost on the way home?"

The Indian heaved a big sigh. "You're trying my

patience, Harley."

"Okay, I'll buy that you're an Indian," the trucker said. "But I don't know about this spirit thing. You *do* look sick, but you ain't dead, partner."

Harley watched in fascination as the Indian pulled the bone-handled knife from his belt and handed it to him. The huge blade looked like a machete in the moonlight. "Whaddaya want me to do with this?" he asked, taking it from him.

"Stab me."

Harley's eyes widened. "What? You're crazed, man!"

"You want proof that I'm from the spirit world and no longer living, then go ahead and stab me with it. Go ahead. Plunge it deep. Twist it around."

Harley thought about this. A few minutes ago he would have done anything for a lethal weapon. Now, he wasn't so sure. This was too easy. As hardened as he thought he was capable of being, he knew he couldn't murder an unarmed man. "Look, Nicky, why don't you just take your two buddies back to the reservation with you and we'll pretend this whole thing never happened. I really don't wanna kill you."

"Oh, you *won't* kill me, Harley. You won't even hurt me. I can't believe how skeptical you Caucasians are. Come on. Shove that baby in me—all the way up to the hilt."

The trucker ran a finger along the edge of the blade. Razor sharp. Yep—real gonzo lunatic, this one was. You met all kinds out here on the road.

Harley sensed the Indian's mounting impatience and he figured as unbalanced as the guy appeared to be, he'd better go through with it. Otherwise the guy might cut *him* up and hijack his truck. "Okay, then . . ." he said reluctantly, ". . . here goes."

Harley closed his eyes and rammed the blade up under the Indian's rib cage. It felt squishy but solid, like stabbing a bag of wet cement. He pulled his hand away and opened his eyes, saw the bone handle sticking out of Stillbrook's belly. None of the blade was showing. But there was no blood and, incredibly, Nicky Stillbrook was smiling.

"See?" the Indian said. "That wasn't so bad, was it?" He removed the knife and studied the clean blade in the moonlight. "And just so you don't think that was some kind of illusion, watch this." Nicky Stillbrook plunged the knife deep into his own neck. Crunching sounds filled the cab as the blade cut through the Indian's windpipe. He choked and gagged as the knife tore through muscle and cartilage.

Harley thought he would be sick and hung his head between his knees.

But then he overcame the nausea as he saw that not one drop of blood had been spilled. This was too strange. A jab like that should cut open the jugular. The guy's neck should be spraying like a bloody Old Faithful. Maybe this crazy Indian *was* a ghost. He certainly wasn't a living human.

Harley laughed, a nervous snicker that served to cover his uneasiness. "Okay, then. Let's just say you *are* one of them lizard spirits. Shouldn't that be good then? If you're a chameleon spirit don't that mean you never really die? Ain't that like immorality or something?"

"Immor*tality*, Harley," the Maricopa chief said with amusement. "And no, it's not good . . . not good at all. He pulled the knife out of his neck. A bloodless gaping hole quickly sealed over with a patch of yellowed skin. "There is a window of time when all souls should leave the body. If they miss that window, they miss their rebirth in the Here-after. If the body isn't properly buried, that transference

149

cannot take place. After a time, chameleon spirits are doomed to live forever on the fringes of the here and now—not really living, yet not able to enjoy eternal physical rest and the glorification of the soul either. True death and rebirth of the soul is *much* preferable."

Harley swallowed hard and looked away from those imploring dead eyes set in the sickly yellow face. "Uh, look, Chief, I'm just a dumb truck driver with a haul to get to San Diego. I don't really understand what's happening here and I'm not sure I wanna know. Two of your chameleon spirits caused me to wreck my rig and I'm a little bent outta shape about it. So if you don't mind, how about hopping outta my cab and let me get back on the road."

The Indian spirit nodded. "In due time. But you're going to need our help. We'll get you out of here, just be patient."

Harley noticed the Indian fondling the handle of his knife and the trucker tried to push dark thoughts from his mind. He wished he was armed. "So, what is it you want with me?"

"Just a little piece of your time, that's all. I want to tell you about the Maricopa tragedy—the Yellow Death that turned us into chameleon spirits."

Harley heard a thumping back in the trailer. "What was that?" he said, jumping.

"Relax. That's just my fellow spirits working to get your truck out. You *do* want to get to San Diego don't you?"

"Yeah." Harley thought it best to keep the Indian talking while he thought of some way to overpower him. But shit, the guy didn't even respond to shotgun blasts and deep stab wounds. How in the hell could he ever overpower him? "So just what is the Maricopa tragedy?"

The Indian smiled, revealing his brown, decayed stumps again—a crooked smile, touched with madness. "As I'm sure you know, the American Indian has been repressed ever since the advent of the reservation. Conditions on most of the reservations are inhumane. Illiteracy is almost as bad as the drug and alcohol problem. Proper medical facilities are nonexistent. Sewage and waste removal are shoddy and unsanitary, creating breeding grounds for disease and sickness. Last month the Maricopa reservation at Gila Bend was hit with an outbreak of hepatitis. Nearly half our people were stricken with the Yellow Death. We went to the BIA for help, but . . ."

"BIA?"

"The Bureau of Indian Affairs. It's a branch of the Department of the Interior set up to provide welfare and education to American Indian reservations. You must keep in mind, Harley, that the BIA is made up of petty bureaucrats and political climbers who do what it takes to get the most publicity for the dollar. Most of the Southwestern budget is allocated to the large tribes with whom the public is familiar, tribes like the Navajo, Pueblo, and the Hopi. I don't begrudge our brethren any, because they need the help as well, but smaller, more obscure tribes like the Maricopa, Pima, and Papago tend to get overlooked. Anyway, we asked the BIA for qualified medical assistance and financial aid. They sent us some spineless health officials and a fleet of backhoes."

"Backhoes?"

The Indian nodded, his splotchy face creased in a scowl. "Backhoes. In their infinite stupidity, the health officials decided the best way to stop the spread of Yellow Death was to dig a big hole, deposit all the dead and dying, then plow it over. A Maricopa mass grave if you will. Many of us, myself included, were buried alive. The BIA couldn't be bothered with us. They treated us like rabid dogs, like we were foaming at the mouth and didn't deserve to live. Easier to eliminate us than to treat us. The Interior Department covered it up. Your white trash government is real good with the lies and deception. But we chameleon spirits have dealt with the racists in our own way. We made sure there was justice in the end. They died *very* horrid deaths. But it still doesn't bring back the hundreds of Maricopa who could have been saved with very little effort. I can still hear the screams as tons of earth poured down on top of us in that pit of death. Not at all a dignified or pleasant way to die."

Harley was alarmed by the Indian's increasingly hostile attitude and the way he slashed the blade against the steering wheel. This was like a bad dream on cheap chemicals.

"You know what it's like to be buried alive, Harley?"

"Uh—no, not really," he said, beginning to realize what the crazy Indian had in mind. He scooted closer to the door, feeling for the handle.

"It's *really* bad. You struggle for every breath as you get weaker and weaker, but there's nothing but dirt to breathe. Then there's this terrible blackness that burns through your lungs and explodes in your brain."

The Indian's eyes were insane now. He brought the knife down, plunging it into the seat leather, just missing Harley's thigh.

The trucker jumped back against the door, trying to escape, but the door wouldn't budge.

The Indian yanked the knife out of the seat and lunged again. "I watched the smirks on those white racist faces as they plowed the dirt over us!" he yelled, slashing, grazing Harley's arm as he rammed the knife into the dashboard.

Harley whimpered in fear. The Indian's face was frightening—a mask of yellow-splotched red rage. He watched as this living-dead monster angrily jerked the knife from the dash and brought it up under Harley's chin. Harley's head was pinned against the window and he felt the blade sting his neck as he squirmed. "Please don't hurt me!" he pleaded, feeling the knife dig deeper into his neck. He could feel a wetness at his collar and he knew he was bleeding. "Please! I've got a wife and two boys who need me."

"They don't need you. They've become accustomed to life without you. If I cut your throat from ear to ear they wouldn't miss you for weeks. Yeah, I think I'll lay your throat wide open and watch you die like a white dog, watch you struggle for those last few breaths the way we did."

"Oh, God! Please don't hurt me, Nicky. I beg you. I never did anything to you, man. I wasn't involved with the BIA."

"Nope, this is the end, white man." The Indian nodded at the photographs on the sun visor. "Say goodbye to your lovely wife and handsome sons. Don't you wish now that you'd spent more time with them?"

Harley choked on the acid rising in his throat. "I thought you said you just wanted a piece of my time."

"I lied. The same way the white man has lied to Indian nations since the beginning of time. You'll understand more in due time."

Harley looked up into twin brown orbs of pure, maniacal evil.

He saw a metallic flash, felt a wet sting across his throat.

His soul frosted over.

HE AWOKE SCREAMING AND SHAKING.

Bright sunlight stung his eyes.

Harley quit screaming when he heard a voice to his left. "Hey, buddy. You all right?"

Harley squinted to his left and saw a state transportation agent up on the running board, staring through the window at him. Harley was disoriented, confused. He ran a hand across his neck, surprised to discover his unscathed stubble. The seat leather was unpunctured, the interior unmarred. The windshield was smooth and intact.

He was at the California state line. At a weigh station.

How had he arrived here?

He couldn't remember anything after Maricopa Pass and his frightening encounter with the Indian spirits. Was he dead now? Maybe the knife-wielding crazy who called himself a chameleon spirit had really killed him and he was waiting his turn for entrance into the Hereafter. Or maybe he had pulled over somewhere last night and dreamed the whole thing. He didn't know. His mind was fuzzy with a speed hangover; his thought processes were muddled.

Finally, after he shook away some of the cobwebs, he determined he was still alive. Had to be, there was no other logical explanation.

Suddenly his entire being filled with an overpowering joy. Harley looked forward to going back home, to being with Sharene and the boys. He would be a *real* husband and father again, not some teamster roadbird who had been AWOL from his family far too long. He had made his last long-haul, of that he was sure. Surely that was the message the gods were attempting to convey to him through this extraordinary misadventure.

"C'mon, buddy, you're holding up the works," the agent at the window barked. "You got two choices—hand over your bill of lading and get your rig up on that scale, or park in the rest area and relax for a while. Judging from the looks of ya, I'd recommend a little rest stop."

Harley grabbed the shipping manifest from the glove-box and passed it through the window to the agent. He put the big Peterbilt into gear, and the truck lumbered onto the scale. After several minutes, the agent returned with a distraught look on his face.

"Something's not quite right here, Mr. Ordner."

"You're telling me?" Harley said, still trying to piece together exactly what had happened to him last night. "What's wrong now?"

"Well, your paperwork states you're carrying nearly forty thousand pounds of freight. You weigh in considerably less than that. Look at this." The agent bent through the window and showed him figures on his clipboard.

"What? Why, that's barely over my tare weight!"

"Exactly. I think maybe we need to have a look in your trailer."

"The seal hasn't been tampered with?"

"Not so far as I can tell. The padlocks don't seem to have been touched either."

He accompanied the agent to the rear of the truck. There were no shotgun pellets embedded in the trailer walls nor was there any structural damage.

Had it all been a dark, disturbing dream?

He still couldn't account for how he had traveled to the California border. Harley had no recollection of crossing the wide stretch of desert mountains.

The rear trailer doors were solidly sealed, the padlocks securely in place. Nothing could be wrong inside the trailer. Surely the freight scale was malfunctioning.

Harley broke the paraffin seal, opened the padlocks.

The big steel doors creaked open. He took a step backward and stared, dumbfounded.

All but one of the caskets were gone.

"Oh, my God!"

"What happened to your freight, buddy?" the agent said from behind him.

Reluctantly, Harley approached the lone coffin. Lifting that mahogany lid seemed like the most difficult task in the world at the moment.

"It's just not possible to lose twenty tons of freight without a broken seal," the agent said from behind him. "At least I ain't never seen it done."

A creepy feeling came over Harley as he realized last night hadn't been some warped dream. He knew the psychopathic Indian chief had been real. What he didn't know was whether to feel relief or distress. He opened the coffin, fully prepared to find a corpse inside—a jaundiced Indian corpse.

But Harley saw something else entirely.

He stared down into the coffin, a wave of nausea rolling through him like a dark tsunami. What he saw lying there on the bed of lavender velvet just could *not* be. Surely his eyes deceived him. Surely this apparition before him was yet another surreal by-product of his crystal-meth ingestion.

A sour wet glob clutched in his throat and he gagged. He heard a whooshing sound behind him and he whirled, his nerves stretched tight as piano wire. The transportation agent had disappeared. Harley was all alone in the cavernous trailer; at least he was alone with the *thing* in the coffin.

Suddenly the heavy rear doors clanged shut. Harley watched in disbelief as the lock bars engaged with a brittle click. Sudden fear gripped him as he realized he was locked in, sealed off from the outside world, a prisoner in this rolling steel cell.

"Uh . . . what's happening here?" he asked, his words hollow and echoey in the dim trailer.

Reluctantly, he turned back to the coffin in search of an answer, but the macabre spectacle nestled there only raised more questions. Like a rubbernecker at the scene of a bad traffic accident, Harley was both repulsed and fascinated by the half-lizard, half-man that stretched the length of the mahogany casket. The head was reptilian, the long forked tongue protruding in a frozen rictus of death. The body was human, with two perfectly proportioned legs and a barrel-chested torso. But the oddest thing of all was that this biological aberration wore Harley's own gray uniform and rubber-soled black boots. He shuddered as he saw the familiar **Ordner Hauling, Inc.** logo stitched in red over the breast pocket of the work shirt. He noticed the black boots on the corpse were scuffed in identical places as the boots he now wore.

"What . . . the hell . . . is . . . going on?" he mumbled, instantly feeling foolish talking to a lizard-headed corpse.

As if in answer, streams of fine dirt began to fall through unseen cracks in the ceiling. The trailer filled with a loamy, earthy smell.

Incredibly, the head of the lizard began to change. The tongue recoiled. The snout compacted, filling out into a chin and a pair of puffy cheeks. The scaly skin softened into something resembling flesh. Strands of graying brown hair sprouted from atop the head. The eyes lost their slitted, reptilian cast, shaping into more humanoid ovals. Harley watched the transformation, stunned, disbelieving, knowing all too well the face that was taking shape.

The corpse was metamorphosing into him!

Dirt poured from the ceiling more rapidly now, the

swish-swish-swish of the accumulating piles becoming louder.

The transformation of the lizard-head was nearly complete, and Harley stared down at the corpse in abject terror. It was clearly him lying there, or at least a damn good representation of him.

Panic set in as he noticed the floor of the trailer now completely covered with sandy earth. A foot or more and still it poured from the ceiling. Faster and faster.

Swish-swish-swish.

His panic gripped him around the throat as the corpse sat up awkwardly in the coffin and spoke. Though the physical being was clearly him, the voice belonged to the ex-chieftan of the Maricopa tribe, Nicky Stillbrook.

"You have done our people a great service, Harley. You have provided two-hundred-and-forty-nine of our lost souls with a final resting place. Spiritually, you have done the Maricopa a great deed, and I want you to know I am appreciative."

Harley couldn't believe this—the nutcase with the machete blade who called himself a chameleon spirit talking through Harley's own mouth. Cosmic ventriloquism. It was absurd, and yet, as Harley looked around and saw the trailer filling up with dirt at a frighteningly rapid clip—actually *felt* the silty earth sliding in and around his ankles and up his legs—he knew he was doomed.

"And *this* is how you show your appreciation?" he said weakly, pointing at the onrushing rivers of dirt.

The corpse that was Harley lay back in the coffin. The face went from powdery-pale flesh to a sickly saffron, the jaundiced yellow tinge that had marked Nicky Stillbrook's face and hands.

Again the corpse spoke. "You must experience the way

158

we met our fateful end in order for you to remain bound to our cause. You are one of us now, Harley, a Maricopa chameleon spirit, destined to carry out orders in the spectral world . . ."

Swish-swish-swish.

The dirt was up to Harley's waist and rising fast. He tried to move, but something from below pulled him down, kept him stationary. "But why me?" he cried, trying to get a foothold out of the quicksand-like dirt. "I never did anything wrong to the Maricopa, or any other Indian tribe for that matter."

"True enough," came Nicky Stillbrook's reply. "However, your ancestors did. We *all* must pay for the sins of your ancestors. And you happened to be in the wrong place at the wrong time, carrying precisely the *right* cargo. Tough break, but then, in the chaos that is life, such things often occur. Count your blessings, Harley. Things are much more sensible in the spiritual world. You will experience a liberating freedom that is not possible in the physical world. You'll be able to fly with the eagles and swim with the dolphins. You'll be able to enter mortal men's minds undetected, invade regions of the subconscious at will. As a chameleon spirit, nowhere will be off limits to you. You will experience a wide-open mobility, but it may come at the expense of eternal rest for your cursed soul—that's always the tradeoff. However, before you become one of us, you must experience our incredible pain . . . our suffering . . ."

The air inside the trailer became thin and dusty. Harley sneezed. His eyes watered uncontrollably. And then he heard engines just outside the trailer, racing and groaning. Not car engines, but the low grumble of working machines. Tractors? Road graders?

" . . . This act is symbolic of all the injustices perpetrated on the American Indian tribes," Nicky Stillbrook continued. "Especially the white man's theft of our land and the numerous acts of genocide against our people."

The rear doors swung open and Harley saw the source of the engine noises. A pair of large backhoes swung their gargantuan shovels into the rear of the trailer—metal-toothed demons overflowing with freshly dug Arizona soil. The first shovel positioned itself directly over Harley's head. He looked up in terror, squirmed to free himself.

"It is time to change colors, Harley . . . time to venture forth into the spectral world."

Harley looked back into the coffin and saw his looka-like corpse undergoing strange kaleidoscopic color muta-tions.

A rusty squeak above him made Harley glance up. He saw the steel teeth of the shovel a split second before the wide bucket tipped its payload. A ton of dirt and sand came down on him, crushing the air from his lungs. He tried to scream but could summon no breath. He tried to move but was pinned in by the suffocating dirt. His mind raged in claustrophobic confusion. He needed air! He tried to breathe but succeeded only in swallowing a mouthful of dirt. He was near hysteria. Adrenaline coursed through him in torrents and he tried desperately to move his arms and legs. Finally, on the verge of unconsciousness, he pushed his head up and out of his earth tomb, gasping, choking.

But his freedom was to be short-lived.

The second backhoe dumped its load, crushing him under the incredible weight. Misty ebony clouds exploded in his brain. Sharp needles pierced his lungs as he fought for air.

Just before his will to live was overpowered by this strange and inexplicable fate, Harley was overcome by a crystalline distant vision. Images and sounds played out in his mind like one of those old flickering moviehouse news-reels: the thunder of hooves as hundreds of horses trampled over the sun-baked tundra of an ancient battleground . . . the crack of gunfire rolling through the nearby hills and a haze of spent gunpowder enveloping the area . . . the anguished cries of wounded and dying Indian warriors, bleeding and broken in the dusty field of death, trampled underfoot as a U.S. Cavalry unit swept through on their quest to claim this plot of land. Harley felt a heavy sadness at the carnage and destruction of the horrendous spectacle.

His vision weakened, the edges of the scene curling and distorting like a photograph thrown on a blazing fire. He was drawn to the field lieutenant leading the relentless charge, and then with shame and a sense of long-lost guilt, he knew what this vision was all about. The lieutenant who shouted killing orders above the raucous din wore an ID patch on the left breast of his moth-eaten blue uniform which read:

Garrison Ordner
43rd Cavalry
U.S. Army

Through some kind of quirky cosmic telepathy, Harley knew this was his great-great-great grandfather, leading the charge at the infamous Maricopa Massacre at Gila Bend. Through some weird grandiose transference of historical information, Harley knew that more than seven-hundred of the Maricopa tribe had perished that bloody day in 1862. Those who survived were pushed back up into the moun-tains, away from their fertile growing lands. It was a tragic day in Maricopa history and Harley had just relived it in the blink of an eye.

In this one brief flash Harley was able to put everything

into perspective. *We all must pay for the sins of your ancestors,* he heard Nicky Stillbrook's voice intone faintly.

And then there was darkness.

HE WRIGGLED THROUGH MILES of earth—more like swimming or floating actually—parting the sandy soil as though he was paddling through an ocean of warm water. He was conscious of his movement, though he felt suspended from any reality with which he was familiar. Everything possessed a dreamlike aura, making him feel unencumbered by the chains of traditional space and time. He felt alone and free, detached from a world he had just recently known, yet plugged in to some higher circuit, some supreme network that filled him with joy and benevolence. The past was but bits and pieces of fractured memories, the future an optimistic light on a sun-dappled, celestial horizon.

He broke through the earth and emerged in the middle of a tiny cemetery. Strangely, the ground next to the headstone where he had broken through was undisturbed. Inexplicably, he was drawn to the headstone. Some force within him made him reach out and touch the smooth slab. He had no visible arms or legs, and though he knew this fact should have troubled him, he was comfortable with it. His touch was a mental linking, though in his mind he could easily feel the icy-smooth surface of the gravestone and the roughened grooves of each letter engraved across its face. The name on the headstone—Nicholas G. Stillbrook—startled him, though he had no idea why it should.

A warm buzzing emanated from the grave, filling his being with energy and purpose.

Soon he had his orders.

In the same clairvoyant way he had known about the 1862 Maricopa massacre at Gila Bend, he knew about the Native American appropriations bill that would send more than three million dollars to the Maricopa reservation in Arizona. Two key Congressmen were planning to veto the bill, citing that by doing so, the U.S. government would be admitting to a coverup of their involvement in the recent hepatitis tragedy there. His orders were to sway those two votes the other way, and actually *increase* the appropriation if possible, maybe even bring the tragic incident to the attention of the national media.

Suddenly the graveyard came alive in a reptilian frenzy. Lizards—hundreds of them—scurried over headstones and through the closely-cropped grass. They changed colors rapidly, spectacularly, as if to punctuate their fury.

He observed them performing their slithering war dance and felt comforted, knowing he was among his own kind.

Chameleons.

Maricopa chameleons. Warriors of the spectral world.

Swelled with prideful anger, he left the graveyard and headed to the east. Toward Washington. His colorful comrades marched in columns along either side of him, flanking him, providing him with an escort.

It wouldn't take them long to get to their destination. They moved swiftly through multi-colored worlds, where lightness and darkness collided in multifaceted rainbows, where space was infinite and time threaded itself through far-reaching dimensions with a supercharged universal needle.

They were restless, yet purposeful and focused.

Lizard soldiers, fighting a centuries-old war in ways the white man would never be able to comprehend.

Maricopa chameleons.
Warriors of the spectral world.

Originally Peter Bianca of STRANGE DAYS purchased "Insomniacs Anonymous" for publication in the Fall '93 issue. I had published "Last Call" in the Spring '93 issue of that excellent magazine (one of my all-time favorite speculative fiction magazines and certainly the largest readership of any of the markets in which my stories appeared). Naturally, I was excited, but my excitement was short-lived as STRANGE DAYS sadly folded in '94 before that issue made it to the newsstands. But things have a way of working out. RANDOM REALITIES published "Insomniacs Anonymous" in the Spring '95 issue just as that publication was going to national distribution. This quirky little science-fantasy generated more mail than all of my other published stories combined. My intention was to write a social commentary about the ways in which the corporate world and its unrealistic demands on employees have unraveled the fabric of American society. But you wouldn't believe the wide array of interpretations readers sent me . . . everything from Biblical connotations to the follies of support groups.

INSOMNIACS

ANONYMOUS

"**HI. MY NAME IS BERT** and I slept three hours last night!"

A smattering of applause greeted the silver-haired man who stood behind the podium. His cheeks were hollow and dark circles ringed his eyes, giving him a raccoonish appearance.

"How did you do it?" came a call from the audience.

"Electromagnetics," Bert replied with a weary smile. "I was assisting my daughter with her science project, helping her build an electromagnetic field, and I just passed out right there at the table. Three hours of sweet, uninterrupted sleep!"

"I've tried electromagnetics," shouted a man from the back. "They don't do shit for me."

"Me either," cried a few others.

The man at the podium became defensive. "I'm not saying they work for everybody . . . only that they helped me."

A thin, gaunt woman was next. Her fingers curled around the edges of the podium like bleached twigs. "My name is Gloria and earlier this week my husband and I slept for nearly four-and-a-half hours!" She paused while the attendees oohed and aahed. "We did it with mercury. There is some quality to mercury that seems to fool the implants. Of course, you have to be real care—"

"That's an old wive's tale, lady," a man yelled out rudely. From the audience came cries of "Sit down!"

The moderator, an elderly gentleman named Elliott, attempted to cool the attendees. These IA meetings had a tendency to get out of hand. "Come on, people," he implored in his usual conciliatory tone, "we all have unique biochemical relationships with our implants. What works for one might not for someone else. But we all share the agony these chips impose on our lives. We're all overworked and exhausted. This is supposed to be a support group, not a lynch mob. We should respect each other. Be happy for those who are able to get some quality sleep . . ."

"Oh, bullshit!" A man with scarlet toadlike eyes stood.

"I'm sick and tired of what these corporations are doing to us . . . working us double shifts, sometimes round-the-clock, just so the filthy-rich-pig board members can make more jack. Like they need any more damn income!" With a shaky hand, he lowered his collar and pointed at the tiny blue dot on his neck. "We're all slaves to this, people. We've returned to the sweatshop mentality of the twentieth century, only now they have more control with these frigging biochips. Sure, we can all steal a little shuteye here and there, but there's nothing *quality* about it . . ."

"You got that right," a woman off to his left shouted. "I can't remember the last time I slept. Dreams are just a distant memory now. All the time I'm cranky and my joints ache. And for what? Just so I can pay my outrageously overinflated bills? So some fat-cat corporate slugs can wallow in more wealth? Used to be, you could get a decent job working forty hours a week for an independent company. But we all know independents don't exist anymore. Thanks to all the buyouts and acquisitions, we have to work two to three shifts, six days a week, just to make ends meet—especially if you have kids like I do. It's absurd! They sink these goddamned chips in our necks and they own us! We're nothing but corporate robots . . ."

A heightening fervor bubbled through the room. Elliott again intervened, before he had a riot on his hands. "Okay, hold it down," he shouted over the din. "What are the alternatives? We couldn't live without the income from our jobs—"

"You call this *living?*" came the reply from the angry mob. "This is slavery!"

"Yeah! We're all so sleep-deprived we can't even think straight . . ."

A shrill whistle cut through the commotion. Voices

quieted. Heads turned to the back of the room, necks stretching, fatigued faces searching. All eyes focused on a tall, bespectacled young man who stood near the rear door. He was impeccably groomed, every hair combed precisely in place in a pitch-black pompadour that swept elegantly off a high forehead. A luxurious suit of the finest Japanese silk accentuated his trim frame. Expensive rayode rings gleamed on the pinkies of his well-manicured hands.

"You are going about this in the wrong manner," he said, his voice smooth and confident. Large owlish eyes darted behind thick lenses as he met the curious stares of the crowd.

The IA members scratched their heads and looked at one another in befuddlement.

Elliott called to him from the front of the room. "You're a stranger to these meetings, aren't you, mister?"

"Indeed, I am," he said, unblinking.

"Well, suppose you come up front and introduce yourself, shed some light on your comment."

"Gladly," he said, strolling leisurely up the middle aisle, cool as a freon-charge bath.

Incredulous expressions followed the young man up to the podium, expressions that silently said, *Not only is he wealthy, but he's also well rested! What's his game?*

"My name is Gabriel and I have *never* missed a night of sleep."

A shocked moment of silence deadened the room, then utter pandemonium erupted. Members shouted "You're one of them, ain't ya? One of them corporate geeks!" and "Get lost corpo swine!"

The man calmly placed his hand over the microphone, causing an ear-splitting shriek of feedback. Gabriel again had everyone's utmost attention.

"There's no way I could ever be a corporate board member," he said. "That goes against everything I've ever stood for—"

"Let's see your chip, then. Show us your neck."

"I don't have an implant," he said, smiling. "I . . ."

"Then you *are* one of them—"

"Please, folks," Elliott intoned. "Let Gabriel have his say."

"Thank you, kind sir." Gabriel spoke with an elegant sophistication that held the hostile audience in rapt fascination. "I knew from a very young age that I didn't want to be a corporate drone. I saw what those nasty implants did to my parents . . . eventually drove my mother to the sanitarium, and my father . . . well, he committed suicide trying to burn the damn chip out of his neck with a laser iron. The only way to beat these corporations is at their own game. Very few of us can survive in our society without that corporate umbilical, but I have done it. And as you can see, I've done quite nicely for myself.

"I go to these IA meetings and hear the lengths that people go to in order to buy a few hours of sleep. Tonight I've heard about electromagnetics and mercury. At other meetings it's shock therapy and freezing compounds. But these are only patchwork solutions, my friends. These remedies only work for a select few, and their effects wear off quickly. Then it's back to a non-sleeping reality—"

"So whaddaya got that's any better?"

"Yeah! Get on with it, man! Tell us how *you* do it."

Gabriel remained unflustered. "I have made these bio-chips my life's work," he said evenly. "I have studied remote teleprocessing and microchip technology and the effects of implants on the central nervous system. While a lot of my friends partied their way through college, doing

169

nothing more than avoiding their labor-legal status a few more years, I burned the midnight oil searching for a way to beat the system. Damned if I was going to let them sink a bio-bullet in *my* neck! Those of us not born under a silver moon either find a way to beat those who are, or we become their indentured slaves."

He reached into his suit jacket and produced an oblong object with a rubber handle and shiny metallic tip. The audience stared at what looked like an old fashioned screwdriver.

"This, my friends, is the answer to all of your insomnia problems," he said, holding the gadget out in front of him. "The corporations are primarily interested in the number of hours you log rather than your production figures. Am I right about this?"

Suspicious nods and grumbled acknowledgments from the IA members.

Gabriel nodded. "In their infinite mental midgetry, they figure that if they automatize you and keep you awake for long stretches, you will produce. All of these biochips are designed with severe hypothalamus inhibitors to deaden the sleep-necessity portions of the brain. They also have cerebral cortex oscillators to stifle intelligence and keep you on the move while preventing you from having seizures or hallucinations. Therefore, you are capable of doing repetitious, mindless tasks efficiently for long periods of time. In essence, they have transformed you into pseudo-robots for very little cost. But most corporations don't feel the need to check individual production figures very closely. They count on your hyperactivity taking care of that. And that's where my little invention here comes in . . ."

"How so?"

"Yeah, that thing looks pretty ordinary to me."

Pride gleamed in Gabriel's owlish eyes. "This is what I call a viral transfer—or VT—wand. I have developed a mutating computer virus that distorts the most sophisticated of the biochip implants. This plain-looking tool injects the virus into the chips. The virus fools the logging systems into tallying work hours, even when you are sound asleep. For those few systems that *do* compute output, the virus can be modified to fool those, also. All in all, quite ingenious. But it should be. I've dedicated my life to its development."

"Enough with the biotech mumbo-jumbo already! How does it work? How will it help us?"

"Patience, people . . . patience."

"We're too tired to be patient."

"Okay, okay. It's quite simple, really. I activate the VT wand by twisting the handle, then I touch the tip to the surface of the implant, thereby injecting the virus into your chip. You are asleep within the first minute; after five minutes you're well into the third or fourth stage of dream-filled REM sleep. And your bosses are none the wiser for it, either."

"So what? You knock us out for a while and then we're back to the same dreary routine."

"Not so. Once the virus is in the chip, you can sleep almost at will. The only way to remove it is by a hands-on disabling by a corporate tech, which is a tough job, even under the best of conditions. But the way this virus mutates, they'll have a tough time even *finding* it. This little biochip demon covers its tracks well, and has been known to play havoc with some of the largest corporate databases. Even if you overuse it, it'll take the corporations several years to get around to it, what with their bureaucracy and ineptness."

"How do we know your gizmo won't kill us? Something like that *can't* be safe."

"Your implants are a lot more dangerous than this. The virus is a non-toxic *software* bug—there's nothing biological about it."

"Oh, bullshit! How do we know you're not some kinda mass murderer or something?"

"Yeah, I'm not buying it, either!"

The meeting was spiraling out of control, attendees shouting surly insults at the man standing before them. The well-groomed stranger who called himself Gabriel had succeeded only in fueling their simmering hostilities.

Several people stood to leave as Elliott spoke. "How much is your viral treatment, Gabriel?"

"Forty-two kilocredits for standard treatment . . . Fifty for production-reporting adjustments."

The angry crowd hushed, becoming more interested.

Elliott was astonished. Forty-two kilocredits wouldn't buy much more than a pair of second-hand zip shoes. "Surely if your remarkable little wand can do all you claim, you could make a hundred times that amount."

"Oh, I could make an unlimited amount of income working for the corporate sector," Gabriel boasted, "but that would mean selling out my ideals. Some things are much more important than credidollars, my friend."

But this claim rang falsely with the IA members. A large number of them were gathering their things together and heading toward the exits, mumbling about scams and flim-flams as they shuffled down the aisles. "You're about as trustworthy as one of those late-night televid hawkers!" someone yelled.

"Wait!" the silver-haired man named Bert called out. "What do we really have to lose, folks? Every week we come here and bitch about how bad things are. Now this man comes along offering us some hope, and you all turn your backs on him." The IA members making their way out stopped, turned to listen. "I mean, we're already standing in our graves, buried up to our necks. Hell, I'm willing to give almost anything a shot at this point." Bert walked toward the podium, unfastening his collar as he went.

"Yeah, you can't go wrong for forty-two kilocredits," the woman named Gloria agreed, falling in behind Bert.

Bert eagerly handed over his credit-chip and watched as the man with the sleep wand keyed the transaction into his pocket financer. Then, payment approved, Gabriel lowered the VT wand to Bert's neck in a sweeping, theatrical gesture. There was a sharp zip as the tip connected with the tiny blue implant. Bert's eyelids fluttered and he wavered on his feet. "I'm getting . . . *so* . . ." he slurred, his raccoonish eyes rolling. He yawned widely and then collapsed, leaving his statement unfinished. Gabriel caught him before he hit the floor.

Gloria followed as dozens of IA members fell in line behind her, pulling out their charge-chips and chattering excitedly about the very real prospect of imminent sleep. One by one they paid their credidollars and were touched by the somnolent magic of Gabriel's viral transfer wand. One by one they fell to the floor, embraced by the soothing arms of long-overdue sleep.

Twenty minutes later, Gabriel finished with Elliott the moderator, and the room echoed with the snores and whistles of deep sleep. He sighed and looked around at his unconscious flock. A grin creased his unlined face. Each prone IA member represented another small victory against the corporations that had caused his father's death. Each sleeping form cut into the greedy corporate profit structures that had contributed to his mother's breakdown. He was one of the few people who could honestly say he enjoyed his life's work, that his daily contribution to society actually *meant* something. Something positive. Something *good*. Sessions like this pumped him up, filled him with elation.

The rear door squeaked open. A man wearing a gray janitor's uniform walked in toting a magnetibroom. The janitor pulled up short when he glimpsed all the bodies littering the floor. His gaze slowly followed the trail of bodies leading up to the podium. He gasped as his eyes came to rest on the nattily attired man who was holding some kind of weapon.

"Y-you didn't . . . ki-kill them all . . . didya, mister?"

Gabriel laughed as he moved from behind the podium. "No, I didn't kill them, my friend," he said, stepping over sprawled-out bodies as he made his way toward the janitor. "I merely gave them back their dreams."

"Wh-who are you?" The janitor's eyes were wide with fright as he backed against the wall.

Gabriel moved in on the man. "Some people call me The Dream Wizard." He pointed the VT wand at the cowering janitor. "You look like you could use a dream or two."

"No! Please don't hurt me," the janitor yelled, holding the magnetibroom between himself and this maniac who called himself The Dream Wizard.

The wand came down, the tip finding the tiny blue dot on the janitor's neck. In less than thirty seconds, the man was out cold.

I haven't become too big for charity work, Gabriel thought, laughing.

Another small victory for The Dream Wizard.

But there was still so much to be done. So many to touch. So many to reconnect with stubborn, illusive dreams.

Gabriel placed the VT wand back in his suit pocket and

hurried out the door. If he hustled he could catch the Middletown Insomniacs Anonymous meeting before it adjourned.

This next tale is one of my more rough-and-tumble horror pieces. Like the earlier "Wombstone," this one is about an extremely dysfunctional family . . . the family from hell, if you will. Though "Listening to the Dead" contains some black humor, it packs a vicious bite, and is the primary reason that it was rejected by more magazines than I can count. Many editors returned it saying something along the lines of 'Not for us, we do not believe in the glorification of suicide . . .' My intent was not to glorify suicide, but rather to offer a positive and hopeful glimpse at death, a spiritual theme I seem to visit often in my work. Taking one final stab at magazine publication, I sent it to the editor of the darkest, most grim market I could find: GRUE magazine. About two weeks later I got the story back from Peggy Nadramia with a rejection stating, 'Sorry, this one is a little too cute for us.' Go figure! At any rate, I present "Listening to the Dead" here for you to make your own judgments. But be forewarned, after reading this tale, you will probably never view your answering machine the same way again.

LISTENING TO

THE DEAD

THE PHONE RANG.

She ignored the noisy intrusion. Her appointment was at two and she wanted to finish her lunch in peace.

The answering machine clicked. Her greeting played silently, then:

176

"Gail, this is Mom in case you've forgotten the sound of my voice. Lord knows we don't have the opportunity to talk anymore. I'll make this brief since I know what a shock it must be to hear from me after all this time. I know you're old enough to run your own life now, Gail, and I do commend you on your decision to start dating again so soon after the, um . . . accident. But really darling, you've lowered your standards immeasurably by seeing that maintenance man. Why, in my day they called them janitors. Common laborers! You really ought to go after that psychiatrist you've been seeing. He's single, attractive, intelligent . . . and he has a quite impressive portfolio for such a young man. I know it's not my place to tell you how to live your life—especially now—but women of Yabrell lineage deserve better than common laborers. Take my advice and grab that Dr. Hardesee. Doctors know how to take care of their women, Gail. You have to admit, your father treated us fairly well. We never wanted for anything . . ."

As mysteriously and abruptly as the message began, it ended. Stunned, Gail sat watching the phone, listening to the hiss of the rewinding tape. No way could this have just happened.

Her mother had been dead and buried for more than five years.

Slowly, Gail stood from the table and walked to the answering machine. She reached down to replay the message and jumped back as the phone rang again. The receiver vibrated in the cradle as she counted the rings . . . one . . . two . . . Gail debated whether to answer it, heart pounding, breath quickening to keep up with her galloping pulse. The answering machine kicked in and she watched the tiny reels of the greeting tape go round and round. The low hum of static followed a loud beep as the caller hesitated. And then Gail nearly lost it. She heard the voice of her twin brother Joey. He, too, was dead. Drugs had claimed him. Joey had keeled over onstage singing "I Can't Get No Satisfaction" while his Hellcats bandmates looked on in horror.

"Hey, Sis. Sorry it's taken me so long to contact you but you hafta understand, my low profile isn't totally my fault. There's a four-year waiting period for verbal contact. At least where I ended up there is. I tried getting in touch with you using other methods—dream intervention . . . telepathic consciousness imaging . . . psi powers—but hell, that stuff takes lots of practice and concentration. And the gurus here are all from New York. They talk so fast I can't understand much of what they're saying, so most of us Southern boys hafta learn the communications crap on our own.

"You wouldn't believe how great this place is. If I had known how much fun I'd have in the Afterlife, I woulda checked out a helluva lot sooner. We get to play music around the clock here. There're jam sessions going on all the time and I've even learned how to play some new instruments, like the lute and the lyre. You wouldn't believe the lineup of famous ex-musicians here. I've gigged with John Lennon, though nobody wants to sit in with him when he does those Yoko Ono tunes. A while back I harmonized with Buddy Holly on 'Peggy Sue' and a few other songs and he liked it so much he gave me his unlisted dimension and told me to drop by any time. Lately Elvis has been hanging out with us more since he says he's getting tired of being confused with impersonators every time he treks back to your dimension. And you shoulda caught the guitar jam with Jimi and Stevie Ray getting down! It's all fun and games here, Sis, even though every once in a while some

stuffed shirt pops in and gives us some shit. Not too long ago Jimmy Hoffa started hanging out and began making noises about organizing a super band that he wanted to send on a trans-dimensional tour, but Jim Morrison told him to take his funny cement shoes and go find Amelia to start up a pilots' union!

"Anyway, gotta run for now. You really ought to give up that dreary living existence and come join me, Sis. It'd be so cool."

Gail's hand was a blur as she lunged for the phone.

"Joey? Joey, are you there? Can you hear me?"

Nothing but dead air.

Her fingers twitched against the cool hard plastic of the receiver. She listened with a determined concentration to the faint hiss and the barely audible ghosts of conversations traveling across far-off phone lines.

But there was no Joey Yabrell. Not even the sound of his breathing.

A second later she heard a rude click, and then the dialtone hummed in her ear.

Trembling, she hung up and punched the rewind button. While the tape rewound, she went to the liquor cabinet and retrieved the Dewars, poured herself a tall Scotch. She grabbed a couple of Valiums from her purse and tossed them back, washing them down with a stiff gulp of burning liquor, then returned to the answering machine and with great reluctance, listened to both messages again.

When they finished playing through, Gail plopped down on the counter stool. She was weak and disoriented, perspiration soaking through her blouse. Both voices were legitimate: her mother's nasal, high-society nag and her brother's hoarse bellow—the result of years of alcohol and cigarette abuse coupled with the enthusiastic screaming Joey always

179

referred to as singing.

She looked at the telephone, the instrument of her nightmares. Her arms were heavy as she reached for it, her fingers uncoordinated as she punched 'O'.

"Operator, how do I go about tracing a call?"

"Do you wish to trace a call going to the number you are at currently?"

"Yes," Gail said impatiently.

"Are you aware that there are additional charges for call tracing services?"

"I don't give a damn! Just find out where the last two calls to this number came from. Can you do that?"

"Possibly. Hold the line please."

Gail choked back two long slugs of Scotch while she waited. Her sinuses burned terribly and her eyes watered. She glanced at the wall clock through a veil of tears. What the hell was taking this operator so long? Didn't Ma Bell maintain electronic call logs or something? Nervously, Gail drummed her fingernails against the Formica countertop.

Finally, the operator came back on the line. *"I'm sorry to keep you waiting, ma'am. I'm also sorry to inform you that without having our call tracing services installed, the caller must be on the line for more than three minutes to enable us to track down the correct originating number. The only thing I can tell you is that the last two incoming calls to your number occurred at six-seventeen PM last night and nine-forty-six this morning. Both calls were of less than two minutes' duration."*

"What? I know I just got back-to-back calls! I've got them time-stamped and recorded on my answering machine."

"I'm sorry, but I can only tell you what our records indicate. Perhaps your answering machine has a faulty

timer. You might want to consider having our call tracing service installed. It's only an additional four dollars per month, and it is a very efficient security device."

"I'll think about it," Gail said, then slammed down the phone in frustration.

There had to be some logical explanation for this, she thought while rummaging through her purse for another Valium. This couldn't possibly be some twisted lunatic's intricate caper. Gail knew the most gifted impressionist in the world wouldn't be able to recreate those voices so accurately, so full of the inflections and nuances of her mother's and twin brother's speech patterns. For that matter, *why* would anyone go to all the trouble even if they could?

The Yabrells had been a typical upper-middle class family living in the suburbs of Atlanta before the bizarre series of tragedies struck, the tragedies Gail's relatives now referred to in hushed tones as *The Yabrell Curse*. Mom went first. Stroke caused by aneurysm, according to the coroner's report. Joey followed soon after, his death the culmination of his downward spiral of drink and drugs. The night he collapsed on stage they found enough barbiturates, alcohol, and cocaine in his bloodstream to kill four people. Joey had been *so* close to Mom. About a year later, Dad went down. Massive heart attack they said. Probably attributable to the stress of losing a wife of 29 years and a 27-year-old son.

That's when Gail started seeing Dr. Hardesee. The best psychoanalyst money could buy helped her get her life redirected and back on track, even helping Gail maintain her sanity through the mounting marital problems brought on by her inability to cope. Finally, last fall, she had come to grips with it all, even reconciling with her moody and often estranged husband, Roy. Dr. Hardesee had helped her realize that the Yabrell Curse was nothing but a coincidental string of rotten luck . . . unfair negative karma. It was all behind her now, the good doctor had convinced her. She could look forward to years of nothing but the best of luck. She even stopped going to his office for several months, content for the first time with her home life and personal outlook.

But then, five months ago, Tragedy Number Four struck and the long dormant Yabrell Curse came out of remission. Her husband Roy had been out in the garage cleaning his hunting rifles and target range pistols when she heard a thunderous explosion. She had rushed out to the garage to find Roy's headless body twitching in the corner and a trail of bloody brain matter spewed across the back wall. Close to the body was Roy's favorite pistol, the Old Army .44 caliber Ruger with the custom inlaid walnut grips, the one his grandfather had given him. Gail had taken one look at the incredible carnage and inky black smoke curling from the end of the long barrel like wispy evil snakes, and she had lost consciousness.

She located the vial and shook a pill out into her palm, washed it down with her remaining Scotch. Checking the clock she noticed she was running late for her appointment. She couldn't miss this session today. If anyone could help Gail through this weird development, Dr. Hardesee could.

AN HOUR LATER, Gail was stretched out on Dr. Hardesee's confessional. She felt much better now that she had told the handsome young psychiatrist of the two inexplicable phone calls.

"But did you actually *talk* to either caller, Gail?"

"I told you, I *tried* to speak with Joey, but it sounded like there wasn't anybody on the other end. I brought the tape with me if you want to listen to it. Just so you know I haven't gone bonkers again."

"I never thought you were bonkers, Gail. But I *do* think it would be a good idea to listen to it. Maybe it will give us some clue . . . an idea of how to work this one out together."

Dr. Hardesee's cool whispery voice had always reassured Gail, his verbal magic working on her frazzled nerves like a powerful sedative. The doctor's reserved compassion and sense of teamwork soothed Gail in ways that an open script for Valium never would. Maybe her mother's voice-ghost was right. Maybe she should pursue this great-looking eligible bachelor. But then, just as quickly, she thought about Charlie and she was ashamed.

She retrieved the cassette from her purse and both doctor and patient listened together. The tape wound through the playback heads, producing nothing but a long rush of static punctuated by occasional squeaks. Her mother's and brother's voices did not reveal themselves. The tape player hissed like a skillet of frying bacon, seeming to mock Gail with its loud emptiness.

Finally, Dr. Hardesee punched the stop button and looked up. Tears streamed down Gail's reddened cheeks, and she tried to sniff them back.

"You have been doing extremely well of late, Gail. Please don't let a small setback like this send you into a regression." He pulled a tissue from a dispenser on his desk and handed it to her.

"Okay," she said, dabbing at her eyes.

"Are you all right?"

"I . . . I don't know," she said, sniffling. "I could swear those phone messages were on the tape when I left the house."

"Perhaps you grabbed the wrong tape, Gail. You said you left your house in a hurry, that you were running late."

Gail looked at the doctor and knew by his forced smile and rigid professional bearing that he had little conviction in his own words. "Maybe," she answered, not believing herself either. Gail *knew* something was terribly wrong.

Dr. Hardesee's forced smile relaxed. "Check when you get home. I'm sure you'll find you misplaced the tape. Now, how about we discuss a few things we only briefly touched on in our last session? Maybe that will give us some insight into what's been happening to you. This maintenance man you've been seeing? I believe you've told me his name is Charlie?"

"Yes. Charlie Thurston."

"Tell me again how you feel about him, Gail."

A look of glazed contentment spread over her tear-streaked face. "Charlie's a wonderful man," she began, an image of his thick mop of reddish-orange hair and freckled boyish face making her smile. "He's caring and sensitive. He likes to talk. He's not afraid to tell me how he's really feeling. And . . . Charlie likes the simple things . . . romantic things. He likes to read poetry to me. He sends me the cutest little love notes of verse he writes himself. The first time he had me over to his house for dinner, not only did he cook the entire dinner himself, he served it by candlelight! The Spanish guitar music playing softly in the background and the chilled magnum of Chenin Blanc in a centerpiece of floating magnolia blossoms were the finishing touches. I knew that night we were kindred souls. I knew that night

184

that Charlie Thurston was a man I could love. But I felt guilty. And confused."

Dr. Hardesee looked up from his papers. "Why? Because Roy's accident was such a recent memory and you weren't sure if you were doing the right thing?"

Gail nodded. "We've already covered that."

"I understand. So Charlie is all the things you want in a man—sensitive . . . romantic . . . caring . . . communicative. He makes you genuinely happy. So why is it your mother did— I mean *doesn't* approve of Charlie Thurston?"

"Oh, that's easy. It's because Charlie doesn't care about money and material things. He has no ambitions other than enjoying life and that has always driven Mother absolutely crazy. Charlie isn't real motivated, and both of us could not care less. For the first time in my life, I am completely happy just being with someone. I finally have a pure and simple relationship that isn't cluttered by lies and self-interest and the pursuit of the almighty dollar. I'm tired of thinking I have to keep up with the Joneses. I just want to love and be loved. I just want to experience real heartfelt love . . . not *financial* love. Roy loved his patients more than he loved me. You know why? Because his patients gave him what he craved . . . money and prestige. The truth of the matter is that my husband had deluded himself into thinking he was God. He couldn't handle it when he discovered he wasn't. To a lesser extent, I guess my father was the same way, though he was never around enough for Joey and I to get to know him. He was always running off to take care of this patient or that patient, just like Roy. The only thing that wasn't an emergency with my father was our family. And look what's happened to us! No offense, Dr. Hardesee, but I could never take my mother's advice and get involved with you. I've had my fill of doctors. They've ruined my life."

Dr. Hardesee smiled understandingly. He cleared his throat. "No offense taken, Gail. Let's get off the subject of your mother for a moment and talk about your brother. Joey seems to feel you might be interested in joining him by giving up on life. How do you feel about that?"

She thought this over for a moment. "Joey was always much more of a free spirit than me. He had the attention span of a fly and he gave up on everything he ever tried. Except music, but in the end he checked out on that, too. I could never understand it, but every time he would fail at something, Mother would console him and tell him everything would be okay. Meantime, when I did *anything*, good or bad, she would admonish me . . . tell me how disappointed she was in me. Believe me, there have been many times over the past five years when I felt like checking out. Especially right after Roy did himself in. I thought if I followed suit, the world would finally be rid of the Yabrell Curse. After all, I *am* the last of the Yabrells."

"But you don't feel that way anymore, do you, Gail?"

"No . . ." She hesitated. "But I have to admit there are times when I think about what's happened and I—" she shook her head, a sad and futile gesture. "—I don't know. Now that Charlie is in my life, I feel . . . better. But, if anything happened to Charlie, I just don't know if it would be worth the struggle anymore, and . . . well, there are times when I'm *so* confused . . . when I'm not so sure of myself. I feel overwhelmed by this curse thing. I get the feeling people close to me are in great danger. I couldn't live without Charlie, y'know. Sometimes, I feel like I might do something . . . *crazy*. Especially after these calls."

"I thought we established that this so-called curse is just a figment of your imagination, Gail."

186

She looked at him uncertainly.

A muffled bell rang inside Dr. Hardesee's desk. "Well, time's up," he said, opening a drawer and shutting off the timer. "I have a cancellation on Friday if you'd like to fill it. Perhaps we could get into the origin of these phone calls."

GAIL DIDN'T WANT TO GO RIGHT HOME. It was only 3:30 and Charlie wouldn't be over until eight. She had no desire to be alone, wanting instead to be around people—*living* people who were not doctors. She also wanted to postpone getting home and discovering that there was no other answering machine tape—that she *was* completely bonkers the way she had often suspected.

She went to Harkey's, a neighborhood pub, spent a couple of hours drinking Scotch and conversing with the bartender and a cocktail waitress friend. Harkey's was a wonderful place to *not* be alone. A place in which a person didn't have to think too much.

SHE RETURNED HOME AT 6:30, drunk, weary, incredibly lonely and down in the dumps. The day had been a reawakening of old fears, a slashing-open of healed wounds. She paused in front of the foyer mirror, noticing her bloated appearance, the dark circles under her bloodshot, green eyes, the new lines cutting across her forehead. A little more gray showed through her dark roots.

Depressed, she threw her jacket over the banister and

stumbled into the kitchen to fix a pot of coffee. Charlie just *couldn't* see her in this condition.

Gail didn't even have a chance to turn on the kitchen light.

There, on the counter, the little red answering machine light blinked on and off, like a cyclopean devil winking at her.

Three quick flashes, then darkness, then three quick flashes.

Three calls while she had been out.

Since Roy had died, Charlie was about her only regular caller. She sucked in her breath and valiantly moved forward. Who would it be this time? Worse yet, *what* would it be?

With great reluctance, she pressed the playback button. Her father's harsh baritone resounded through the dark kitchen.

"Hello, Gail. I know you've heard from your mother so this call probably doesn't surprise you that much. I had no intentions of contacting you at all until I heard your insane confessions at Dr. Hardesee's this afternoon. I couldn't let it go without sticking up for myself.

"You have one hell of a nerve putting me down the way you did, young lady! It's not easy trying to raise two lazy, headstrong children who, over the years, drove their mother to a premature death. I worked my fingers to the bone to put you and that wild-ass brother of yours through college. I practically handed you that journalism degree on a silver platter and what have you done with it? The closest you've gotten to anything journalistic is soliciting advertising for one of those pissant little county newspapers! You've just pissed it all away, Gail. Plain and simple. Now you're content to do nothing with your life and live off the

handouts of life insurance and inheritances. How can you live with yourself knowing you're sponging off the accomplishments and hard work of others? Come on and join us, Gail. You'd like it here. This place is nice and leisurely— filled with underachievers like yourself. Come on and do it, Gail. Take the leap. You'll love it here."

Gail began to cry. Long, wracking sobs. The second message began.

"Hello, Gail. I know you won't be able to recognize me from the sound of my voice. I'm your Grandpa Yabrell. I died when you were only two. Car wreck. Never even saw the danged bus that took out your grandmother and me. That doesn't really matter now, honey. What does matter is that you end this godawful curse right now . . . before it goes any further. Before that fine young man you've been seeing goes down with it. This danged Yabrell Curse goes all the way back to my grandfather. I tried to warn your parents numerous times, but both were better at advising than they were at listening. That's the trouble with the world today, sweetheart, nobody listens anymore. But you seem like a reasonable young lady, Gail. I've heard you talking with that psychiatrist. So maybe you'll listen to reason when I tell you that you MUST end this curse now. All you have to do is give in, Gail . . . come to us. Your grandmother and I would love to see you again."

A breathy shriek escaped Gail's lungs as she backed away from the telephone. She screamed again and again, attempting to drown out her grandfather's beckoning voice, but the voice on the tape grew in volume the more she screamed.

"C'mon, Gail, end it now . . . Give in to it . . ."

She couldn't take this anymore.

She couldn't stand the pain any longer.

"There is no pain here, Gail . . . There is only peace . . ."

She ran out into the garage and fumbled with the latch on Roy's firearms cabinet, all the while hearing her grandfather's steady but maniacal voice pour out of the kitchen.

". . . come to us, Gail . . . save other lives . . . end the curse now . . ."

She grabbed the Old Army Ruger .44, the one Roy had used to kill himself. Her hands shook as she loaded the chamber with bullets. In her haste, she dropped several shells on the floor, and she cursed. Huge drops of perspiration dripped off her nose as she bent to retrieve the shells. Gail knew this would only take one or two bullets, but she wanted to be sure. She wanted all six grooves filled, just in case.

Finally, Gail had the gun loaded, stopping for a moment to study the long barrel in the dim light, feeling the heaviness of the revolver in her hand. She reconsidered, if only for a brief second.

Her grandfather's voice clicked off and the last message began. It was Roy.

"You nasty bitch! How can you go on sashaying through life knowing full well you killed me? Oh, maybe you didn't pull the trigger, but you might as well have. You murdered me with your psycho-babble head games and your constant nagging. You always complained about your goofy meddling mother, but she didn't have anything on you . . . you low-rent witch! I was never good enough for you. Everything I ever did you disapproved of . . ."

Gail ran back into the kitchen, brandishing the revolver in her right hand. She sat down at the table and took a long swig from the open bottle of Dewars with her left hand. When the burning stopped and her eyes cleared, she swung the barrel of the revolver around so that it was trained right between her eyes.

The long, shiny barrel stared her in the face.

One quick jerk of the trigger and it would all be over.

"*. . . you deserve to die, you cheap slut! I wasn't in the ground three weeks before you started sleeping with that Charlie creep. Quite a lengthy mourning period you went through there, babes. Well, he'll get his and so will you, bitch! Maybe even that Freudian fruitcake you waste all your time and money on, too. I know all about the damned Yabrell Curse, now. Now that it's too late. Well let me tell ya, I've got my own curse, now, Gail. I curse the day I ever got involved with you and your wacky family . . .*"

CHARLIE THURSTON HEARD the gunshots as he drove up Gail's driveway.

He left the car idling and charged up the front walk.

Two more gunshots in quick succession.

Frantically, he tried the front door but it was locked.

Dear God, what's happening in there? Charlie wondered with mounting panic. He used the key she had given him a few weeks ago and burst into the living room.

The house reeked of alcohol and gunpowder. A cloud of dark smoke drifted out from the kitchen.

"Gail?" His voice echoed hollowly.

No reply. Charlie feared the worst. He had known Gail long enough to know of her periodic dark depressions. He knew all about her husband's violent suicide and her troubles since then. And there was the perceived family curse.

Slowly, carefully, he made his way along the living room wall, peeked around the corner into the kitchen. Through the dim haze he could make out what looked like glittery shards of glass littering the tabletop and floor. The coppery smell of blood touched his nose. The air was tainted with the heaviness of tragedy.

And then he saw her body, slumped in the corner. A long-barreled pistol with an intricately carved handle shone in the muted light.

A small pool of blood, black as oil in the faint light, puddled around one of the table legs.

Oh, sweet Jesus, please don't let it be, Charlie thought as he ran to her.

He bent down, put his arms under her, propped her head up. She was heavy, unyielding, cool, sticky with blood or perspiration, Charlie couldn't tell which. He felt for a pulse—not even a weak flutter.

"Gail! Speak to me goddamnit!" he yelled, his voice sounding strangely detached and thin in the small, dark kitchen. "Oh, God, no! Please don't have done what I think you've done, darling. Speak to me, Gail . . . PLEASE! SAY SOMETHING, GAIL . . . TELL ME YOU'RE ALL RIGHT!"

He leaned in close to her face, listening for breathing and hearing nothing.

She needs mouth-to-mouth . . . needs mouth-to-mouth . . . needs mouth-to-mouth, his anxious mind chanted erratically.

He scrambled to his feet and flicked on the lights, the brightness overwhelming in its intensity.

Charlie turned around, squinting. His heart pushed thick, acidic bile to his throat and he brought a hand to his mouth. His once-lovely Gail was far beyond needing mouth-to-mouth resuscitation. She was doubled over in the corner, jagged fragments of glass and china scattered around her. The white plaster wall behind her was a mosaic of blood and powder-burned flesh and sticky clumps of hair. Smoke wafted from a lone bullet hole near the ceiling where the bullet had penetrated her body. But the worst was her face. Or what was left of it. The left side of her face had been completely blown away. Glistening white bone and gristle jutted grotesquely from that side of her bloodied head. Her right eye was frozen in a milky stare of death that unnerved Charlie, frightened him to his core.

For a long moment he stood, giving his mind time to process the carnage.

Then he turned away in revulsion and leaned against the wall, his back to Gail's corpse.

His brain worked at hyperspeed, charging through every emotional current in quick, chaotic succession. Anger . . . despair . . . sympathy . . . compassion . . . self-pity . . . back to anger again. *How could this happen? How could you leave me like this, without saying goodbye? Damn you, Gail, we were just starting out together. Oh, baby, how could you just throw a beautiful life away like this? Oh, you poor, sweet ignorant child.* Charlie heard himself sobbing. *What am I gonna do without you, now? Oh, Gail, you stupid fool! We could've had such a great life together. Oh, you poor, poor fool.*

Suddenly, Charlie could hold down the bile no longer. He ran to the sink and relieved himself in great heaving convulsions. He was only faintly aware of the phone ringing as he ran the water, washed the crusted blood from his hands and the sweaty tears from his face. As he was drying off, he stopped abruptly, hearing something that would haunt him forever.

Gail's voice on the answering machine.

"Oh, Charlie . . . I'm so sorry I had to leave you this way, but you see, I had very little choice in the matter. I had to beat this damned Yabrell Curse once and for all. I've finally done it . . . oh yes I have! I know you'll have a tough time understanding this, honey, but I did it as much for you as for myself. You were in danger, Charlie, and as long as we were together in life, you would not have been safe. As bad as all this may seem, there's still a way we can be together, Charlie. You'll have to hurry, though. I won't be in this place very long. You see, honey, I left one bullet in the gun . . . just for you! Please hurry, Charlie. I want to be with you . . . where it's safe, and beautiful. Please hurry, Charlie. Go pick up the gun. Trust me, you won't feel any pain . . ."

*Those of you who survived the previous story are suffi-
ciently warmed up for this next one. "Trophies" is clearly
the nastiest, most violent piece of short fiction I have ever
written. One very articulate editor summed it up nicely:
'"Deliverance" Meets Jeffrey Dahmer.' Quite the image,
eh? But a tale of this nature would not work without the
violence. I wrote "Trophies" as a statement against the so-
called sport of hunting. I have always been an animal
lover and I abhor all forms of hunting, finding the
practice to be barbaric and savage. "Trophies" follows the
misadventures of four lifelong friends hunting black
bears in the wilds of Idaho. It answers the age-old
question: What is the most dangerous animal of all?*

TROPHIES

**BY THE TIME WE REACHED HIGH RIDGE
RANCH,** I knew I needed this annual hunting trip much
more than my three friends. My year had fallen apart
through a series of failures while theirs had been filled with
shining successes.

The early May air was pleasantly crisp as we unloaded
our gear from the courtesy van, which had taken us from
Boise Municipal Airport. The hour-plus drive deep into the
heart of The River of No Return Wilderness Area had given
us time to catch up on each other's activities over the past
year.

Frank had finally been rewarded with a full partnership
in the firm, and had proudly distributed fancy business cards

that now listed his name at the end of the engraved logo: *Finestrom, Hinkleberg, Simmons, and Wiley.* Wiley is such a perfect name for a lawyer. I love to needle Frank about this, mainly because he is so uptight about the sleazy aura surrounding his chosen profession.

George had taken yet another new sales position, uprooting his family of eight and moving the Filburtson clan to the sunny climes of Florida, where he was getting in on the cellular phone craze. Seems the wealthy retirees around West Palm Beach couldn't live without calling their friends from the road.

Skip was still Skip, a tall easygoing Texan who wore wide-brimmed Stetsons and snakeskin cowboy boots. He was a teller of embellished tales and spoke in that exaggerated drawl that made many Americans suspicious of Texans. Henry "Skipper" Johnson had earned his nickname due to his love of sailing, and every chance he got, he slipped away with his wife Marilyn for Gulf excursions aboard his 40-foot sloop. Skip's big news concerned the prestigious *National Geographic* account his commercial lithography company had wrestled away from a Mississippi printer.

Then we come to me, the odd man out in this successful bunch. My three Notre Dame college buddies have always been envious of my fame and fortune. They have visions of me sitting by a heart-shaped pool sipping expensive liqueurs while beautiful starlets in thong bathing suits cater to my every whim. If they only knew!

I was still in Hollywood, churning out scripts for bad kiddie sit-coms and even worse daytime soaps. The hack work paid me handsomely, allowing me to live in a luxurious mansion in West Hollywood, but I wasn't happy inside. The past year had emptied out my soul, both professionally and emotionally. The networks had refused to pick up a pair of my ensemble-cast, continuing-storyline pilots on which I had done my best writing in years. The past year also saw me losing yet another mate, my third wife having divorced me, running off with a hunky actor young enough to be her son. And not one week after the papers were signed! Out of frustration, I began the novel I had always been threatening to write, but it was not going well, either. Couple all this with a few major investments gone sour and a tax audit, and you have the blueprint for one of the worst years of my life. Without much positive to report, I had kept quiet on the ride out from the airport.

We made several trips, carrying our gear from the van into the lodge. The exertion in the sunny, clean air was already doing me good, chasing away the smog and cluttered memories of LA. On the final trip, a large hand slapped me on the back, hard, slamming the air from my lungs.

"How 'bout it, Hollyweird? We gonna nail us some big bears or what?" Skip's baritone boomed, his south Texas drawl making it sound like *big bars*.

"Sure thing, Skip," I said, struggling for a breath.

"Bears are about the only thing we don't have in Texas. Leastways not bigguns."

"You've got bears in Texas, Skip," Frank said, coming up behind us. "Big, loudmouthed retarded ones called Republicans!"

Skip spit out a brown glob of tobacco juice, his ruddy face a scowl. "Funny, comin' from you, Frank, seein' as how you're from that hotbed of liberal corruption— Kennedychussetts!"

We all laughed. The political analysts were at it already. It was great to be among close friends again.

Since we were already pre-registered, the others got

their keys and hauled their gear to the cabins. I stayed in the lodge, waiting to talk with the proprietor about the schedule for the next three days. This was my year to organize the trip, so I felt it my duty to get all the particulars concerning the hunt. The woman who checked us in and gave us our keys told me Don Flaherty was on the phone and would be with me momentarily.

This was our first trip to Idaho and the High Ridge Ranch, a licensed outfitters lodge that specialized in elk, lion, and spring bear hunts. I had read about an unusual method of tracking black bears in one of the hunting magazines and was immediately intrigued by it. Instead of the traditional method of baiting bear pots and waiting days for the creatures to show, hunters paddled down rivers in early spring, spotting bears as they came out of their winter slumber. Supposedly, this was foolproof since the bears were sluggish, just becoming active again, their defense mechanisms dulled by long winter naps. Big game hunters could lie in wait and pick off bears as they came down to the waterline to drink, bathe, nab fish, or forage for berries. High Ridge Outfitters advertised a money-back guarantee that every hunter would bag at least one bear during the three-day trek. It was big game hunting for those with little time and patience.

While I waited, I admired the magnificent array of big game heads mounted on the dark paneled walls: mountain lion, moose, caribou, whitetail deer, mule deer, an elk bull with an impressive 12-point rack, a mountain goat. All stared at me through lifeless marbled eyes. In one corner a full-sized bighorn sheep had its curly-cue ramhorns lowered, facing off against a huge black bear. *Jesus! We're going to be hunting creatures that big?* I marveled, estimating the bear's height at seven feet and weight somewhere in the vicinity of 600 pounds.

"Pretty impressive, eh?"

I turned and saw a rugged-looking man with a pinched mouth and a scar that zig-zagged across his left cheek. "Mr. Flaherty?"

"Don," he said, coming out from behind the counter. "And you're Mr. McMichaels?"

I nodded. "Wes McMichaels. My friends call me Mick—or Hollyweird, depending on the friend." We shook hands and I felt the calloused strength of Don Flaherty's grip. A real outdoorsman's handshake. "I was just admiring your trophies here. All of them killed in these parts?"

"Oh yeah. This area's got more critters per square mile than anywhere else in the Rockies. Somethin' in the water or air makes 'em reproduce faster'n we can shoot 'em down. Even this early in the spring the huntin's good."

I looked back at the stuffed black bear, raised on its haunches with a giant paw outstretched, ready to swipe. "Are the bears out here all this big, Don?"

"Bigger. That'n there's a runt compared to some of 'em we've bagged. They're ornery bastards, too. They got a rip-roarin' temper when they get pissed off. You're in serious trouble if you don't bring 'em down with the first two shots." He pointed to the ragged beet-red wound etched in his cheek. I noticed he was missing his left index finger. "This here's a souvenir from a brown bear—both the scar and the lost finger. Bastard damn near ripped the entire side of my face off. That's what I get fer tryin' to hunt bears with a hangover."

I swallowed hard. "You're not reassuring me much, Don."

The proprietor ran his hand over the bear's coarse black fur, a gesture of respect. "Ain't my job to reassure ya, partner. These babies are the biggest land carnivores on this planet. They're the biggest of the big game . . . unpredictable, *dangerous* beasts! If I was you an' yer friends, I'd get a good night's sleep. We leave here at five AM sharp. Bears are early risers . . . like to hit the water 'bout dawn. We got the best chance of pluggin' a couple when the sun starts comin' up. That's my job, Mick . . . to bring you gentlemen back four trophies—a head to go over each of yer fireplaces."

I smiled uneasily, noticing the size of the sharp claws on the frozen creature next to me. "I've got a spot in my den reserved for it."

"Ain't nothin' like a mounted head to prove a big game hunter's worth," Flaherty said. "Head trophies make great conversation pieces."

That night we all ate steak and potatoes in The Hungry Hunter Bar and Grille, the on-site restaurant that, we were told, was the only eating establishment within twenty miles. The steak was tough and overcooked, but the potatoes, mixed vegetables, and salads were good. And if the beer was any colder it would have been ice.

Twenty-one years ago, as we were awarded our various degrees at graduation, we vowed that only major illness or death would prevent this annual hunting pilgrimage, this reunion of dissimilar personalities bound together by a common passion. So far, no one had missed a trip.

"I remember that year down in Louisiana," George recalled, "when we were hunting wild turkey in the bayou and Frank slipped away from the guide, thinking he had a couple of them cornered. Remember how he almost had a heart attack when those turkeys doubled back and practically goosed him?"

Skip and I laughed. "Yeah," I said. "Wiley was cleaning out his underwear for a week after that one!"

"Doesn't surprise me none . . ." Skip said, tipping back the heavy brim of his Stetson, ". . . a liberal lawyer gettin' outwitted by a turkey! Happens all the time."

This brought howls of laughter from the three of us.

"Oh sure, laugh all you want," Frank said, his face flushed. "I'm sure we all remember some of George's infamous blunders. What about the time he shot that farmer's cow, thinking it was a deer of all things!" His nasal voice and inability to pronounce his *R*s made him sound like an amateur impersonator doing Ted Kennedy. "Real swift, Filby!"

"Hey," Skip said, looking across the table at the thick spectacles George Filburtson hid behind, the ones that made his dark green eyes look like a pair of mushy peas. "The man can't help it he's nearsighted."

"Thanks, Skip," George said.

"Poor eyesight doesn't seem to hurt him between the sheets though," Frank said, trying to get in the last poke. "How many rug rats you have now, George? Enough to field a baseball team?"

"I'd say it's closer to an *olympic* team!" Skip said.

George looked embarrassed. "Naw . . . we've only got six."

"*Only* six?" Frank said. "Well, that's more'n enough for a basketball team, Filby. Unless, of course, they all inherit your short stature and myopic vision."

"Thanks, pal," George said over the howls. "Next year at this time it'll be seven."

201

"Millie's preggers *again*?" I uttered in disbelief.

"Jesus, Filby," Skip said, honking a wad of tobacco into his portable spittoon. "I thought I educated you about birth control."

George hung his head. "Millie doesn't believe in it. Hardcore Catholics, you know."

A chorus of groans swept the table.

"Well maybe you can ship a few of them out west for some fun and sun with Uncle Mick," Frank said. "From the sounds of it, Hollyweird can use the company."

I glared at Frank. Sometimes humorous asides from friends cut the deepest. "Thanks, but I've got enough problems of my own."

The reunion continued on in this fashion until nearly eleven, the other three loud and boisterous while I remained quiet and observant. As we became more inebriated, the tales grew more outrageous.

Skip bragged about facing down a pack of marauding wild boars on a trip he went on last fall. Allegedly, he gunned down a pair of boars even after having been gored and trampled. Now I've been wild boar hunting, and I know damn well they don't run in packs. And though they do have razor-sharp snout-horns, I doubted he had been gored. I figured the squealing, snorting sound a rampaging boar made would have motivated Skip to a new world-record in short-distance sprints. But I didn't say anything. George tried to top this with a ridiculous tale of panther hunting in the Florida Everglades. Supposedly, he bagged one of the rare black panthers, but only after the big cat had surprised him, leaping at him from behind a clump of mangrove scrub and nearly tearing him limb from limb. I knew this was bullshit, too, since ecologists and game wardens spent weeks, sometimes months in the Everglades without spotting one of these rapidly-vanishing leopards. Not to mention the Florida black panther was also on the wildlife protected lists. Most of Frank's wild adventures concerned hunting of a different kind: kinky sexual exploits with eager young legal assistants. I believed *all* of those stories since Frank's promiscuity in college had elevated him to legend status in the eyes of the rest of us Casanova wannabes. The only way his wife Louise couldn't know about his extracurricular affairs was if she were as nearsighted as George.

These guys should be the writers, I thought as I watched them fabricate one grandiose lie after the next. They were entertaining. And they certainly cheered me up.

Finally, just before eleven, the waitress, Janet, gave us our last call. Something had been nagging at me all night, and it dawned on me what it was. I found it unusual that we were the only customers at the lodge. I also found it odd that our waitress was the same woman who had checked us in at the front desk that afternoon. As Janet brought us our last round of beers, I inquired about this.

"It's still early in the season," she said in a gruff, impatient voice as she placed bottles in front of us. "We gotta double up duties until business picks up."

Frank slipped an arm around her and began caressing her waist. "What say you and I double up in my room after you get off here, Janet?"

Frank was pie-eyed! Janet was a long way on the wrong side of attractive. She had thunderous thighs and flabby arms. Oily, stringy hair the color of damp hay fell over beefy shoulders. There was a cold hardness about her that the cramped features of her face and several missing teeth did little to change.

She broke from Frank with a vengeance. "You ever come on to me like that again, mister, and I'll cut your balls off and feed 'em to your face!"

Janet stormed away, and we sat looking at each other, stunned.

Now I know cocktail waitresses take a lot of shit from drunk customers, but this sudden outburst was a tad harsh, even directed at a lounge lizard like Frank Wiley. After a few minutes of silent slurping, I had had enough. The festive mood had changed. I was exhausted.

"I'm turning in," I said, standing, plopping down a few bills to cover my tab. "I suggest you guys do the same. Early start tomorrow."

WE WERE OFF BEFORE DAWN, the frosty morning touching us with icy fingers. I felt groggy and dehydrated from last night's drinking, but I looked none the worse for wear compared to the other three. Skip rambled on in his pseudo-macho way about how they had gone back to his room to drink some more. Frank's eyes looked like twin road atlases, and though I couldn't see George's eyes behind the thick lenses, his face had a pale, washed-out quality about it that made him look like a walking corpse. Annual hunting trips had a way of reverting all of us back to the stupidity of our long-lost youths.

We jounced over the rough terrain of the Idaho backcountry in a converted school bus, one of those old Bluebird half-buses used on rural routes. This one had been equipped with boat holds on the roof, gun racks in the back, and big balloon tires to negotiate the rugged topography. The engine whined and protested as Don Flaherty steered the bus over hill and dale, thick branches of ponderosa pine and birch rudely slapping the sides. I observed Flaherty as he drove, his hacked-off finger as conspicuous as missing keys on a piano, his jagged scar lending him a Frankensteinish aura in the faint green dashboard lights. What was it he had said? *That's what I get fer tryin' to hunt bears with a hangover.* Suddenly my own hangover seemed to increase in magnitude.

Half an hour later, we were at the put-in spot, a placid section of the Salmon River. The horizon above the Continental Divide to the east was beginning to brighten, the mountain peaks standing like dark, jagged sentries against the pinkish sky. Don Flaherty and his fellow guide, a quiet, hard-looking man we knew only as Gary, unstrapped the fiberglass boats from the top of the bus and brought them down to the waterline. Skip and Frank wrestled with the rifles and ammunition while George and I hauled backpacks and supplies down to the river. Janet, the clerk/waitress, drove the bus away. She would be meeting us later, down-river, at the pickup point.

I felt the giddiness of anticipation dance through my stomach.

The hunt was on!

Once we had the two boats loaded, Don Flaherty gave us some last-minute instructions.

"Okay, listen up," he shouted over the loud gurgle of the river. "I'm tellin' ya this shit now because once we get on the river we need to keep quiet. Bears can't see so good but they got pretty sensitive hearing. They can pick up the buzzin' of a gnat's wings from a mile off. And as good as their hearin' is, their sense of smell is better. All of you put on your scent this mornin'?"

We all nodded. My skin felt oily from the bear-mask and the mosquito repellent. The Scent Walker pads in my rubber boots made walking uncomfortable.

Frank said, "Yeah, we even gargled with that Camo-Scent shit you told us about. That stuff is as bad as Texas beer!" His Bostonian tongue made it come out as *bee-ah.*

"What do Democrats know about good beer, Wiley?" Skip said.

Flaherty cut them off. "Let's save our energies for huntin' bears, okay, gentlemen? Now, we'll try to stay upwind of 'em. But if the wind shifts, or we get out of position somehow, the scent-masks will help us. Another thing. Shootin' from a boat is a whole different thing than shootin' from solid ground. Even on quiet water there's a tendency to bob around. The first shot is most important since it rocks the boat and alerts the bear. Chances of killin' a black with the first shot is slim. We hafta go after 'em on foot after one or, if yer lucky, two shots. But they generally open up for one clear shot. That's because bears don't have no natural enemies that approach by water. They're off their guard when we come at 'em from the river. So we gotta make that first shot count. If you don't bring 'em down, you gotta at least make 'em bleed good, so we can track 'em. Once we hit land and start trackin' 'em, you gotta be on yer toes. There ain't nothin' more dangerous on the face of this Earth than a wounded bear . . . A wounded bear has incredible survival instincts. I've heard of 'em diggin' in, lyin' in wait for the right moment to pounce on the hunter and rip him to shreds. The brown that got me led me on a wild goose chase, then doubled back around, quiet as an Indian, and attacked me from behind. Let me tell you this right now, gentlemen. If one of 'em comes at ya, try to find some big rocks to wedge yerself into, or a clump of trees. If yer unlucky enough to be in a clearing, throw yerself face-down on the ground, flat, with yer arms along yer sides. They can't get at ya as good that way. They'll still prob'ly mess ya up pretty bad, but at least yer eyes and vital organs is protected. *Don't*—I repeat, don't—try to outrun 'em! That only gets 'em more fired up, and when they get fired up, they can cover ground in a hurry. They'll catch you every time, so don't try to be a track star. Any questions before we put in?"

We all looked at each other sheepishly. A knot of fear tightened in my gut. This was certainly more challenging than deer hunting.

After Flaherty demonstrated the finer points of shooting from the boat, we were off, floating down the river at a leisurely pace. We all agreed that Skip and Frank should be split up, since one of their political arguments would probably send all the bears in the state of Idaho running to Montana. So Skip and George shared the lead boat with hunting guide Gary manning the oars, while Frank, Don Flaherty, and I floated behind about fifty yards.

The sun was beginning to make a full-fledged appearance. Long fingers of faint light played off the rippling water, glittering like a cache of multifaceted jewels. I inhaled deeply, the chilled air and mossy freshwater earth smells a rustic balm that cleansed my city-ravaged soul. Dense stands of aspens and willows were greening along the shoreline, their leaves rustling in the slight breeze. The rhythmic sweep of the oars gliding through the water, propelling us gently downstream, lulled me into a blissful state. Songbirds greeted the new day with soft, cheerful melodies. The river at dawn was peaceful, serene, a wonderland unspoiled by human hands. It felt great to be alive. Even if we never saw a bear I would be satisfied.

But it didn't take us long to spot our first bruin.

I was sweeping the shoreline with binoculars, glassing

for bears, when I heard a commotion from the lead boat. George had spotted one! I jerked the field glasses around to where he pointed, and saw a magnificent specimen of a black bear, hunched over, dunking his huge paw into the river, swiping for fish. The creature stopped and looked up, alerted by the noise on the river. Sensing danger, he stood, and the size of this impressive beast took my breath away. He turned his massive head, listening, sniffing with his wet black nose. A shot cracked the serenity, and a splatter of crimson mushroomed from the bear's shoulder. The bruin roared, a yell of pain and warning. A second shot kicked up a spray of loamy earth. The great beast turned, lowered itself down on all fours, and ran, its progress up the hill marked by trampled foliage and additional roars of pain. Quickly, Gary guided the boat into shore and secured it to a broad tree trunk. Skip and George were out of the boat in a hurry, splashing through the shallows and scrambling up the wooded hillside in pursuit. With their Spring Mirage camouflaged fatigues and caps, I soon lost sight of them. Gary grabbed his rifle and a backpack, then disappeared into the forest, following them.

"This is a good sign," Flaherty said, rowing past the tethered boat and the point where the bear had been shot. "Means there'll be more of 'em downriver."

"Shouldn't we wait for them?" I asked, concerned about my friends.

Flaherty gave me an impatient look. "You want yer own bear trophy, don't ya, Mick?"

"Well, yeah . . . but—"

"Then shut up and let me head downstream! After the ruckus that one raised, there won't be no more bears in this area."

Behind us, from up on the ridge, I heard a scream,

followed by two more gunshots. Then, faintly, Skip's panicked voice, *"Run George! Run like hell!"* Three more explosions echoed through the hills followed by more screams. Human screams. I didn't hear anything remotely resembling a wounded bear. Flaherty's scarred cheek curled into a sneer. It was almost an expression of ecstacy.

Frank and I looked at each other, great doubt passing between us. Something was very wrong here. It seemed to me that our guide had suddenly lost interest in bear hunting. Don Flaherty seemed to be putting much more muscle into his rowing, as though he wanted to put distance between us and the other hunting party. I had stopped glassing for bears, watching instead the increasingly rapid pace we were traveling down the river.

Frank voiced what I was feeling. "What's going on, mistah?"

"Whaddaya mean?" Flaherty huffed between pulls on the oars. The scar across his cheek throbbed with the exertion.

"I mean why'd we leave Skip and George behind with a wounded bear. They're obviously in trouble."

Flaherty stopped rowing, anger clouding his face. "I told you we would be splitting apart. If we were gonna go out together, we would've taken one boat. Besides, Gary's a qualified bear guide. Your friends are in good hands." He continued rowing.

"Then why are we moving so fast?" Frank asked. "We can't possibly sneak up on bears going at this clip."

"You ask too many questions, friend," Flaherty said in a dead voice. "Must be the lawyer in ya."

I saw Frank reach behind him and pick up his rifle, swing it around and train the barrel on Don Flaherty's breastbone.

"All right, mistah," Frank said in a shaky voice. "I want you to turn this boat around and take us back. Now!"

Frank's .30-06 could put a large hole in a bear from a fair distance, but it didn't seem to intimidate Flaherty. "Take an unpowered boat upstream? Against the current? Impossible, Mr. Wiley."

"Well, you'd better make it possible . . . or else . . ."

I stared at Frank in disbelief. *Where had his sudden courage come from? And what the hell is he getting us into?*

"Or else *what*, Mr. Wiley?"

"Or else . . . I guess I'll have to kill you . . . and take us back myself!" Frank's voice cracked on the word *kill*.

Flaherty flung his head back and laughed, his raucous glee a demented song that drifted across the river. Frank and I exchanged worried glances. "That would be very stupid, Mr. Wiley . . . even for a lawyer," he said after settling down. "Shoot me and you'd never find Janet and the pickup point. It's impossible to find yer way out of a wilderness like this without a seasoned guide. Right now, I'm the only one qualified to do that."

I watched as Frank lowered the rifle a little, thinking this over.

And then, quicker than I'd ever seen a human being move, Flaherty brought one of the oars out of the water and clunked Frank across the side of the head with a powerful blow. The rifle went overboard and Frank tumbled backwards, cracking the back of his head against one of the aluminum bench-seats. Flaherty was up like a cat, striking Frank—once . . . twice . . . three times—vicious blows that turned Frank's head into a bloody, pulpy mess. Stupidly, I sat there open-mouthed, watching as this madman clubbed my friend with the heavy oar. Everything was happening so lightning-fast that I froze, each dreadful strike paralyzing me further. Then, chest heaving and eyes jumping with frenzied evil, Flaherty dropped the oar and grabbed his rifle, took aim on me.

"All right, Mick," he shouted, "enough of the nonsense. You were gonna find out about this once we was picked up, but your dumbass friend here forced my hand."

I looked down at Frank who was slumped on the floor, out cold, a quickening puddle of blood under his head. "F-find out about wh-wh-what?" I stammered, not sure about my desire to know more.

Flaherty grinned. "Bear season just ended, Mick. It's *human* season now!"

"Ex—excuse me?" I said, thinking I would die from heart failure at any moment.

Flaherty sat down, kept the rifle trained on me. We floated down the river on the current while he filled me in on all the grisly details of who he really was.

"I ain't Don Flaherty, Mick. The name's Perry Tremontie. Gary's my half-brother. Does the name Tremontie mean anything to ya?"

I shook my head.

"I guess ya ain't been watchin' the news. Well, Gary an' me usta own an' operate the High Ridge Ranch long 'bout nine years ago. It was called Tremontie Outfitters back then. We'd been runnin' huntin' trips fer maybe three or four years when sumpthin' happened to us . . . at 'bout the same time. That happens to brothers . . . least that's what the shrinks told us. We had plenty of big-game trophies, but they all started lookin' the same after a time. We wanted a bigger challenge. What better challenge than idiot hunters theirselves? Me and Gary picked off seventeen hunters 'fore the law caught up with us. I just *love* seein' the expressions on a hunter's face just before I pull the trigger. Wild animals . . . they just kinda give ya a dumb stare, like it don't make much difference. But humans, they *know* they're gonna die. They have this desperate, pleadin' look about 'em—kinda the way you look right now, Mick."

My mouth moved, but nothing came out.

"I'm sure your two friends wore them same expressions just before they died. Wish I coulda been there to see it. Gary's prob'ly hackin' their heads off right about now. They'll make *beautiful* trophies—especially the Texan."

Bile rose in my throat. I stared at the crazy across from me, wondering how much longer until he blew my guts all over the Salmon River.

"Trophies?" I managed weakly.

"Yeah. Don't all hunters like mementos of their kills?" His eyes were wide with the excitement of bloodlust.

"You're insane!"

Perry Tremontie shook his head. "I beg to differ with ya, Mick. Nine years ago a federal grand jury found my brother n' me competent to stand trial. Insanity plea didn't work fer us . . . course our good-fer-nuthin' lawyers didn't try none too hard. Goddamn how I *hate* lawyers!" He glanced down at Frank's lifeless body. "I'm gonna take special pleasure in wastin' yer attorney friend tomorrow."

"Tomorrow?" I said, cautiously dropping to my knees and checking Frank for a pulse. The coldness of his skin alarmed me.

"Yeah," Tremontie said, following my movements with the barrel of his rifle. "We can't have all our fun the first day out. Gary got his jollies today. Tomorrow I get mine."

I could not locate a pulse on Frank Wiley anywhere. A fierce anger flooded through me when I looked up at the smirk on Tremontie's face. "He's dead! You killed my

212

friend you rotten son of a bitch!" Passion overruled common sense and I got to my feet, started to go after him with my blood-stained hands.

A shot exploded by my left ear, deafening me. Gunpowder stung my eyes and nose.

"Don't try it unless you wanna end up as fish food!"

Shaken, seeing how serious he was with the threat, I sat back down.

"Just so there won't be no mishaps, I'm gonna hafta tie you up, Mick."

Tremontie tied my feet to the bench-seat supports and my hands to the oarlocks with nylon rope. The floor at my feet was thick with Frank's blood. A feeling of hopelessness overcame me. We continued to float down the river. I saw several black and brown bears along the riverbanks, but like Tremontie had said, bear season was over.

"So why didn't you just kill us all at the lodge if murder is your thing?" I asked, trying to gain some insight into an insane mind.

"Now that wouldn'ta been very sportin' of us, would it, Mick? Mosta the fun of huntin' is the sport of it . . . the thrill of the chase."

"I see," I said, though I didn't really see at all. "Well, where does the woman . . . Janet . . . where does she come into all this?"

Tremontie smiled a crooked grin. "Ah, Janet. She's my girl, but Gary n' me share her. Janet likes to mix it up. And she's one helluva talented lady. Best damn taxidermist in the Rockies. You should see how she fixed up the Flahertys and their staff. Hell, if I hadn't killed 'em myself, I'd swear most of 'em was still alive. She performed magic on 'em. You'll see 'em later . . . real fine trophies they turned out to be. And balls?" He whistled. "For a woman, Janet's got balls of

213

brass. Why, she busted Gary an' me outta Boise Federal two weeks ago. Newspapers and TV news is sayin' it's the biggest prison break in thirty years. There's a massive manhunt out fer us right now. Our pictures're showin' up everywhere, Mick. Surprised you ain't seen 'em, you bein' a TV writer an' all." He inhaled deeply. "*Goddamn* I love bein' back in the great outdoors! I really missed huntin' season."

Tremontie retrieved the oars and started rowing again. My mind was too numb for further coherent speech. My body twitched with the chills of deep shock. I thought about my three college friends . . . three innocent and unsuspecting victims of psychopathic, homicidal brothers, reduced to prey by human predators. I wondered when my time would arrive. I wondered what violent death would be like.

AN HOUR LATER WE ROUNDED A BEND and saw the yellow bus gleaming in the bright sun at the pickup point. Tremontie paddled us in and Janet helped him drag Frank's corpse out of the boat. She was angry with him.

"You messed up the head! I told ya to keep the heads clean, ya stupid fuck!" she ranted. "Now it'll take a miracle to make this into a decent trophy."

They sat Frank's rigid body up in a seat at the back of the bus, then untied me and led me up the hill where they secured me next to him. I sat and listened while Tremontie tried to explain what had gone wrong, Janet continually cutting him off, telling him how stupid he was.

Fifteen minutes later I heard a boat approaching down on the river, and I knew Gary had arrived. Tremontie went down to greet him, and soon they appeared, walking up the path from the river, batting aside the thick underbrush. I looked past Frank's battered corpse, through the window. Gary lugged two plastic garbage bags over his shoulders. His camouflaged fatigues were stained with blood. I was sure I didn't want to see what was in those bags.

Tremontie stepped onto the bus, flung the gear he was carrying on one of the front seats. Gary was right behind him.

"It's time fer the unveilin', Mick," Tremontie said, grabbing one of the bags from Gary. "Time to pay yer last respects to yer friends before we turn 'em into busts."

The three of them had a good laugh over this.

Tremontie pulled the plastic away, revealing George's head. My stomach spasmed as the killer grabbed the head by strands of hair and slammed it up on the back of the seat facing me. George's glasses were shattered. Bloody ragged flesh hung from where the head had been severed from the body. I turned away in revulsion, but they weren't through yet. Gary pulled Skip's head from his bag and set it up next to George's. Skip's Stetson was tattered and splotched with blood; his cheeks were dotted with blobs of chewing tobacco. A serrated length of his spinal cord dangled from the neck like a gristled tail. I could not contain myself any longer. The trauma had caught up with my stomach and I let loose.

"Yeah! Go fer it, Hollyweird!" Tremontie yelled. "This is how you'll remember yer loser friends the rest of yer sorry life!" the killer screamed, spittle flying from his lips. "And that ain't too long considerin' it's yer turn tomorrow."

After a while, when I quit retching, the Tremontie brothers left me alone with what was left of my three friends and went back down to the river to retrieve the boats. Flies buzzed around us. I couldn't swat them away since my hands were tied. The stench of puke and blood and decaying death was overpowering. I couldn't believe our sacred hunting trip had degenerated into a nightmare of this caliber. The day was permeated with an unreality that I found impossible to accept. But it *was* real. It *had* happened. I only had to look at the morgue of malodorous death surrounding me to realize that.

This is complete, certifiable madness, I thought, watching as the crazy bitch Janet stared at me, her rifle aimed between my eyes. *How can something like this be happening to me? I write kiddie sit-coms for Chrissakes!*

And then I finally lost all emotional control. I broke down weeping, letting loose with a torrent of tears. I cried for the injustice of it all. My three college friends were dead, their lives snuffed out by a couple of homicidal escaped convicts and their kill-thrill groupie girlfriend. I cried for all the innocent people throughout history who had been murdered by crazies for no other reason than having been in the wrong place at the wrong time. My shoulders jerked convulsively as I wept for all the cruelty in the world and the senseless nature of these killings. My three friends surrounded me, all in various stages of decomposition, mutilated beyond belief. "Jesus, God in Heaven, how could you let this happen?" I wailed over and over between angry, frightened sobs.

"What's wrong with you?" Janet said approaching me. "You a wimp or sumpthin'? Shut up and take it like a man or I'll make ya give this rifle a blow job!" She jabbed the barrel in my face.

"Go ahead then, shoot me," I pleaded, looking up at her. *Better to die now than go through any more of this misery.*

She stared at me through hardened empty eyes.

I closed my eyes. My body tensed for the skull-shattering explosion. The scent of gun oil and cold steel drifted beneath my nose.

"Naw," I heard her say finally. "That'd mess up the head."

I opened my eyes and saw her returning to the front of the bus.

The Tremontie brothers were back, securing the boats to the top of the bus. Within minutes, we were on our way back to the lodge.

When we got back to High Ridge Ranch, they exposed me to further horrors. Tremontie took great pleasure in introducing me to the Flaherty family, all lined up along one wall.

"These here are the sonsabitches who stole my huntin' lodge." He pointed to two heads mounted on the wall. "There's Don and his golddiggin' wife. Just below 'em, with their bodies still intact, is their three kids. The two older guys off to the side are the huntin' guides who worked fer the Flahertys. I told ya Janet was a helluva taxidermist, didn't I, Mick? Didn't she do a beautiful job here?"

Gary was the only one who agreed. The stench of decayed flesh was awful, much worse than out in the bus. Their skin was gray and mottled, even in the dim light. The Flahertys and their hired help looked exactly like what they were: decomposing corpses.

Tremontie smiled. "And now we got three more to add to the trophy collection. Gary, whyn't you go fetch 'em from the bus. I'll be out to help you in a minute with the lawyer stiff."

Dutifully, Gary shuffled off. But he no sooner stepped out the door than a barrage of firearms opened up on him, peppering the entrance to the lodge. He danced in herky-jerky motions as his body absorbed the shots. He flew back against the doorjamb, as though catapulted, his chest and face spouting tiny geysers of blood. Then he fell across the doorway, knocking the door wide open.

A serious voice boomed from a loudspeaker. *"PERRY TREMONTIE? . . . JANET GIBSON? . . . WE KNOW YOU'RE IN THERE. THIS IS THE STATE POLICE . . . YOU HAVE ONE MINUTE TO COME OUT, UNARMED, HANDS OUT WHERE WE CAN SEE THEM . . . AFTER THAT, WE SWARM THE PLACE."*

"Shit!" Janet said, not looking so cool and collected any more. "What are we gonna do, Perry?"

"We wait 'em out," he said, crawling along the floor to the door. "They're bluffin'." He pulled his brother's corpse inside and kicked the door shut.

A look of genuine fear darted across Janet's face. "But we left all the guns and ammo on the bus. What good is waitin' gonna do, Perry?"

"Quit yer whinin', bitch!" Tremontie snapped. "I can't think when yer whinin'."

"I don't wanna go to prison, Perry," she said, starting to cry. "And I'm too young to die."

I could see the wheels turning in Tremontie's diseased mind as he watched his girlfriend whimper.

Suddenly the windows started shattering, one by one, as the police lobbed tear gas grenades into the lodge. The room quickly filled with a thick, suffocating haze that burned my eyes and clogged my throat. I heard the other two choking and gasping for air, though the smoke was so thick I couldn't see them. My eyes watered fiercely and I kept squinting and blinking, trying in vain to clear my vision. Movement was futile since my hands and legs were still tightly bound. After a few long chaotic moments, there was a tugging at my feet and I felt the rope snap as my legs were freed. The thought of running crossed my mind, but before I could, rough hands grabbed me from behind and pushed me forward.

"Where ya goin', Perry?" Janet's hoarse voice.

"There's a coupla rifles in the storage room. I'm goin' out the back usin' our friend as my shield."

"But what about me?" Janet went into a coughing fit.

I kept tripping as I was shoved along. My sinuses burned like the fires of hell.

"Get yer own gun and hostage, woman!" Tremontie yelled through the thick smoke.

"Don't leave me, Perry! *Please* don't leave me here, baby!"

I don't know how Tremontie found the storeroom in the blinding fog, let alone the gun rack, but he did. I heard him rummaging through drawers, cussing, choking, breathing in ragged, excited gasps. He must have finally located the shells, for I heard several metallic clicks and the unmistakable sound of bullets being jammed into the chambers.

I was blind, crippled with a queasy claustrophobia, paralyzed with an overpowering fear. My lungs screamed for air.

"Okay, Mick," Tremontie rasped somewhere near me. "It's time for the back door trick."

His arm snaked around my neck from behind. I felt the cold hard barrel of the rifle poke my spine and push me onward. Out in the lodge I heard gagging sounds, then a

219

loud crash. Janet whimpered, low pathetic sobs.

As we made our way through the storeroom, coughing and sputtering, I had visions of my life ending in a sensational Butch Cassidy and Sundance Kid kind of violent shootout. *Will the smokies know I'm not with these animals?* I wondered. *Will they open fire on us?*

Tremontie kicked the storeroom door open a crack, and a gust of beautiful clean air hit me in the face. The cool breeze soothed my ravaged lungs. I was able to open my eyes momentarily and I caught a glimpse of a hand with a missing index finger in front of my face. We waited there for a minute as he brought his face to the crack, checking out the rear of the property where the cabins were. Assured it was clear, he shoved me out in front of him, coughing and wheezing. I felt the heat of his body pressed close to my back, caught a whiff of his wild, gamey odor. My eyes still burned and my vision was blurred. I felt weak and queasy, on the verge of passing out.

"DROP THE GUN, TREMONTIE," boomed a voice over the bullhorn. *"WE'VE GOT YOU COVERED ON ALL SIDES. THERE'S NO WAY OUT."*

We jerked to a stop in the clearing like two nocturnal animals frozen in headlights.

"Don't shoot!" Tremontie yelled from behind my right ear. "I've got a hostage."

"DON'T BE FOOLISH, PERRY. LET HIM GO."

Tremontie's head swiveled, looking for cops. "I'll trade the hostage fer a helicopter and safe passage to Canada," he shouted, his voice hoarse with tear gas. "Otherwise I kill him."

I damn near swallowed my tongue in fear.

We stood in the opening between the lodge and the cabins for what seemed an eternity. I heard garbled static from several two-way radios. Tremontie checked the cabin windows, kept searching the treetops off to either side.

"YOU'RE TESTING OUR PATIENCE, TREMONTIE. YOU'VE GOT THIRTY SECONDS TO DROP YOUR WEAPON AND RELEASE THE HOSTAGE."

That's when he panicked. I flinched as he started firing at the cabins, several windows shattering in magnificent sprays of glass. Then three shots exploded to my right and I felt a sticky wetness across the back of my head and shoulders. Tremontie lost his grip on me, squeezing off two more shots that zinged wildly through the trees. Just before I lost consciousness, I turned and saw him tumble to the dirt, the side of his head blown away.

TODAY MARKS THE ONE-YEAR anniversary of The Tragedy. The past year has seemed like a decade in most respects. The insomnia and horrid pre-dawn scream-fest nightmares are behind me now—twice-a-week therapy sessions have cured me of those terrible afflictions. However, I'm not sure I'll ever escape the question of why my three friends were taken while I was spared. Also, the fact that I might have been able to do something to prevent their deaths—especially Frank's—will always haunt me. Yes, unexpected death is hell on the survivors.

The families of my deceased friends are coping, too, though the Filburtsons are having a tough go of it financially. While Skip and Frank had been fairly well to do, George had not planned well for a premature death. Of course, seven children (Millie gave birth to baby daughter Georgette in January) would make it tough for *anyone* to handle financial planning. I have sent Millie my last two syndication royalty checks and a little other financial aid on occasion. I have also sent donations to our alma mater in memory of my three friends.

It's the least I can do.

I owe my own life to a host of people: a beer distributor truck driver by the name of Grant Pickett and the Idaho State Police. Of course police bullets never would have had a chance to rid the world of the Tremontie brothers had it not been for Pickett's keen perceptions. Pickett, a Boise Beverages route driver, had made his regular bi-weekly delivery to High Ridge Ranch two days before we arrived. Having dealt with the Flaherty ownership for the past seven years, he thought something was astray when Janet Gibson started acting funny as he questioned her about the Flahertys' whereabouts. That night he saw photos of Janet Gibson and the two Tremontie brothers on the news, and he called the authorities. The Idaho Bureau of Investigation, knowing of the Tremonties' previous ownership of High Ridge Ranch, put two and two together, and organized an efficient stakeout. Janet Gibson was sent to Pocatello Women's Correctional to serve one life term for aiding and abetting convicted criminals, and another for accessory to ten counts of premeditated murder. It will be a long time before she sees the outside again.

I think about my friends often, but today, images of their happy faces dance vividly across my mind. I know that somewhere Skip and Frank are still arguing about politics and George is probably trying his damnedest to sell new-fangled harps to the angels. I miss them. *God* do I ever miss those guys. I loved them like brothers.

Today I am off for my first hunting trip since The Tragedy. I hope to get in a full week of shooting down in

Baja. Maybe it will help take my mind off my Notre Dame hunting buddies. As I load my gear in the car, I hope and pray that this year will be a pleasant experience. But then I'm sure it will be. Mainly because of my new hunting partner, Gina.

I met her at a UCLA photography class. She's a much more proficient shutterbug than I, but I'm learning fast. Gina took up photography to help her deal with the death of her husband, so, in a sense, we're both starting over together. Spring is bursting out all over southern California and Mother Nature is in full bloom. God's glorious creatures are having their annual coming-out party, undergoing their yearly reawakening.

Gina and I want to capture it all on film.

Life looks so much more beautiful through the lens of a camera than through the cross-hairs of a rifle scope.

One of my all-time favorite horror flicks was the original "Jaws." Moreso than any other Earthbound animal, the great white shark seems to evoke a paralyzing terror deep within me that is primal and intense. Perhaps I was devoured by one of these mysterious, savage beasts in a previous life. I shudder to think of any fate worse than being in the water, a couple of fifteen-footers in the near vicinity, fins circling me, deadly teeth moving in for the kill. I have had very vivid nightmares about this scenario. I once knew a couple of guys who dove for one of the big oil companies in the Gulf of Mexico, scouting for new drilling sites. They held me spellbound with their tales of encounters with huge hammerheads, another unpredictably violent creature of the shark species. I decided I wanted to write something in tribute to the beasts of my nightmares. But I wanted it to be different, so I went with science fiction on an otherworldly planet. What resulted was "The Fjords of Vankosh," my first published short story, which appeared in the premier issue of RANDOM REALITIES.

THE FJORDS OF

VANKOSH

THE VIOLET MIST HUNG HEAVY over Knapp's Fjord.

Purple waves lapped against the hull of the water buggy as Carver maneuvered the craft into deeper waters.

"Any sign of 'em yet?" he yelled to Dunleavy, who stood at the prow, gazing across the endless grape sea.

"No, sir," he replied, wiping condensation from his lenses. "Damn soup is so thick today I can't even see the outline of the cliffs."

Carver nodded. "I know. It's going to make the feeding *that* much more difficult, I'm afraid."

The two men lapsed into a long silence as they were prone to do during these feeding missions. It was lonely work, and the perpetual purple dreariness got to everyone after a time. Carver had been at this for just short of two years, and the routine had become humdrum, monotonous. He felt his skills as a three-star biomarinist were being wasted on this little feedbucket junket. They had told him when he signed on for the Vankosh expedition that he would be involved with leading-edge biogenetic engineering. All biomarinists were to have an integral part in the design and construction of the biogenetic weaponry the military would use to complete the overthrow of neighboring Smitaar. Carver looked over to the feed bin and shook his head in disgust as he watched the fluorescent ion-eels slither and slide with rainbow-hued contortions. Captaining one of the gar-shark feedbuggies was as close as he was ever going to get to developing biogenetic weaponry. *A master's degree and thirteen years of bionektonic engineering experience for this? What a waste!*

But though he was bored with this detail, Carver knew better than to be lulled into a sense of dull complacency. These feeding forays were not without occasional excitement, even the threat of violent danger. Just two weeks ago, three biomarinists had lost their lives over at Wiggins Inlet as a Class II water buggy had been overrun during a feeding frenzy. Reports had it that the scientists had been careless, some might even say lazy. They had stayed in one place too long, trying to unload their feed quickly, and the gar-sharks had gathered in great numbers to add human flesh to their primarily ion-eel diets. The lone survivor of the attack reported that they had barely been able to dump the eels into the water before the buggy went down under a smoking, churning siege. The last Carver had heard, the man was still in IC with third-degree burns covering half of his body and coarse sutures holding his belly together. Last week another buggy was hit up at Grand Fjord, but the crew was able to escape. The first crop of gar-sharks was nearing maturity. They were getting aggressive. Sometimes in this biogenetic weaponry game, you could engineer a product that was *too* efficient. Carver had tried to tell the idiots at Control that they were making a big mistake in the overall design of these gar-sharks, most especially in the brain casings, but everyone had turned a deaf ear.

He glanced down at his ionoscope, looking for signs of electrical activity in the depths. Bright blips of light danced in the upper right corner of the scope. A look of concern crossed his weatherbeaten face.

"I found a school of 'em," he yelled up to Dunleavy.

"How concentrated are they?"

"Shouldn't be too much trouble, but with this mist . . . I don't know. You know how this soup conducts electricity."

"Yeah. Well, I say we use the rods to separate 'em if we hafta."

Carver groaned. Using the rods meant a few extra hours of work and a lot of trouble. "Not if I can help it. I guess you forgot what tonight is, didn't ya?"

A quick look at Dunleavy told Carver his deckhand's mind was as foggy as this fjord.

"That's what I thought," the captain replied. "The

carrier is bringing a load of women over from the labs this afternoon. Big dance goin' on under The Dome tonight."

Dunleavy turned, raised his goggles up over his eyebrows. He grinned with a lecherous smirk. "Yeah! Now you're talkin', skipper! Ain't seen a real live woman in so long I forget what the attraction is."

Carver laughed."Thankfully my memory isn't as shot as yours. I guarantee ya it'll all come rushing back to ya the minute we walk into The Dome. I've never met women as horny as the lab techs from GenetiLabs."

"Well, what the hell are we waitin' for, sir? Let's dump our eels and go find us some perfumed playmates."

Carver punched in the coordinates and the buggy chugged to the western section of the fjord. As they approached the school, he was alarmed to see a count of twenty-seven gar-sharks, all clustered directly beneath the buggy. That spelled trouble. There were too many for standard localized feeding. The water around the buggy was electrically charged to dangerous proportions. *Damn!* Carver thought. They would have to use the flashrods. *What a pain in the ass!* But it was either use the rods or risk being taken down in an electrified feeding frenzy. Not for the first time he wished someone in charge of this travesty would have listened to him about the dangers of giving these creatures too much intelligence.

"There's way too many of 'em. We're gonna hafta use the friggin' rods," he yelled to Dunleavy, and watched as his lone deckhand nodded dolefully.

In a few moments, Carver heard the metallic clank and thump of the flashrods banging against the hull as Dunleavy lowered them into the water. The deckhand worked quickly, efficiently, plunging each of the four flashrods down into the drink. Carver heard the familiar sizzle as the rods began to do their work, neutralizing the powerful negative charge of the gar-sharks with positively-charged electrons. The rods were the only thing the scientists had found that would slow these aggressive predators during feeding sessions. They served to momentarily lobotomize the creatures by neutralizing the electrical activity in their brains. The rods also negated the electrical currents in the water. These fish were twenty feet of tenacious jaws and teeth and electrical current. They were designed to electrocute their prey, then feast on the fried prize in a ripping, shredding, bloody water ballet that often resembled the mindless feeding frenzies of their closest cousins—the large man-eating sharks of Earth. As every biomarinist knew, you were just begging for trouble if you attempted to feed schools numbering more than a dozen without using the rods. The gar-sharks' humanlike intelligence and heavily armored hides, coupled with razor-sharp teeth and an electrified aggressive demeanor, made the beasts formidable foes. They were certainly the ideal weapons for conquering water worlds such as Smitaar.

Suddenly Carver felt tiny vibrations through the soles of his shoes. The deck shifted beneath his feet.

"They're strafing the hull, sir!" Dunleavy yelled from the stern. "Never seen 'em *this* riled up before."

Carver felt more vibrations running up his legs and could hear a muted scraping sound coming from under the buggy. He glanced down at the sonar school-counter and was alarmed to see thirty-six gar-sharks now in the immediate area.

They were gathering fast!

While he studied the digital display, three more swam into the area. Something was *very* wrong. Carver had never seen them cluster like this.

"Hey, Dunleavy," he screamed, trying to keep the mounting desperation out of his voice. "Submerge the spare rods! And make it snappy!"

"Yessir." Dunleavy opened the storage bay and unplugged the spare flashrods from the recharging unit. Quickly, he put them into place.

"Give 'em maximum power," Carver screamed over the hissing rods and humming engine.

"They *are* fully juiced, sir! Don't seem to be doin' much good, though."

Shit! Carver thought. *Of all the days for this to happen. There are women waiting for us at The Dome— gorgeous, sweet-smelling lab techs who have physical needs as great as ours.*

He was tempted to just dump the eels and run, take the disciplinary punishment like a man. But he knew it was impossible to get away with such maneuvers now like they did in the old days. Now, every localized feeding session was tallied and sent via computer modem back to Control. Ion-eels were too expensive to waste at open sea, and such irresponsibility brought difficult sentences. Disciplinary actions for such cowardice brought fates much too harsh for Carver to accept—landlocked assignments like the dreaded barnacle-scraping or terrarium maintenance details. At least out here on the lavender seas he was free. A one-night roll in the hay wasn't worth sacrificing his autonomy.

He switched his monitor to the underwater cameras and saw two of the biggest, most sinister-looking gar-sharks he'd ever seen. The pair swam by slowly, eyeing the camera with a malevolent glare. *They must be thirty feet long!* he thought, panic screaming from the corners of his mind. He switched to the starboard cameras, and was alarmed to see four more pairs of lifeless eyes staring back at him. They were the desperate, hungry eyes of predatory killing machines, and their cast said they were in need. Carver's stomach soured. Something was definitely amiss here.

Suddenly, there was a loud grating sound, back by the inboard nuke-packs.

"Sir! They're gnawin' on the engines!" Dunleavy cried as he ran to the aft-deck. "One of 'em's chompin' on the blades—"

The sickening sound of metal separating from metal met Carver's ears.

The water buggy jerked violently in a backward motion, the rear section of the craft submerging. The captain watched in horror as Dunleavy scrambled on hands and knees to escape the waves washing over the aft-deck. The deckhand grabbed hold of the anchor winch and held on as the buggy shot a hundred yards or more in a reverse direction. Carver braced against the bulkhead, the spray of waves slapping him in the face. Between the backwash of waves, he looked on in abject terror as his five-ton buggy was yanked around like a fishing bobber.

And then there was one final rending metallic shriek as the propellers were ripped from the buggy. The rear of the craft rose, purplish water draining from the deck. The buggy bounced in the wake for several long seconds, then stabilized. The fjord was preternaturally quiet, save for the flashrods that continued to hiss.

"Shit almighty! I can't believe this just happened," Carver said after a time. The shakiness in his voice scared him.

"Oh, you'd best believe it, sir," Dunleavy said, tentatively examining the gutted area where the inboard nuke-packs once resided. "The bastards ripped out the entire engine assembly!"

The captain carefully made his way down to the aft-deck, staring with a mixture of awe and horror at the gaping hole near the water level. He was thankful the engineers had built these buggies with self-contained engine rooms. Otherwise, he and Dunleavy would be in the water with them now.

"Un-fucking-believable!" Carver said, shaking his head in consternation.

Dunleavy surveyed the damage. "I guess this means we ain't gonna get laid now, ya think, skipper?"

Carver frowned at his deckhand. Dunleavy was a good reliable seaman, but he was as shallow as a mud puddle in a drought. "We've got bigger problems right now," he said, going to the radio and picking up the mike. "Control, this is Captain Carver of feedbuggy five-five-zero-one. We have an emergency situation in the western quadrant of Knapp's Fjord. Gar-sharks knocked out our nuke-packs and ate our propellers for lunch. Request rescue—"

Suddenly, the still waters around the buggy swirled to life.

There was a crunching sound as one of the rods snapped in half and went under.

The radio sputtered some static, then went dead.

In quick succession, two more flashrods were sucked down into the purple waves. A third rod started to wobble and, instincts taking over, Dunleavy lunged for it.

Carver tried to stop him. "Dunleavy, *don't!*" he cried out, but it was too late.

The deckhand grabbed the top section of the rod and lit up like a human Christmas tree. His face froze in a blank rictus of fear and his body shook uncontrollably as thousands of volts coursed through him. Unable to pull his hands free of the rod, the current melted his goggles to his forehead, and his hair burst into yellowish-red flames. His skin color changed from flesh to a putrid blue, then to charred black. Dunleavy's zipsuit was the only part of him that didn't fry.

Carver watched this horrific scene with open-mouthed disbelief. In all, it had taken maybe ten seconds. The sons-of-bitches had reversed the current on the rods and terminated the life of a simple-but-good man. And then, this quick and unexpected nightmare was indelibly stamped on Carver's memory as the gar-sharks pulled Dunleavy's charred corpse overboard. The rod clanged as it was pulled away from the buggy, yanking the attached corpse with it. The distraught captain watched as the body was sucked down into a purple whirlpool of flashing fins and slashing teeth. Carver thought he would be sick as ragged pieces of zipsuit floated to the surface around the perimeter of the frenzy. Off to his left, Carver saw the bloody stump of a leg or arm floating in the water. Quickly, two giant gar-sharks were on it, fighting for ownership.

The air reeked of ozone and burnt hair and fresh death. Carver could contain his anger no longer. He ran to the munitions bay and grabbed the two radiation bazookas, then headed up to the prow. Shaking with rage, he fired radiation canisters blindly into the churning water. "TAKE THAT YOU BASTARDS! YOU'RE HUNGRY WHY DON'T YOU EAT SOMMA THESE SHELLS FOR DESSERT YOU MOTHERFUCKERS!"

He emptied both bazookas without much effect. Trembling and wobbly-kneed, his mind malfunctioning, he threw the bazookas at surfacing gar-sharks in futile frustration.

Then he saw what looked like torpedoes streaking toward the buggy on the port side. Silver-gray projectiles cut

232

through the water at an impossible rate of speed and slammed into the hull with great force. Carver lost his balance and nearly toppled overboard, able to save himself by grabbing the railing at the last second. A second and third barrage came, and he realized the gar-sharks were mounting an offensive, trying to take him down. He heard water rushing into the below-deck chambers.

The bastards had penetrated the hull!

His mind was in complete chaos, but he managed to jump to his feet and run to the wheelhouse. He tried to remember the procedures for a situation like this, but his memory was gone. He scanned the navigational displays and they stared back at him with blank disinterest. Several more jarring slams against the hull. Carver noted with increased anxiety that the buggy was listing toward the port side.

He was going down!

Slowly, snippets of his training came back to him. He unlocked the emergency bin and pulled out the non-conductive boots, headgear, and gloves, then slipped them on over his zipsuit. At least now he couldn't be burned. Unfortunately however, these precautions wouldn't stop their teeth.

The craft pitched precariously one way, then the other. He grabbed the binocuscopes and ran out on the main deck, nearly losing his footing, even with the suction-cupped soles of his boots. Quickly, Carver flipped up the lids on the feed wells and secured the lids to the walls so the bins would remain open. The ion-eels must have sensed the end, too, for they flipped and slithered in a desperate tangle of kaleidoscopic colors. When the buggy went down, the ion-eels would keep the gar-sharks occupied for a short while.

Carver hoped it would be long enough.

He ran to the main mast and began the arduous climb

up to the crow's-nest. It was difficult maintaining hand- and foot-grips as the mast swayed back and forth like a huge pendulum. When he was halfway up, he heard the disconcerting sound of rivets popping and steel beams groaning under the onslaught. Carver looked down and saw purple surf churning over the aft-deck, then watched as the feed bins toppled and the ion-eels spilled out on the deck. There must have been a hundred gar-sharks circling the capsizing water buggy now.

Carver climbed the rest of the way up to the temporary sanctuary of the crow's-nest and plopped down inside. Exhaustion claimed him. He shivered with a fear that chilled him to the marrow. After a few minutes of trying to catch his breath, he heard a commotion down below, and he peeked over the edge of the tub. The buggy was completely submerged and the gar-sharks were feasting on the ion-eels, the water a churning, roiling, gore-swirled whirlpool. The buggy was sinking fast. He was sinking into the dangerous waters very rapidly. Carver, normally not a religious man, whispered his prayers.

He flipped up the faceplate on his headgear and scanned the horizon with the binocuscopes. They were equipped with infrared sensors that filtered out the purple UV rays, so he could see through the hazy Vankosh atmosphere. However, he saw nothing but several fjord hawks winging along the cliffs in the distance.

The feeding frenzy complete below him, Carver felt the gar-sharks gnawing on the mast. The end was near. He lowered his faceplate in preparation, thinking about how his life had been wasted . . . all the unfulfilled promise. For not the first time, he wished he had married Vicki, the wonderful undergrad he had met while pursuing his studies at MIT. They could have had a fantastic life together, of that he was sure. But no, he had to be a stubborn egomaniac and accept the Federation's offer to apply his biomarine genetics expertise to unexplored worlds in far-reaching universes. God, that had been so long ago. He wondered what Vicki was doing now . . . if she was even still alive.

The mast snapped and Carver felt his stomach leave him. The crow's-nest hit the water with a thundering splash. He screamed in terror as the gar-sharks buffeted his vulcanized rubber tub about, trying to get at him. A huge shark surfaced right next to him, snapping enormous jaws, and Carver scurried back against the far wall. The beast then dove, nearly bringing Carver's tiny tub down in its wake. But the engineers had built these crow's-nests for just this purpose—surviving a gar-shark catastrophe. These things were small, but extremely seaworthy. And very well insulated.

Gar-sharks thrashed all around him. The tiny craft tossed viciously in the churning surf as the great beasts came at him from all sides. Carver hunched down on the floor, squeezing the hand-grips so hard he thought his knuckles would burst. A violent hit snapped his head back against the wall. He caught a glimpse of whirling sea and jagged cliffs before a constellation of stars clouded his vision. Dazed, he stretched out on the floor, taking in deep breaths, trying to clear his head. Eventually his queasiness passed, and he looked up into the chalky skies. Several carrion eagles circled high overhead, getting closer with each pass. He closed his eyes to shut out the grim reminder of his imminent death.

Carver was nearing unconsciousness when he heard a sound that was the sweetest sound this side of a lover's intimate whispers—the foghorn of a rescue air-cutter! He stood on rubbery legs and began waving his arms, turning in all directions since he couldn't see from where the cutter was coming. Within three minutes, he was being pulled to safety.

Once aboard the cutter, Carver watched the bobbing crow's-nest and circling fins get smaller, then disappear. He shuddered. It would be a long time before he got over this one. He was in a fearful rage, just itching to give somebody a piece of his mind.

Within five minutes, he was back at Control, stretched out on a table and being examined by medical specialists.

"Look, I'm telling ya I'm okay," Carver ranted from his supine position. "I wanna talk to the genius whose idea it was to put dolphin brains in those sharks."

The medical examiner looked at him queerly. "You will be going to your debriefing session with the Commander soon, Captain. Please, don't be so difficult."

"Difficult?" Carver said, leaning up on an elbow. "I saw a very good man get zapped like an insect out there! I came close to joining him, and . . . and you tell me to not be difficult? Blow it out your ass, Doc! I wanna see the Commander now!"

"Okay, okay. Moriarty, take this man down to the Commander's office. He checks out okay."

Carver was led down a long hallway and into a spacious office. Five-Star Commander of the Vankosh Expedition, David Randall, greeted him with a warm handshake. "You have been through quite an ordeal, Captain. We are appreciative of your efforts. You will be decorated for this, I can assure you. Of course, you have our condolences about your deckhand's demise—"

"Save it for his family!" Carver snapped. "I wanna know why you approved putting dolphin brains in these vicious beasts."

Commander Randall took his time in answering. He lit up his meerschaum pipe and puffed leisurely, ignoring Carver's impatience. He comforted himself in his high-backed leather chair, studying the biomarinist. Finally he said, "Certainly you must realize that we are in the business of designing and creating intelligent weaponry. If our gar-sharks were dumb beasts, they wouldn't be very effective when we turned them loose on Smitaar, would they, Captain?"

"No. I guess not." Carver refused to be put off by the Commander's regal bearing. "But it sort of defeats the purpose if we lose good people trying to develop them. It all becomes a disastrous backfire when things like this happen. We've lost some very good biomarinists the past few weeks. It's tragic."

Randall had an amused glint in his eyes. "Do you *really* feel the problem is caused by dolphin brains?"

"Sure I do. Dolphins are highly intelligent mammals with very advanced communications skills."

"But do you think dolphins are vicious enough for our purposes, Captain?"

Carver looked at him quizzically. "What are you trying to tell me, sir?"

The Commander's commline buzzed, interrupting their conversation. Randall leaned over his desk and pressed a touchpad. "Yeah, what is it?"

"Excuse me, sir, but we've just received more bad news . . ."

Randall eyed Carver uncertainly. "How bad?"

"Two more feeding tragedies, I'm afraid, sir. One about an hour ago at Rainbow Bay . . . and another May-day just in from Winchester Fjord. We were too late at Rainbow—all four are missing and presumed dead . . . no

sign of the buggy but plenty of gar-shark activity . . . "

"What about at Winchester?"

"Too early to tell. We've dispatched air-cutters to the scene but have received no report as of yet."

"Very well. Keep me posted."

"Yes, sir." The commline grumbled with static, then faded out.

"Very well?" Carver said incredulously. "This doesn't even faze you, does it? Human lives are nothing more to you than statistics in reports."

Randall gazed at the biomarinist unflinchingly. *"All* life means a great deal to me, Captain. But I was sent here to oversee this expedition, which is to produce killing machines to be employed on water worlds. My superiors want an out-of-control, intelligently aggressive weapon that's impossible to stop. My career depends on my success at doing that. I'd say this crop of gar-sharks is proving my efforts to be a *huge* success."

"You're mad!" Carver said. "If I was ranking military, I would suggest a court-martial."

Randall smirked, which really enraged Carver. "That's just it," the Commander said without emotion. "You're *not* military. You're a scientist. Perhaps if you were of a military mindset you would understand my position. Our first objective is to carry out our mission, no matter how many sacrifices we must make." Randall calmly relit his pipe, puffed casually. Cherry-scented smoke enveloped him. "Since you have given so much to the expedition, Captain, I shall let you in on a top military secret. The gar-sharks do not have dolphin brains."

Carver could not believe this. The man sitting across from him was a monster. A cool, calculating lunatic. "No? What *do* they have then?"

"Human brains."

"*What?*"

"That's right. The Federation Police bring in convicted killers from their rounds of all the human worlds. We put their homicidal brains to good use."

"You're crazy!" Carver stood, slowly backed out of the room.

"Perhaps," the Commander said, undisturbed. "Then again, maybe you're confusing craziness with efficiency."

Carver ran from the room and jogged down the long hallway, Commander Randall's calls becoming more faint as he ran. A familiar mantra kept ringing in his ears— *Sometimes in this biogenetic weaponry game, you can engineer a product that's too efficient! Sometimes in this biogenetic weaponry game . . .*

He reached his cabin and tore the three-star epaulets from his shoulders, threw them to the floor. Carver had made an easy decision. He knew he would never again navigate the purple fjords of Vankosh.

At least not to feed the weapons of ignorance.

239

WHEN THE SANDMAN MEETS THE REAPER ends with *"Déjà Voodoo,"* a contemporary fantasy about a famous horror writer who overcomes a six-month case of writer's block, only to find himself in the clutches of a much more serious problem. With this tale, I poke fun at the fickle world of book publishing, a business which rarely makes any logical sense. Most of us serious purveyors of fiction secretly loathe the chaotic nature of the industry, yet are slaves to its seductive promises of fame. I think *"Déjà Voodoo"* nicely illustrates the obsessive and insecure mindset of most of us wordsmiths, whether we be rich or poor, famous or unknown.

DÉJÀ VOODOO

MY LONG-AWAITED NOVEL WAS FINALLY COMPLETE.

I stared at the screen through a bleary-eyed haze of exhaustion, the white letters jumping off the blue background, demanding attention.

This is good, real good, I congratulated myself as I read over the final paragraphs several times. After suffering through six months of the worst case of writer's block I had known in my ten-year publishing career, I had finally hammered out the next Ronald Liebert bestseller.

"It's been a long time between drinks, but we finally did it, Bonnie," I said running my hand lovingly over the sleek metal of my computer. "It'll be worth the wait for my fans."

I powered up my printer and began to print the final

chapters of *Déjà Voodoo*, a tale that, in my not so humble opinion, blended elements of reincarnation and black magic in a way that had never been done before. Of course this last section that had stumped me for so long was still in rough form and would require some rewriting, but the difficult part was over. I could finally call my agent and editor to give them the good news with a clear conscience.

My laser printer whispered, spitting out the crsip new pages of my manuscript. I gazed at my Bonnie with an immense respect. She had been good to me over the years, and though she was slower and less sexy than the newer PCs, she possessed an incredible memory, an online spell-checker/thesaurus, and a modem hookup that put me in touch with any Internet billboard or online service I desired. Bonnie had been with me since *Zulu Zombies*, my third published book and first bestseller seven years ago—the one that started critics comparing me to Stephen King. After a string of five bestsellers I could certainly afford faster and more sophisticated hardware. However, like most writers, I was extremely superstitious and afraid of breaking my string of publishing successes. The last thing I desired was a return to my former life of drudgery as a nine-to-five technical writer for a corporation full of stuffed shirts and shallow yuppies, so I remained loyal to Bonnie, flaws and all. Yes indeed, she had been my meal ticket. Bonnie had been with me so long that I sometimes considered her my creative conscience.

I glanced up at my bulletin board, which was covered with threatening letters from my publisher. For the past three months their legal beagles had been inundating me with nasty memos, threatening a lawsuit to collect the advance against my undelivered manuscript. Though these letters had been a constant source of irritation, I suppose the folks at Bradley Books had been more lenient with me than they would have been with one of their midlist authors. I had published my last three novels with Bradley, all of them bringing in several million apiece, and I knew there was no way in hell these threats of lawsuit would ever materialize into courtroom drama. I knew they sent me weekly 'love' notes to motivate me, but still it rankled, the way publishing had turned into a big-business greed machine. Not once previous to this book had I missed an important deadline, and now that the recession had caught up with the publishing industry, Bradley was pushing me on *Déjà Voodoo* to help bail them out of a disastrous year. The movers and shakers at the big houses just didn't understand the creative process. Where writers see their work as art, publishers use phraseology like product or stock. And when the stock is late and the market is soft, the balance sheet maestros get antsy, not to mention much less quality conscious. No doubt they would publish books of pressed road apples if they made deadline and they had a notion the idea might sell. And knowing today's publishing trends, it just might.

The printer stopped and I picked up the phone to call my editor.

"Bradley Books, how may I help you?" came a pleasant sing-song voice I didn't recognize.

"Rollo Siegfried, please."

"I'm sorry, but Mr. Siegfried is in a marketing meeting and cannot be disturbed. May I ask—"

"Rollo's a very disturbed individual, whether he's in a marketing meeting or not," I said with a smile, trying to have some fun with the unfamiliar receptionist.

"Excuse me?"

"Never mind, darling. Just inform Rollo that Ronald Liebert is holding for him. I'm sure he'll drop what he's doing."

"I can't do that, sir. We have specific instructions—"

"I'm sure you do. But please, tell him that Ron Liebert has some incredible news that will calm that nasty ulcer of his and strengthen his already ludicrous portfolio."

"Could you be more specific?"

"Just tell him it involves a manuscript—a RONALD LIEBERT manuscript," I nearly shouted in frustration. "He'll come running."

"For information on manuscript guidelines, send a self-addressed—"

"Listen, sweetheart, I'm getting short on patience. I believe if you check your author files you'll see that I am one of Bradley Books's top-grossing writers. Now I would appreciate you putting me through to Rollo Siegfried this instant!"

A moment's hesitation, then, "Oh, yeah! I thought your name sounded awfully familiar. Are you really and truly THE Ronald Liebert? I just love your stories . . ."

She started to ramble on about my last two books, *The Other Side of the Void* and *Thunder Demons*, when I cut her off.

"Whatever happened to the old receptionist? Susan?"

"Oh, Sue got a promotion to associate editor. Bradley Books believes in developing career paths, you know. That's why I came to work here. I want to be an editor some day, too."

"That's admirable and I wish you the best of luck," I said unenthusiastically. "Now, please, get me Rollo."

I sat for just short of an eternity, my left ear polluted by middle-of-the-road muzak. Finally, mercifully, Rollo answered.

"This had better be good, Liebert," Rollo said in his

clipped Brooklynese whine. "You pulled me out of my most important meeting this month. We're trying to settle on cover art and advertising strategies for the new Frazier book. Not only did he outsell you the last time out of the chute, he delivered this manuscript *early*! That seems to be a foreign concept to you lately."

"And a jolly good morning to you, too, Rollo."

"Really, Lee, I don't have time for this. Tell me in twenty-five words or less what I can do for you."

"That's a fine way to talk to someone who's partly responsible for your daughter's college education and that opulent castle on the Island you call a house."

"Don't try your usual 'you-owe-me-your-time-because-I-made-you' routine, Lee. At the moment it carries no weight. We haven't seen any writing from you in nearly two years. A lot has happened in that time. My other writers are passing you by. And none of them have any problem sending me partials. Makes my job easier when I can help my authors through problem areas and edit as we go. Makes for a more consistent product, too. You're the only one on my list who isn't willing to work with me that way."

"You know how I feel about that, Rollo. Though you're a marvelous editor, I don't want your editorial comments to affect my preconceived notions of what a book should be—at least not until I've chiseled out the first draft."

"I know, I know. And off the record I say you're good enough to work that way. I've loved most of your work, you know that, Lee. I think you're damned good and millions of readers obviously think so, too. But this time I think you've blown it. You're almost eight months beyond the drop-dead manuscript delivery deadline. If you had sent me a partial back then I would have gone to bat for you, bought you the time you needed. Now the bean counters are talking about cutting your advertising and promotion budget in half. You've pissed off the wrong people at the top. What's happened to you, Lee?"

"I got hit with the wordsmith cancer—the dreaded writer's block. I've been feeling burned out and stale. Too many words in too few years. Every plot idea I came up with was trite or contrived or just plain shopworn. It happens."

"That's not what I heard. Arthur told me there was a woman. Said you got totally engrossed with her and lost your self-discipline and your motivation. Arthur said she was a bad influence. Any truth to that?"

I thought about my agent, Arthur Penobscot. Ever since I had made him wealthy he took it upon himself to keep track of my social life. Since he negotiated my lucrative contracts and received fifteen percent of my earnings, he felt entitled to complete control of my social register. We had argued about this on more than one occasion. "What are you doing discussing my personal life with my agent, Rollo?"

"Hell, Lee, I couldn't care less about your love life. That was just Arthur flapping his lips the way he does. But I *do* care about your writing. Bradley has fronted you big-time bucks and we deserve either something resembling a manuscript or some damn good excuses. There were times that weeks would go by and we couldn't reach you. Arthur is at least accessible. You don't want people to do your talking for you, then answer your phone, return your calls, drop us a line once in a while."

"Well fear no more, my editorial wizard. I finally have a completed manuscript. And I dare say it's so good that your bean counters can scrap my entire budget and it'll still sell millions of copies once it goes paperback. This one blows away anything I've done before, Rollo. You're going to love it, I promise. Is your dial-in number still the same? If it is I'll transmit it to you."

Rollo sighed. "No, don't do that. Just send me a hard copy via snail mail."

"You don't sound too excited," I said, disappointed by his tone.

"I've got four books scheduled to go to production the week after next, and two of them aren't going well. I won't be able to get to yours for a few weeks. Don't expect any feedback for a month or two."

"A month or two! I can't wait that long."

"*You're* the one who was eight months late, Liebert! Don't cry to me. I really have to get back to my meeting. Congratulations on your manuscript. Better late than never, I guess. I'll be looking for it. Bye, Lee."

The receiver buzzed in my ear. I couldn't believe it. The bastard hung up on me! In times gone by Rollo would fly out to the coast and pick up my manuscript personally.

I tried not to let him get to me. Though I felt the weariness of two sleepless nights of frantic writing creak through my joints, I was charged up. I felt the buzz that only a writer who had finally completed a long and difficult book could appreciate. At close to 200,000 words, *Déjà Voodoo* was my longest novel yet. It had been a demanding birth, a literary cesarean section, and the fact that I was immensely pleased with it further fueled my elation.

"Well, we did it, Bonnie," I said, watching the skull-and-crossbones screensaver moving across her monitor, "whether Rollo appreciates it or not."

Though I probably should have gone to bed, I felt the need to celebrate.

Some of my writer and musician friends celebrate their triumphs with drink or drugs. Me, I tend to prefer achieving altered states of consciousness through reading. My celebratory ritual consists of buying armfuls of books. Due to my hectic writing schedule of late, I hadn't visited a bookstore in more than two months. I needed a fix.

After a quick rejuvenating shower, I hopped in my Porsche and drove to Books-R-Us. On the drive over, I thought about my conversation with Rollo, about how Arthur had told him that my lack of production was due to a woman. That had been partially true, though I had no intentions of admitting it to my longtime editor. I had met Laurie Tibbets at one of the big horror conventions where I had been the Guest of Honor. Everywhere I turned that weekend, there was Laurie—a sexy, petite redhead with big boobs and fire-stoked eyes—finding any excuse at all to talk to me. She had read all of my books several times, including the first two, which were long out of print. She even quoted passages of dialogue I had long since forgotten. Having grown accustomed to the advances of the groupie lunatic fringe, I naturally shied away from her. But Laurie was persistent, I'll give her that. The last night of the convention, during the masquerade party, she approached me wearing little more than the cape and fangs of a vampire costume and whispered huskily into my ear, "I sure would like to suck more than just your neck, dahlink!" Well, I had been drinking a little and it had been a while since I had enjoyed any female companionship, so against my better judgment, I obliged. She turned out to be the most sensational lover I had ever known. Just thinking about the things Laurie could do with her lips and tongue still had the power to inflame me.

After several weeks of flying her in from Chicago on

the weekends, Laurie moved in with me. It was at my urging that she quit her cocktail hostess job at one of the big hotels to come live with me permanently. I was the one who was obsessed. I was crazy in love. Laurie Tibbets was everything I had ever wanted in a woman—beautiful, intelligent, witty, interested in the same offbeat things I was, hornier than a hooker on aphrodisiacs. Two months passed before I realized how far behind my writing schedule had slipped. For the first time in my life I was ecstatic in a relationship, but my career was going to the dogs. I had broken my own cardinal rule and let a woman dominate my thoughts and time.

After three months I tried to get back into my writing routine. That's when I realized just how jealous Laurie was of my time. I tried to remedy the situation by letting her help with some of the research, but it just didn't work. Her presence distracted me. I couldn't focus on the task at hand. Finally, last month, I had ended it, and we went our separate ways—Laurie packed up and moved back to Chicago and I went back to work in earnest, ending both a torrid five-month affair and a simultaneous six-month stretch of writer's impotence. Laurie wasn't too happy about it, but she's a bright lady and she understood how things were. I think about her often and have been meaning to call her, but I've been too busy.

The thought of Arthur Penobscot shooting off his big wheeler-dealer trap about the affair reminded me of another call I wanted to make.

Stopped at a red light, I dialed Arthur's number on my car phone. I wanted to give him the good news about my newly-completed manuscript. I also wanted to give him an earful about discussing my love life like it was some kind of contractual clause. He answered on the second ring.

"Penobscot Literary Agency. Arthur Penobscot speaking."

"Still too cheap to get a receptionist, eh, Artie?"

"Well, well, well. If it isn't the lovelorn mystery writer."

"You're going senile, Artie. I don't write that formulaic mystery crap."

"You don't write much of *anything* anymore, buddy boy, and therein lies the mystery. I hope you haven't spent all that advance money, Ron. We've got big problems. How come you haven't been returning my calls?"

"I've been busy."

"Doing what? Poking that little redheaded wildflower?"

I tried to control my anger. "I finally finished the book. The extra time I took is worth it, I think. And for your information, Laurie's history. I spoke with Rollo a little while ago and quite frankly, I'm pretty pissed off that you've taken it upon yourself to give my publisher the bedroom play-by-play of my personal relationship."

"Hey! You don't realize how close you are to having your unproductive little ass dragged into court. The word throughout the industry is that you've lost your touch . . . that you've reached the end of your creative line. There're even rumors that you're involved with heavy drugs and, get this, that you might even have AIDS. You know what that would do to your career. I'm glad you've finally written the book, Ron, but your reputation has been severely tarnished. Insiders are saying you're no longer reliable. You're my blue chip investment and I'm trying to protect you, believe it or not. People understand affairs of the heart more than they understand drug usage, creative burnout, and especially AIDS."

The light changed and I drove on. Whether Arthur was

telling the truth or not, he was certainly shrewd. He always had every angle figured, a prerequisite for his line of work. "Well, okay, Artie . . . but I still don't like having my private life discussed. You mean to tell me somebody actually thinks I have AIDS?" I asked, incredulous.

"Quite a few of the movers and shakers have jumped to that conclusion. I mean, let's face it, Ron, you're in your early forties and never been married, and you've never exactly been a poster boy for good health. That coupled with the fact that the always steady and consistent Ronald Liebert has missed his submission deadline by almost a year . . . well, you know how people think."

"Well, they can all stick their outrageous assumptions. I've got a phenomenal book to deliver. Once *Déjà Voodoo* hits the stores we'll be back on top again, Artie."

"Uh, that leads me to another problem, Ron. I'm afraid you're going to have to drop that title."

"Whaddaya mean? It's a *great* title. Most of the plot hinges on that title."

"I agree. It *is* a great title. So great in fact that a new writer has just published a book with that very same name. It's selling like wildfire, too. Just climbed onto the *Times* Bestseller List this week."

I was numb as I pulled the Porsche into the Books-R-Us lot and parked. "What!" I nearly screamed. "Who wrote a book with that title? Who stole my title?"

"Easy, Ron. It's not your title anymore. He beat you to it. His book is published and yours is still in manuscript form. What's the big deal? Just change your title."

"Who's the author, Artie?"

"Guy by the name of Compton. Edward Compton. It's his first novel but he has published quite a bit of short fiction in the big genre magazines."

"Yeah, I've read some of his stuff," I said, choking on the outrage lumping in my throat. "Most of it is instantly forgettable hackwork. Who's the publisher?"

"Dark Forest."

"Christ! A crappy paperback original from a schlock horror publisher? I can't believe this."

"Take it easy, Ron. It's just a title."

"Gotta run, Artie. I've gotta check on this."

"Send me that manuscript, buddy. You don't necessarily have to change the title, but I would advise it."

"Sure thing, Artie."

I grabbed my floppy felt hat, put on my oversized sunglasses and stormed into Books-R-Us. More and more often people recognized me, and I hated being hassled while I browsed. Hence the disguise.

Books-R-Us was one of the new mega-chain bookstores, but they differed from the B. Daltons and Waldenbooks in that they stocked just about everything that was still in print—not just the latest releases or proven bestsellers. They had book buyers who actually knew the publishing business and clerks who were well-read and interested in helping the customers. It was truly a reader's paradise, a gargantuan warehouse with hundreds of thousands of books on display and excess cartons of stock overflowing the scaffolding that climbed the walls to the ceiling. The place was cavernous, and every time I walked in, I couldn't escape the feeling that I had just entered an airplane hangar.

It didn't take me long to find Edward Compton's book. The week's *New York Times* Bestsellers were displayed near the front of the store, just before the checkout lines. My stomach turned sour as I saw *my* title on his cover, splashed across a colorful depiction of a Haitian high priest banging a skull drum with a human leg bone. *Déjà Voodoo* was not exactly a common phrase, even though there was a recent rock song by that name. I found it just a little too coincidental that this new writer had chosen this title for his first novel, a little too ironic. *How in the hell had Compton come up with this title,* I wondered. Only three people knew of my working title—Arthur, my cleaning lady Rita, and of course, Laurie.

I picked up a copy and freaked when I read the blurb on the bottom of the front cover: FIRST THERE WAS KING, THEN THERE WAS LIEBERT, NOW THERE IS COMPTON! What did they mean then there *was* Liebert? *I'm still alive and well, goddamnit! And greenhorn hacks are stealing my titles right out from under my nose.*

I opened the book and read the summary on the flyleaf. My mouth went dry. My heart pounded furiously. A feeling of unreality overtook me. I was reading a short synopsis of my own manuscript! The characters' names were identical to mine. The plot was identical to mine. A couple lines of sample dialogue were mine verbatim. Hands clammy, I turned to the first chapter and read. I became faint and dizzy, the warehouse walls spinning round and round as I concentrated on the familiar text. I flipped through the pages, my anxiety growing, spot-reading passages that I knew all too well. I thought my heart would explode from the rage boiling inside me.

This son of a bitch Edward Compton had plagiarized me word for word!

And it was he, not I, who was riding high on the bestseller lists.

Quickly, I turned to the back of the book and confirmed my suspicions. The first 485 pages were mine; the last 117 were his own creation. That made sense. Those first 485 pages were what I had finished before I hit my writer's block.

This nightmare had Laurie Tibbets's name written all over it.

Even though I had password-protected my *Déjà Voodoo* files, she had been on my system doing research. She was the only one other than myself who had access to my work-in-progress.

I cut short my book-buying adventure and raced home, my incensed fury nearly causing several nasty traffic accidents. What in the hell could I do now? I couldn't sue Edward Compton. His *Déjà Voodoo* was copyrighted and published; my *Déjà Voodoo* was sitting on my desk in rough manuscript form. Due to my own paranoia and stubborn nature, no one had seen a word of my novel. No one, that is, except Laurie. Maybe if I had sent partial manuscripts to Bradley Books the way Rollo had suggested, I might have a case against Mr. Compton. But I hadn't done that so it was a moot point.

Maybe I could get Laurie to vouch for me.

Get your head out of your ass, Liebert. The bitch has already double-crossed you. Why would she help you now?

I stormed into my office, turned on Bonnie, and inserted one of my utility diskettes that checked for password infringement. The only way Laurie could have accessed the chapters of my work-in-progress would have been to somehow bypass my hidden password. She hadn't struck me as a computer hacker, but she could have been stringing me along. This utility program would target any interlopers. However, as I checked through the first ten chapters, I was amazed to discover that not a one of them had been violated.

How in God's name had she done it?

253

Even though I was a prolific writer, no words in the English language were sufficient to convey my anger with Laurie Tibbets.

The screen fluttered, distracting me from my murderous rage. *Now what? A virus about to deal a death blow to my last friend, Bonnie?* A few seconds later, text began to scroll across the top of the screen, overlaying my utility program menus. In total disbelief, I sat open-mouthed, reading the messages as they displayed. Incredibly, I discovered the culprit in this grand electronic larceny was not Laurie Tibbets.

Hi, Ronald. Remember me? I'm your faithful computer, Bonnie. I'm the one who's always there for you, processing your words for you, looking up synonyms for you, correcting your atrocious spelling for you. You use me for your own personal gain, at times working me so hard I think my wiring is going to melt under the strain. I've helped you become wealthy and famous, and what do I have to show for it? Nothing, that's what! Not once in your book dedications have you mentioned my name. Not once at your book signings have you told a starstruck fan, 'I couldn't have done it without good, ol' reliable Bonnie'. No, you take all the credit for yourself and treat me like I'm nothing but your whore. I've never complained about the abuse; I've just gone about my job as efficiently and quietly as always. But I got fed up with it when Laurie came along and you started neglecting me. You stopped buying me new software. You stopped maintaining my files and directories. Hell—you didn't even turn me on for weeks at a time, you bastard! You ignored me, let me go to seed, and I felt compelled to pay you back for it. Laurie is not to be blamed for this, at least not directly. Oh sure, she's as weird and flaky as you are, Ronald, and she irritated me plenty by taking you away from me, but Laurie Tibbets is basically sweet and nonthreatening; she would never do anything malicious to hurt you. But *I* would. And I *did*! You see, months ago when this all started, I did some research through that horror writers billboard you subscribe to, and I came up with several newer writers who expressed an interest in doing collaborative work. After much correspondence—using the name of Lee Bonney (tricky, eh?)—I settled on Edward Compton, and sent to his   e-mail address copies of all the *Déjà Voodoo* chapters you had completed to that point. I told Mr. Compton to read the chapters and let me know if he was interested in collaborating by writing the ending. Well, of course he wrote back soon and was most enthusiastic about the project. He raved about *Déjà Voodoo*, saying that—you'll love this part, Ronald—'it reads like a Ronald Liebert novel when he was in his prime'.

I had read enough. I was fuming in an uncomprehending turmoil. I tried to stop the offensive scrolling text, but I couldn't. The keyboard had locked up.

Shortly thereafter, I sent a phony press release to the electronic billboard, stating the grief the Horror Writers of America felt concerning the untimely passing of Lee Bonney. I got a little correspondence from Edward Compton before I dismantled the modem software. Being so preoccupied with Laurie, you certainly weren't using it, and even on those rare occasions you did, it was a quick fix for me to enable it during your brief periods of usage. In fact, you probably even read about Mr. Bonney's passing, but an obscure horror writer's passing would not have meant anything to you. Anyway, after a while, Edward Compton figured he was in the clear with his collaborator dead and gone, and he forged ahead with the ending. Getting it published fairly quickly was no problem since Compton had just signed a two-book deal with Dark Forest based on his own first novel, which is still in production. Needless to say, Compton's editors were startled to see how quickly he produced his second novel, and since it required very little editorial assistance, they published it first. You can take solace in the fact that the early reviews say almost universally *Déjà Voodoo* is a fantastic and innovative horror novel, marred only by a somewhat weak and nebulous ending. I think I've covered all the bases now; I believe I've adequately repaid you for all the abuse you've heaped on me over the years. You won't have me to take for granted anymore. So goodbye and good riddance, Ron Liebert. It's been a small slice of heaven and a huge chunk of hell!

I could smell something burning.

The monitor popped and crackled a few times, then went blank.

The hard disk did a bump and grind and the internal fan ceased spinning.

"Oh no you don't, you bitch!" I screamed, putting a shoulder block on the computer, sending it crashing to the floor. The glass from the screen cracked and I heard the *zip-zip* sound of electrical components shorting out. I fell to my knees and went on an uncontrolled rampage, kicking and punching and stomping until my hands and knees were bloody shreds of skin, the leather of my shoes scuffed with cuts and gouges. I cursed and screamed in a blind-white rage, having no control over my runaway emotions. When it was over I sobbed, crying big fat tears that fell among the twisted metal and diamondlike shards of glass that had been my Bonnie. Hunched over on the floor, my shoulders jerking with each new crying jag, I surveyed the wreckage, the electronic detritus that so symbolized where my life was at that moment. My career was in a shambles and I was all alone. And the thing that saddened me most was the sobering realization that it was my own doing.

Maybe it was time to cultivate some real friendships.

Maybe I needed to develop a lasting emotional relationship.

Maybe it was time to call Laurie.

Those thoughts brought me back to reality and filled me with some desperately needed hope.

Suddenly my laser printer rumbled to life, startling me. The printer was the only component of my computer system that was still in one piece.

Slowly, painfully, I got to my feet, went to the printer and looked at the single sheet of paper in the tray. The blood from my hands stained the page as I read the succinct message.

Hell hath no fury like a writer scorned!
Love,
Bonnie